"YOU'VE GIVEN SO MUCH TO MY WHOLE FAMILY."

Philip's voice was tender and patient. "But I'm a man, Emily. I need you to start giving to me, too."

"I don't know what you mean." The sudden stiffening of her body made her words into a lie.

"Oh, yes, you do. This discussion is long overdue."

"Do we have to talk now? It's Christmas and I don't want to argue."

"Emily." Philip spoke her name softly and gripped her shoulders, pulling her to him. "Look at us. Look at where we are in our lives. Think of how far we've come together."

Emily was silent for a long time before she spoke, and when she did, there were tears in her eyes.
"You're right," she said quietly. "It's finally time for us both to start truly giving to each other. And what better day to start than this special day?"

ABOUT THE AUTHOR

A former copywriter herself, Debbi Bedford has a life that in some ways has taken the same path as her heroine's. After publishing her first Superromance, *Touch the Sky*, Debbi put her writing career on hold to start a family with her husband, Jack. Today they are the proud parents of year-old Jeffrey, to whom this book is lovingly dedicated.

Books by Debbi Bedford

HARLEQUIN SUPERROMANCE
154–TOUCH THE SKY

These books may be available at your local bookseller.

Don't miss any of our special offers. Write to us at the following address for information on our newest releases.

Harlequin Reader Service
901 Fuhrmann Blvd., P.O. Box 1397, Buffalo, NY 14240
Canadian address: P.O. Box 603,
Fort Erie, Ont. L2A 5X3

Debbi Bedford
A DISTANT PROMISE

Harlequin Books

TORONTO • NEW YORK • LONDON
AMSTERDAM • PARIS • SYDNEY • HAMBURG
STOCKHOLM • ATHENS • TOKYO • MILAN

Published December 1986

First printing October 1986

ISBN 0-373-70239-6

Copyright © 1986 by Deborah Pigg Bedford. All rights reserved.
Philippine copyright 1986. Australian copyright 1986.
Except for use in any review, the reproduction or utilization of
this work in whole or in part in any form by any electronic,
mechanical or other means, now known or hereafter invented,
including xerography, photocopying and recording, or in any
information storage or retrieval system, is forbidden without
the permission of the publisher, Harlequin Enterprises Limited,
225 Duncan Mill Road, Don Mills, Ontario, Canada M3B 3K9.

All the characters in this book have no existence outside the
imagination of the author and have no relation whatsoever to
anyone bearing the same name or names. They are not even
distantly inspired by any individual known or unknown to the
author, and all the incidents are pure invention.

The Superromance design trademark consisting of the words
HARLEQUIN SUPERROMANCE and the portrayal of a Harlequin,
and the Superromance trademark consisting of the words
HARLEQUIN SUPERROMANCE are trademarks of Harlequin
Enterprises Limited. The Superromance design trademark
and the portrayal of a Harlequin are registered in the
United States Patent Office.

Printed in Canada

You are
at first
my friend
leading
me
through today
with a stronger hand,
a greater faith,
than I could find myself—
Reaching
  Stretching
    Handing me
    my
      shining
        distant Promise.

—Debbi Pigg Bedford

This is dedicated to Mother and to my Jeffrey, my son, for all the two of them have given me—a faith in myself and a purpose for living, my past and my future, the simple continuity brought forth in all God's promises.

Special acknowledgment and thanks to Alice B. Uehling, known lovingly as Abu to all her adopted children. It is she who, with the formation of her nonprofit company Mothers-In-Deed, turned mothering into a full-charge, managerial, professional career and liberated hundreds of women back into their homes.

There are literally thousands of families around the world that are indebted to her, to her work, to her dedication to children. And for the inspiration, the giving, of this story, I am indebted to her, too.

CHAPTER ONE

IT WAS LATE SEPTEMBER in the blacklands of North Texas, one those blatantly sunny days when autumn hung crisp and cool in the air, one of those breezy days that hinted of sweaters, hot apple cider and football games.

Emily Lattrell half walked, half ran, north on Dallas Parkway. She was as sunny and bouncy as the day itself as she made her way toward the cedar-etched professional building that housed Petrie, Simms and Masterson, the advertising agency where she worked.

Emily had a round full face with large eyes the color of maple syrup. Her nose was short and slender, just a touch turned up on the end, and her lips were full, almost forming a bow. She smiled often, and the overall effect—her round transparent brown eyes, her tiny nose, her defined, almost heart-shaped lips—was that she looked somewhat like a china doll. Emily wore her wheat-blond hair in a blunt cut that hung midway between her chin and shoulders. She kept it curled on the ends, probably more than was currently fashionable, but she liked the soft look it gave her.

She was wearing a silk dress today, striped in shades of taupe and cream and gray. Emily wore a gray scarf tied in a knot at her waist and matching low-heeled pumps. She carried a gray leather envelope purse tucked securely beneath one arm. The strand of eggshell pearls around her neck had been a gift from her father on her birthday last June, and they were perfect for her, especially today, because they picked up a confident gleam in her eyes that hadn't been there very long.

Emily worked as an account executive and copywriter at Petrie, Simms and Masterson. Arriving at the office, she walked to her desk, pitched her purse inside a drawer, checked her secretary's desk for messages and then peeked through the glass partition that separated the creative boardroom from the hallway. Her immediate supervisor, Lloyd Masterson, was still chatting with Tim Johnson, a photographer. When Emily's employer saw her, he motioned to her to enter. She opened the door and slipped in quietly behind Tim as he was speaking. "I don't see any problem shooting the full length of the bus interior. I'll try using my wide-angle lenses. When it comes time to do the layouts we'll have lots to choose from."

"Just be sure you don't lose the proportions of the bus," Masterson cautioned as he glanced up at Emily and gave her a welcoming nod. "We can only fill half the rows of the bus with people, if need be. You can always shoot from halfway down the aisle."

Emily was already shaking her head in disagreement. They were discussing the DART account—the Dallas Area Rapid Transit—and Emily felt strongly about it. That was one of the hazards of working in the advertising industry. They sold their ideas. But Emily's ideas and her boss's ideas were not always the same. "The proportions of the bus don't matter at all, Lloyd. It's going to be the people who count in this campaign, not the stylized photography." Emily respected Lloyd Masterson. He had taught her almost everything she knew when it came to practical, hands-on knowledge of the advertising industry. He insisted on being thorough with his accounts. But Emily wasn't afraid to debate ideas with him.

Lloyd flipped a pencil into the air and watched it land a good five inches to the left of the ashtray he had been aiming for. "You're wrong, Emily. But—" he said, pausing to smile "—remember that major dissension is good for the client. There's nothing that will kill a good creative session any faster than total agreement. Too bad you didn't get here sooner. Maybe some of your ideas might have stirred Petrie and Simms up a bit. All our ideas were so cut and dried this morning. That always worries me."

Emily was pleased by his compliment. She knew he didn't take her work lightly, and he wouldn't have flattered her if he had not been totally sincere. Lloyd Masterson always proved himself brilliant when it came to developing concepts that could be turned into viable ad campaigns. She had been his protégée for six years now, ever since her graduation from the University of Texas department of business administration, and she knew she owed Lloyd more than she could ever repay. That was one reason she was becoming gutsy lately. She wanted all their campaigns to be perfect, to be brilliant in every detail. For years she had been content to conform to Lloyd Masterson's ideas. But she knew that she owed him more than mere conformity now. She owed herself more than that.

The product of Emily's working relationship with Lloyd now was a meshing of both their ideas, a union that made both Emily's and Lloyd's original concepts stronger. The two of them had turned into a marketing duo worth reckoning with. Lloyd Masterson was proud of Emily's talent, proud of the things he had taught her, proud of the way she had learned them.

He frowned at the photographer and waved one hand, pretending impatience. "Go ahead and break for lunch, Tim. I'll call you when we've gotten this thing figured out. At this rate—" here he cast a knowing look at Emily "—it may be midnight next Tuesday before we can make any final decisions about the proportions of the bus."

"Like I said," Tim replied patiently, "I can bring all the wide-angles I've got. If you can find models willing to sit still long enough, I can take just about every shot you can think of."

Emily grinned at Tim. He had never once raised his voice to remind them that he was the professional photographer in the group.

Tim shrugged his brown leather camera case onto his shoulder and hastily let himself out of the room. It was long past lunchtime.

"Okay." Lloyd turned back to Emily after the door closed. "Why don't we spend a few minutes going over your ideas?" He had a two-fold reason for the suggestion. He was eager to hear her ideas. They were usually good. But he also wanted to show Emily that he had confidence in her. She had come to him with a good bit of enthusiasm and an appropriate degree from a good university. But she hadn't had much more than that. Lloyd hated to admit it, but he had almost not hired her. She had seemed so frightened, so timid, at first. Something about her had won him over, though, something he had seen in her eyes. He had looked at her and seen raw honesty and strength and something else that suggested she knew how to survive. So he had taken her on. And he had never regretted his decision. It had taken him time to build her confidence but he had, slowly, by asking her opinion, by giving her increasingly challenging clients and by disagreeing with her ideas. She was a joyous, talented woman, and her lack of faith in her talents had seemed strangely at variance with her abilities.

"Let's zero in on some of the important aspects of this campaign and see what you can come up with," Lloyd said, pulling his thoughts back to the present.

"Fine." Emily paced past him. "What's first?"

"The copy," he answered, "which has already been approved by the client."

Emily nodded.

Lloyd continued. "The headline will read, 'Things you can do on a bus you can't do driving a car.'"

"Lloyd," Emily said as she paced the room, "tell me what the primary goal is going to be for this campaign."

Lloyd checked his notes. "'To increase ridership on the Dallas Area Rapid Transit System by thirty-five percent,'" he read aloud.

"And how is this approach going to accomplish that goal?" Emily smiled at him, and Lloyd realized too late that she was carefully leading him on. He admired her for it, though. It was an effective marketing tool that he had taught her, and she was using it against him well.

Lloyd picked up another pencil and began flipping it into the air. "It will accomplish the goal by helping potential bus riders think of new reasons why they should be riding the bus instead of sitting in a line of stalled cars on Central Expressway."

"Precisely." Emily plopped a manila folder full of notes onto the table and it landed there with a victorious *thwack*. "And we do that by depicting people on the bus..."

"By depicting how they can best benefit by the time saved riding the bus every morning." Lloyd didn't let her complete her sentence. She was coming close to dangerous ground now, a spot where they didn't agree. And he already knew it. "We need a man working furiously on a personal computer, a secretary taking dictation from her boss, a woman journalist with a notepad..."

"Those people are boring," Emily interjected bravely. "They don't appeal to me."

"They will appeal to our target market. Businessmen and women are the people we want to influence here. We need to make them realize how valuable their morning transit time can be. I want them to see this ad and feel that they're wasting their time when they next find themselves stalled in a traffic jam. I want each of them to feel a great stab of guilt because they aren't already accomplishing things. We're trying to appeal to a hardworking, conservative group of people here."

"Not necessarily so." Emily leaned over the table, placed her weight on her elbows and stared at Lloyd full in the face. "I'm a businesswoman, too. And I want to see something that sparks my imagination. I want to see something that makes me think, that inspires me, that makes me laugh. Every time I look at that ad, I want to see something new, something I haven't noticed before. I want it to make me consider riding the bus for new reasons. Ad campaigns and public service announcements have been throwing all the old reasons at me for years now. And I haven't responded to them. I'm still driving my car to work and battling Central Expressway every morning."

"These new ideas," Lloyd began, chuckling good-naturedly. "What might they be?"

"Fun things." Emily ran her fingers through her hair. "Outrageous things. Risky things." She began to pace the room furiously now, the way Lloyd knew she did each time she became so entranced with an idea that she forgot herself. He toyed with the idea of flipping a pencil at her to break her stride, but he decided it would be too mean for a time like this. "I'd like to see a bride throwing a bouquet out of the bus window and waving goodbye to the bridal party. I'd like to see her groom sitting beside her on the bus seat and giving her a passionate kiss while his mother scowls disgustedly from the seat behind him and holds up something horribly important that he's forgetting to take on his honeymoon... like his toothbrush or his eyeglasses or his underwear." Emily paused to take a breath and Lloyd opened his mouth to say something, but he didn't get the chance. "I'd like to see a ten-year-old boy wearing a snorkel mask and fins just peeking over the back of one of the seats. He can be obviously impatient for the bus to stop so he can get off and go swimming at the city pool. And I'd like to see a man in a jogging suit—"

It was Emily who didn't get to finish her sentence this time. She was so intent on the bus ad that she didn't notice the boardroom door swing open. A man had been standing outside the glass partition for quite some time now, listening to her. He didn't mean to be eavesdropping, but it had long since passed time for his luncheon appointment with Lloyd Masterson. Lloyd had seen him there and had motioned to him to step inside the room. The man had been holding the door open for a few minutes, entranced with Emily's ideas. Feeling playful, he couldn't resist finishing just this one sentence for her.

"I'd like to see a man in a jogging suit standing on his head in the driver's seat while he drives the bus with two very large bare feet."

Emily gasped and wheeled around, facing the stranger. At first she didn't know what to think of the interruption. But the man was smiling at Lloyd, so he obviously was supposed to be here. Emily decided to play along with him. She grinned. *What an absolutely absurd, wonderful idea. I should have thought of it myself.* She could change the headline copy to read: "Fighting Dallas traffic can be as frustrating as standing on your head."

"I like it." Emily did her best to appear serious, and she was thrilled when she saw the worried look on Lloyd's face. "This idea opens up an infinite number of new possibilities. Of course, it might be hard to get the right angle in the photo, so the guy's feet would still be in proportion. What do you think, Lloyd?"

Lloyd was relieved when she let a touch of sarcasm intentionally slip into her tone. For a moment, he thought Emily might actually have been serious. She loved to pounce on new ideas. But he saw that this time she was only teasing him. And he was pleased that she felt comfortable enough with him to do so.

"I think," Lloyd said as he stood up from the office chair where he had been sitting, "you should meet Philip Manning. Excuse her, Philip." Lloyd turned to the man who still stood in the doorway. "She's had a rough day."

For a long time, Philip Manning just looked at Emily without saying anything. She saw a strange expression flit across his face, amusement, coupled with sadness. Emily was instantly sorry she had spoken so impulsively. He obviously wasn't used to such spontaneity. As she stood there, embarrassed, he finally spoke. "I'm the Manning Commercial Real Estate and Investment account." He glanced back at Lloyd. "I hope you don't mind me barging in like this. I had no idea you and your staff were still in creative session. Your secretary wasn't at her desk."

Lloyd glanced at his watch. "I lost track of the time. I'm sorry."

"Don't worry about it." Philip waved his arm in a casual gesture of dismissal and then glanced once more at Emily. "I enjoyed viewing one of your famous creative sessions. The bus account is going to benefit from all this. I can only hope that the two of you argue just as effectively when working on my proposals.''

There was a pause in the conversation, and Emily knew she should have taken advantage of the moment to interject some dry, witty comment. But nothing appropriate came to mind. She could only look at the man who stood before her. Philip Manning. There was something powerful about him, as if he had been born to be in charge of things. Although he was about six feet tall, physically he did not seem like a large man. But Emily knew of the stature he held in the business community. Perhaps because of that, he seemed to fill the room as she stood watching him. The company he had conceived and had coaxed into success, Manning Commercial Real Estate and Investments, Inc., was one of Lloyd's most prestigious accounts. Emily already knew, as she moved forward, extended her hand and introduced herself to him, how much she respected Philip Manning. The Dallas business community was atwitter over his triumphs. His successes intimidated her, and for a moment, Emily wanted to turn and run out of the room, away from him.

His eyes caught her and held hers. At first they'd been clear, the color of ice blue, with a steely glint of confidence in them. But now there was something else in them, too. Something guarded. When Philip Manning looked at Emily, his eyes darkened.

"It is nice to meet you." Philip nodded when Lloyd introduced her, and then he turned back to her employer. "Since we've missed our lunch, let's do our business here quickly. I have to get back to the office," he said, looking at his watch. "I have a showing scheduled in twenty minutes."

"I apologize, Philip." Lloyd glanced ruefully at Emily. He hoped he hadn't jeopardized one of his best accounts. Manning was a kind man, but he was demanding where his business interests were concerned.

Philip nodded in acceptance of the apology as he strode toward Lloyd. "I want to talk to you about the copywriting on this brochure, Lloyd." Emily had turned to leave the room, but she froze when she heard his words. He was holding up a brochure she had written. "I need to put together a portfolio about the person who wrote this."

"Is something wrong with the copy, Mr. Manning?" Emily frowned. She was a relentless perfectionist when it came to the work she produced for the agency.

"Emily wrote the brochure, Philip," Lloyd explained.

Philip turned toward Emily. "I like your copy," he told her. He laid the brochure flat on the table beside her and pointed to the second paragraph. "Explain why you wrote this."

Emily glanced over her work and searched for an obvious answer to his question. He was pointing to a paragraph about the sales associates at Manning Real Estate. The copy said that his sales associates were seasoned professionals, that they benefited from and complemented one another because they sought to draw on one another's knowledge of the real estate market and industry.

"That question is too broad for me to answer," Emily said as she turned to face him. "I'm not sure I understand what you want."

Philip laughed, a warm, kind laugh, and leaned toward her. "I want to know why you used each specific word. Did you write this the way you did because there is a basic marketing formula that says my clients will respond favorably?"

Emily thought for a moment before she commented. "There are several definite marketing techniques I used in this brochure. The things Lloyd told me about your company showed me you place great stock in people. Your confidence in your own people is a positive, inspiring thing. I had no choice but to use it as a marketing ploy. It is a very effective one."

Philip Manning studied her with approval. "I'm sponsoring a marketing seminar for my sales associates next week. There will be several specific workshops, many of which my own associates will be leading. At one of these workshops, I want to introduce the marketing tools your agency has produced for Manning."

"That sounds interesting," Emily said.

"Good—" Philip grinned "—because I want you there, Emily."

"You do?" Emily's voice faltered. What did he want her there for? "I'm certain I could learn quite a bit."

"You misunderstand." Philip couldn't hide his amusement. His blue eyes twinkling, he said, "I don't want you there to learn, Emily, I want you there to teach. Actually, I had in mind Lloyd leading the workshop and then quietly introducing his copywriter. But I'd like you to do the workshop. Would you be willing to tell my associates how they can best present this brochure to each potential client?''

Emily couldn't speak for a moment. A professional presentation about the brochure she had written? How could she explain the creative process responsible for the words she had chosen? Certainly, she could explain the marketing tactics she had used. But she chose words because she liked the way they sounded, the way they blended together to form a rhythm, a harmonious idea. How could she present marketing statistics about something she had created because it pleased her? On the other hand, Emily knew her work had impressed Philip Manning. And she did know how the brochure should be presented. She knew the specific points that should be emphasized each time a Manning sales associate placed a brochure in the hands of a potential client.

As Philip Manning and Lloyd went on to discuss the aspects of a new project for the Manning account, Emily jotted several key words down on a notepad. Speaking at the seminar would be an exciting challenge. It also scared her to death. She wanted to refuse, but there was something about Philip Manning, something about the trust he had already placed in her, that made her want to comply. The way he had sensed the small subtleties in her choice of words for the brochure, the way he approved of her choices, made her want to take a risk for him. And it made her want to risk something for herself.

Emily sat beside both of them for a while, in silence, while they talked. And then, finally, when the two of them turned their attention back to her, she nodded. "Okay," she answered somberly. "I'll do it."

"Are you certain?" Philip was concerned. He had seen her hesitation and it had surprised him. He had meant the invitation to be something of a compliment. He hadn't meant to put her on the spot. He touched her just lightly on the elbow, to reassure her. And Emily felt a warm tingling travel the length of her arm. And when she answered him, she was thinking it was strange that here he was, so successful yet still so kind and down-to-earth.

"Yes," she told him quietly looking into his intense ice-blue eyes. They darkened once more before she gave him a cheerfully determined smile. Emily wondered why.

CHAPTER TWO

PHILIP MANNING WAS FIGHTING Dallas rush-hour traffic once again. As far as he could see down Central Expressway to the south, there were lines of cars and trucks and motorcycles, all of them reflecting the blinding fierceness of the searing Texas afternoon sun.

It occurred to him as he gazed on down the endless rows of fenders that there was not one single city bus among them. Maybe he should have taken the bus today. He smiled to himself. He was one of those conservative businessmen Lloyd and Emily had been discussing. And when he thought of Lloyd and Emily, his mind traveled immediately to the marketing seminar next week. There were still a hundred loose ends to tie up for the two-day workshop. One more guest speaker. Extra folding chairs for the front meeting room. The podium for Dr. Larsen's opening presentation Wednesday morning.

He needed to make a list for his assistant. Things always looked manageable to Philip when he wrote them down and made them into lists. Lists made him feel as if he was totally in control. And he liked that feeling.

There were several things Philip had taken control of this week, several things he was extremely pleased with. Emily Lattrell was one of them. There was something about her that he liked. Something apart from her obvious attractiveness.

Emily was a beautiful girl with an impish grin, flouncy bobbed blond hair and huge dark eyes. If Philip had seen her walking past him on the street, he definitely would have turned around to watch her pass. But he was thankful he had met her at Petrie, Simms and Masterson. There was something unusual about Emily Lattrell that set her apart from other beautiful women he had known. She had a compacted energy, mixed quite nicely with a touch of insecurity, that caught him off guard. Philip had walked into Lloyd Masterson's boardroom and felt as if he was being introduced to an unbridled pony.

She was direct and spontaneous. She let her words dash out and tumble over themselves. He liked her haphazard presentation style. And that was only the beginning. Emily's copywriting in the Manning brochure had won first place in a competition sponsored and judged by the Dallas Advertising Federation. Lloyd Masterson had been notified of the award three days ago. He had suggested Philip present the plaque to Emily as a surprise at the end of her marketing presentation. It would lend even more credibility to the things she said and it would give her the recognition she deserved. The entire workshop would have exactly the same directness, the same spontaneity Philip sensed was so much a part of Emily. He was looking forward to hearing her speak.

As Philip drove south of Dallas on the freeway and mentally surveyed the seminar checklist, traffic around him dispersed. He was out of the city. *Breathing room,* he thought. *That's what this drive always offers me.* He had taken this route so many times now that he didn't need to watch the scenery. He could name the landmarks with his eyes shut. The Brookshire Inn. The Country Store and the Shell gas station. The turnoff to his brother's farm on the right. He took it, and seven minutes later he pulled in across the front cattle guard. As the car grated to a stop in the gravel driveway beside the massive white clapboard house, Philip could already tell that nothing had changed. Everything about this beautiful place was subdued now that his sister-in-law, Amanda, was gone. Everything was quiet and closed, as if life on the farm was slowly grinding to a predestined halt.

Nine months ago, Philip recalled, the white lace curtains in every window on the west side of the house would have been flung wide open so everyone inside in every room could see the fiery Texas sunset across the blacklands. The sunset was just one of the things about living in the country that Amanda Manning had always held dear. She was forever talking about the meadowlarks warbling from across the pasture. She always picked the sour native Texas grapes that grew wild on the rickety grape arbor his brother, Clint, had laboriously constructed for her the year they'd married. And how she had loved the geraniums she always kept in yellow plaster pots on the second-story balcony that ran the length of the spacious white wooden porch below it.

"Uncle Philip!" a boy's voice called from the front porch and Philip moved forward to greet his nephew,

Greg. In Greg's fifteen years, the boy had already grown to be so much of a man, he reflected. Philip hated to admit it to anyone, but of all three of Amanda and Clint's children, Greg was his favorite. Greg had been his firstborn nephew, and he was the closest thing to a son that Philip would ever know. It was a sad thought but an honest one. Philip was thirty-two years old, almost thirty-three, and for many reasons, he had decided that marriage was not for him. It was a matter of trust. He had opened himself up once to that kind of love a long, long time ago. And even though he was a forgiving man, this one particular wound was still festering. Every time Philip did his best to put the past behind him, something would happen to remind him that his heart hadn't healed, and there he would be, wishing he could forget. So he had long since decided to remain married to his real estate investment firm. His deals were his sons and his daughters. And that made Philip Manning love the people closest to him, his younger brother Clint and Amanda and the kids, all the more.

Philip carried so many memories of them all, from long ago, before Amanda's operation, before things had become so incredibly complicated. He would never forget the October when Greg was six, when Amanda and Clint had gathered the family together to announce that there was going to be a new baby soon. Four-year-old Lisa had been excited and adorable, but it had been Greg who had made the day extra special, proudly displaying his knowledge of where babies come from.

"That new baby is in Mommy's tummy," he'd told everyone assuredly, and then he had marched over to Amanda, climbed into her lap and put his ear against her abdomen.

Just then, Amanda's stomach had growled, and she'd looked up sheepishly.

Greg had been overjoyed. "I can hear the baby!" he had shrieked. "I can hear the baby in Mom's stomach and he's in there driving a car."

Driving a car still seemed like one of the most exciting things in the world to Greg. Philip wasn't surprised now to see him holding up two hands covered with axle grease. "Dad and the girls are inside. I'd hug you, but I don't think you want this stuff all over your good suit coat."

"Very perceptive kid." Philip grinned. "I'll take that hug later, though, after you've scrubbed those hands. What vehicle are you operating on this evening?"

"The Studebaker." Greg nodded in the direction of the wooden garage that doubled as a storage shed. "I'm trying to put in a new steering column, but it isn't going very well. I keep finding ball bearings all over the floor, and I don't have any idea where they're coming from."

Philip chuckled. "Sounds like you could use a good auto mechanic."

"I could," Greg called back over his shoulder as he started across the yard toward the garage.

Philip stood for a moment and watched Greg walk away before he pushed open the screen door and went inside. The front room was dark and empty, but from somewhere upstairs he could hear a Mister, Mister song blasting on a stereo. At least Lisa was home.

"Where is everybody?"

"We're in the kitchen," Philip heard his brother call back. "We're washing dishes."

When Philip entered the room, Clint turned to him immediately. It took a moment for his younger niece, Bethany, to do the same. Bethany had been born with a hearing defect in both ears. No one had known anything was wrong until she was almost a year old and her pediatrician had become concerned because she wasn't trying to imitate sounds. Clint and Amanda had worked with her deafness ever since then, and she had gone to a special school where she had learned to sign with her hands and then to read lips. By the time she was in the third grade, her teachers had decided to channel her back into the mainstream of public schools. She had caught up so quickly that even the kids in her class hadn't realized she couldn't hear. She was nine now, and she could read lips and understand almost every word that was being said. And when she saw her uncle in the kitchen, she ran and hugged him.

Philip had grown accustomed to speaking slowly whenever Bethany was in the room. He didn't really need to do that anymore for her, but it had become a habit. Even now if there was ever a big word he wasn't certain she knew how to spell, he would bend down beside her and lovingly take her in one arm and sign it for her. "Hey, kid," he greeted her as he bent beside her. "Jumping Jehosophat," he said, signing the words. He had taught her how to spell "Jehosophat" when he'd visited the week before. "You are growing. Aren't you twenty years old yet?"

"Nope." She giggled as he squeezed her to him. It was a silly question but one that, in a complicated way, was appropriate for Bethany. She had taken it upon herself to become the little mother in this family. During the months that had passed since Amanda's operation, Bethany had purposely taken on the burden of an entire household. Now it seemed to take immense effort to get her to laugh. She planned meals and washed dishes and acted thirty-five, and both her father and Philip were worried about her. It was a rotten deal, a little girl taking over the job of a homemaker.

"Did you see Amanda today?" Philip asked his brother somberly. *Amanda. That doesn't even seem like her real name,* Philip thought. But it was what the family called her now. Clint had taken to calling her Manderly as he had grown to love her. It had been a term of endearment then, but it had suited her. The name echoed her spirit, her laughter and the silly nonsense songs she had loved to sing to the children when they were young.

Clint had not called her Manderly since her operation eight months ago. The name was for someone as vivacious as his sister-in-law had once been. It scarcely seemed suitable for the woman who lay in a coma in W. C. Tenery Community Hospital.

Amanda had gone to the hospital one morning to have minor surgery. And the surgery had been successful. But Amanda's physicians couldn't stop the bleeding afterward, and her body had gone into shock almost immediately—despite the seventeen units of blood they had given her. She had fallen into a coma. The child care she had arranged and the frozen dinners she had left for Clint to microwave during the three days she was supposed to be away became permanent. She wasn't coming home. And so she became Amanda to everyone in the family again. Not their mother, Manderly. Clint had had to sit down and sign the spelling of Amanda to Bethany, who cried almost as hard as her father.

"I see her every day. A nurse lets me in before visiting hours every morning. That way I can read to her before I come home, get the kids up and start working." Clint reached out to his younger daughter and pulled her to him. Since his wife had been gone, he'd become very demonstrative with his children. Holding one another frequently had become their way of holding the family together.

"Is she responding to sounds at all?" Philip's voice was gentle. He didn't know how much he should say in front of Bethany. He did know that she was strong, too. They had all been.

"Yes," Clint said firmly. This morning he had been reading to her, and she had flinched. It was a small movement in her right arm, and the doctor suggested it was an unconscious reflex. "I have to take that as a positive sign. I have no other choice. She's coming back to us. Maybe tomorrow. Maybe a dozen years from now after the kids have graduated from college. I know she wants to come back to us. And I know I'm strong enough to help her."

"Are you?" Philip was concerned about his brother. Clint looked even more exhausted, more gaunt and gray, then he had looked just after Amanda's ordeal had begun.

"Yes." Clint's tone was firm once again. He was getting used to this concern from everyone. His family. Amanda's doctors. His business colleagues. But he had no other choice than to remain strong. He was the children's father. And on the day he had married Amanda, he had vowed to love her, protect her, be there for her, until the day she died. She was his life. "I am. I have to be. I need her."

Philip hugged Bethany once again and took the dish towel from her. "You're a great kid, Bethany." He glanced pointedly at his brother. "I'm glad somebody's around to take care of your dad. He gets this crazy idea sometimes that he has to carry the whole world on his shoulders. By the way, where's your sister?"

"She's upstairs." Bethany looked worried. "She's mad."

"She isn't mad at all of us," Clint reassured Bethany without preamble as he placed a stack of hand-painted plates back in the cabinet. "She's only mad at me. She's sulking up there." Clint turned to Philip and grinned. Philip was relieved to see him smiling again so quickly. "She's trying to make me feel guilty for something I refuse to feel guilty about—acknowledging the small but very pertinent fact that, yes, at thirteen years of age, she's still a child."

Philip laughed. "I keep forgetting how much I knew about the world when I was thirteen. What is it she knows more about than you do?"

"The junior high field trip to Austin. It's next week. A big group of kids is going on a Greyhound bus. They're touring the state capitol building and then spending the night at a camp. I think she's too young to go off on a trip like that. I might consider it if I could go along as a chaperone. But I just can't get away from the other kids and leave Amanda and my work that long."

"How's work coming?" Philip was keeping a close eye on his brother's real estate listings. He and his brother had the same instinctive feel for finances, properties and investments. They had inherited their talents from their father, Bryce Manning, who had been a successful stockbroker in Houston for many, many years before his death. Philip was thrilled to see Clint becoming successful. At a time in Philip's life when pursuing his own career had been a driving force, he had watched while his brother gave it all up to fall in love with and marry Amanda. Amanda, his brother's beloved Manderly, had wanted so desperately to live away from the city and Clint had agreed, after a month of indecision, to move his real estate practice to Amanda's family farm near Waxahachie. Living in the country the way he did, Clint could not maintain the cronies, the constant contacts, that were vital to a flourishing real estate career. He had made himself remain satisfied with the subdued career of a residential broker in the quaint Texas town. For years most of his listings were farm acreages and Depression-era drafty houses lined with gingerbread trim.

The boundaries of Dallas were slowly moving southward, bringing with them an entirely new group of clients for Clint's Waxahachie real estate firm. More and more businessmen wanted to work in the city but to live away from the frustration and the urban frazzle of hordes of people, traffic and skyscrapers. As Dallas encroached on Waxahachie, a commuter life-style was becoming plausible for more and more people. The young professionals were moving to Waxahachie in droves, and they were purchasing the properties indicative of their flourishing careers. Clint was selling huge acreages with executive homes, tennis courts and swimming pools. It was success Clint had deserved for a long time. And because of Amanda's illness, the timing was ironically perfect. He kept a storefront office downtown, but he did most of his work from his study at home. That way he was home for the children.

Philip felt some sort of intense need to help his brother, to give him strength, to help him find the things that could be salvaged from his broken way of life and sustain him as he put his life back together. "You've done well," he commented as he watched Clint thumbing through an album of real estate listing photographs. "You need to have something else to hang on to besides the possibility that Amanda might wake up tomorrow. I'm glad to see you dealing with something you have more control over."

Clint turned toward his brother and studied his face. Clint's face was expressionless. Clint knew Philip was losing hope. Philip ran his life the same way he ran his business. Everything was written down in lists in indelible ink. "It isn't that easy."

"I know." Philip's voice was low. And then he changed the subject. "So tell me about Lisa. What's going on with your middle kid?"

"I wish I knew." Clint shook his head. "She scares me. She's like this miniature Amanda that is sometimes a woman and sometimes a dumb little kid. She's furious with me most of the time, and when I try to find out what's wrong she runs upstairs and turns on her stereo. Sometimes I think the Communists invented heavy metal rock music. It is a definite defense for teenagers against telling anyone what their true thoughts might be." Clint leaned his head back and looked blankly at the ceiling. Then suddenly he winked at his brother. "I don't mean to give you the wrong impression. Me and the kids...hey...we're doing fine."

"I thought so." Philip was grinning now, too. Clint's good humor would help him present this new idea. "That's why I brought you this. Don't get mad," he added quickly. "It's just a suggestion." Philip pulled a two-color brochure from his inside suit coat pocket and dropped it on the desk beside Clint's real estate album. If Clint agreed to try the service he was suggesting, it would take some of the pressure off where the kids were concerned. "The lady who runs this business rented office space from me today. We got to talking while she was signing her lease. I told her about you and the kids, and she suggested I pass on one of her brochures."

"What is this?" Clint was bewildered as he fingered it. "Absolutely Moms? Sounds like this lady has an interesting idea. But Philip, why are you showing this to me? Bethany might benefit from it, but I doubt seriously that my two teenagers need a nanny service."

"Read the brochure," Philip urged. "This is not a nanny service. These gals are sharp. Many of them were career professionals who opted for a life taking care of children, in a very nontraditional way. They are well educated—some of them even have Ph.D.'s. You just said yourself that one of your teenagers is still a child. And these ladies don't scrub floors. They join the family and act like adopted mothers for as long as you need them." Philip had been worrying about how to introduce this idea to Clint ever since Abbie Carson had signed her lease contract. Abbie's company was a national one, even international, but she was just opening her Dallas offices. And elsewhere, her ideas had met with tremendous success. "These women come to your house as actual substitute mothers. They communicate with kids and they dole out hugs and they bake brownies."

"You can buy brownies at a bakery."

Philip was undaunted. "These moms chaperone school field trips," he informed his brother. "They cheer at Little League baseball games. They spend time with one kid so you can spend time with another. You might even have time to get your hands greasy with your son out there on that Studebaker."

"Now you're really grasping at straws."

"I'm not," Philip stated dryly. "You need this. It's time all of you started letting someone else take Amanda's place, even if it is just paying somebody to come here and bake brownies."

"There's no need for anyone to take Amanda's place," Clint snapped. "She's my wife."

Philip had known this discussion was going to be difficult. "You owe it to yourself and to the kids to have someone here taking some responsibility for this household. It would get the kids used to having someone around the house again. And that would open a great many doors for you... even if you don't want them open at this point. If Amanda does come home soon, you don't want her to find her household in a total shambles, do you?"

"Maybe you're right." Clint was still staring at the ceiling.

"Of course I'm right." *Now,* thought Philip, *I'm getting somewhere.* "Call this lady," he urged, not quite so gently this time. "I'll bet she matches you up with some spunky gray-haired grandma who turns all four of your lives upside down."

"I don't know." There was a strange conspiratorial grin on Clint's face, as if he was going to tell his brother some interesting personal secret. "Do you think if I called this lady, this Abbie Carson, she might find an Absolutely Mom who knows how to pick out—" Clint lowered his voice further "—bras?"

Philip raised his eyebrows. And then he lowered his voice, too. "Don't tell me! Why do you need to know that?"

"It's Bethany," Clint whispered. "She came in here the other day and asked me if I'd go shopping with her."

Philip couldn't help laughing. He was certain that Clint had never imagined himself in this situation before. And neither had he.

"Quit laughing." Clint plopped his chin atop his palm. "She really thinks she needs one. And she wants me to help her pick out her first pair of panty hose, too."

"Can't she just go to the store with her friends and try that stuff on?" Philip was just as bewildered about those feminine things as his brother was.

"I don't think so." Clint shook his head seriously. "You have to read the package and measure yourself and decide whether you're a B or an A or an F or something." He rolled a pencil across the surface of his mahogany desk. "I really do need help on this one."

Philip waved the Absolutely Moms brochure in Clint's face. He was laughing again. "You had better call Abbie Carson. Soon."

"Maybe I will." Clint snatched the brochure from his brother's hand. "Maybe I will."

And this time, when Philip hugged his brother and the two of them stepped back and continued laughing, Philip thought how much he loved them all. Amanda was everything to Clint, but Clint and the kids were everything to Philip. After all his real estate deals and his successes were said and done, these people and this place were all he had to hang on to.

CHAPTER THREE

FIVE DAYS LATER, as Emily Lattrell made her presentation at the Manning Commercial Real Estate Seminar, her metamorphosis took place just as Philip had predicted it would. Emily forgot about the podium, the people and the applause. It was as if she was in a creative session again, pacing around the stage at the front of the room because she was too exhilarated to stand still. She let her ideas emerge and playfully take shape willy-nilly, and the wonderful part of it was that her ideas were good ones, effective ones. The faces in the audience melded together to form one face, one smiling new friend. Then, when Emily turned to make her way down the stage steps to rounds of applause, Lloyd rushed up to the stage and stopped her and handed her an award that she didn't even know she had won.

And after she was finished, people she didn't know kept grasping her hand, introducing themselves and complimenting her on the presentation and her writing and her award. It was a heady experience. And as Emily made her way through the milling people and the shaking hands, it occurred to her she ought to find Philip Manning and thank him.

There were times when Emily was shy, when she was frightened to approach people who seemed so much more important than she was, but she was making a constant conscious effort to overcome some of that timidity. If she didn't thank Philip Manning now, she might have to call his office later, maybe even stop by and see him, and that would be much, much harder for her.

Emily searched for Philip Manning in the crowd. She decided to take the proverbial bull by the horns. Her father had taught her to do that. Her father had taught her many things. He had taught her to be persistent, to be a success by caring about people. As Emily had grown up, she had watched her father make a success out of the United National Bank of Decatur. She had watched him do it by doing much more than just offering the most contemporary banking services in the small North Texas town. She had seen him come out of his office to greet Mrs. Sliegner when she was making a twenty-dollar deposit into her husband's savings account. He would have treated someone making a $20,000 deposit exactly the same way.

When United National had to deny a loan to an applicant, Emily's father made an appointment with the applicant and explained why. And since he had been involved in banking long before automatic teller days, he had made certain each of his tellers kept a basket of lollipops and a box of dog biscuits to distribute to children and dogs respectively when a customer came to the drive-up window with other members of the family in the car. Martin Lattrell had made it his business to believe in people.

It had been Emily's mother who had been so habitually untrusting. Two or three times a week, she would remind Martin of how gullible he was. "I had a cocktail with Marge Fletcher at the club this afternoon," Emily had heard her tell her father one evening. "Marge says your bank loaned $120,000 for the Bridger project. I can't believe you would speculate like that, Martin. A shopping mall in a little town this close to Fort Worth and Dallas just isn't feasible. You're going to lose it all. I can feel it. I can't believe you'd do this. John got turned down by three major banks before he came to you."

Emily's father did lose some money in business dealings, but his faith in others had never dealt his bank the fatal financial blow that his wife was certain would come. Instead, the citizens of Decatur kept his bank alive with their twenty-dollar deposits, and finally, twelve years after United National had been chartered, Martin Lattrell had awakened one morning to find that he was an overnight success. The bank had flourished into an establishment with well over $63 million in assets. He had been featured in a small article on page fifteen in the *Wall Street Journal*. And the citizens of Decatur had elected him to serve as president of the Decatur Chamber of Commerce. He had done it. And he had achieved his ambitions strictly by caring about people. He hadn't even neglected the people he cared for in his own family.

The only thing that had suffered in the creation of Martin's success had been his relationship with Emily's mother. And United National had had nothing to do with that. Alcohol had done the damage.

Emily's mother was an alcoholic. She had been stricken with the disease ever since Emily could remember. At first Emily had been too young to understand her mother's strange anger. It had been like living with two people, one who was unhappy but loving and one who was angry. Emily's mother would be gone for hours, and then she would come home and Emily would lie awake in her bed for hours listening to her mother shout at her father. There were times she was afraid to go to sleep for fear she would dream about her parents killing each other. And when Emily's younger brother, Jimmy, got old enough, he had the same nightmares. As she thought back over her childhood, the memories of those nights seemed to stretch on forever, Emily in her bare feet and her flannel nightgown sitting on Jimmy's bed, stroking his shoulders, telling him not to cry. And when Emily had grown older, she sometimes asked her mother why she shouted, why she threw things and broke things. And Emily's mother hadn't remembered.

"That didn't happen, Emily," she would say firmly, her lips pursed. Her answers were stern and, now that Emily herself was an adult, she had to admit they were probably honest, too. She had asked her mother so many times why she did this or why she did that, and her mother had had no idea what she was talking about. She had been in a stupor. So Emily had learned not to talk to her. She had learned to feel guilty for something she didn't understand. She had learned as a child how difficult it was to share her feelings with anyone.

It was almost a relief when Emily returned home from the University of Texas on her first vacation from school to find that her parents were divorcing. Her mother was moving to an apartment in Fort Worth and entering an alcohol rehabilitation program. And Martin was going to do his best to get on with his own life. Emily had dared to hope again.

But Emily's mother bounced from one alcohol program to another, and two years later, Emily began to face reality. Alcohol had drowned the very essence of a person who must have once loved her. And although she tried to rationalize her feelings, Emily felt as if in some way she was responsible. Perhaps if she'd been different, her mother could have confided in her, or loved her more, or... And even if she knew it wasn't logical, Emily felt she owed her father a debt that she could never repay for fighting so hard to keep his family on an even keel all those years. But she still felt like a rudderless vessel, blown back and forth all her life by a force she didn't understand and had probably somehow invoked. There were times alone, when, if she stopped to think about her past and her family, the guilt and insecurity threatened to overwhelm her.

That was one reason Emily depended on her career. She needed the competition, the gratification, the awards of advertising. They proved something to her, that she was okay, that she would survive. But no matter how hard she tried, the cold marketing profit graphs and the gold plaques with her name on them couldn't chase away all her grief and her feelings of inadequacy. She felt as if she had failed her mother somehow, at a time when it had counted the most for both of them, when she was a child. And that profound failure was something she couldn't talk about. It was something she desperately wanted to hide.

There was a hand-stitched baby quilt up in the attic that Emily's mother had sewn during the nine months when Emily had been on the way. It was covered with tiny brown cross-stitched teddy bears flopping and tumbling over their own heads. Below them, in the center of the quilt, Emily's mother had backstitched a poem she'd written in bright royal blue letters:

Good night, sleep tight, my sweet baby bear.
The man on the moon keeps you in his care.
He embraces the night, beams a starlight smile
Beckons you to follow him a milky way mile
On the back of moonbeams I once flew—
And now that journey I leave to you.

There were times now when Emily would drive home to her father's house in Decatur, and when nobody knew it, she would pull the old quilt out and finger its stitches and think of how much love had gone into them. Then she would go with her father and sit beside him in the third-row pew at church on Sunday morning. The whole time everybody was singing and the preacher was giving his sermon, she would sit motionless, her slender fingers locked inside her father's firm strong ones, thinking about a mother's love that she couldn't remember and trying hopelessly to understand where it had gone.

Other people saw Emily's confusion with herself and her emotions as insecurity, insecurity that Emily had to overcome time and time again. She did so now as she searched the meeting room for Philip Manning. She didn't have to search hard to find him. He was standing in the doorway greeting his sales associates as they exited the room. People were milling around him, and he was shaking hands and nodding and looking satisfied. It was obvious to anyone watching that he was in command of this show. There was something magnetic about the man. Even a stranger at the seminar would have guessed he was someone important.

Emily stood in the crowd for a moment and watched him before she called out his name. She watched as he smiled at one of his associates. It was a broad, casual smile that produced tiny wrinkles at the corners of each eye. The lines on his face, the creases that ran from his nose around each corner of his mouth when his grin was at its widest, added definition and masculinity to Philip's already handsome face. His chocolate brown hair was swept softly back from his temples to reveal a hint of pepper gray among the brown. Even the style of it, cut short in a precise curve around his ears and across the nape of his neck, made him look distinguished and larger than life to her.

Philip's eyebrows were just a touch darker brown on the inside of each arch, and the coloring there seemed to draw his eyes together and to expand them. Philip had a way of watching the person he was talking to and never diverting his eyes, as if the present conversation and the person in front of him were the only things capable of commanding his attention. Emily noticed that the intensity of his eyes seemed to draw people out again and again.

Finally she called out to him. She plopped her notes on a folding chair with a determined smack and wove her way toward him.

Philip's ice blue eyes locked with hers as she glided toward him, smiling, carrying the gold plaque tucked beneath one arm. Her grin broadened as she approached him. "You're the one who got me into this." Her words sounded flippant, but her heart was beating so fast that she felt breathless. She was putting on a beautifully timed act for him, one that she had honed to perfection during the past years as an advertising executive. She didn't dare let him see how nervous she was. "It looks like you're the one I'm going to have to thank for it. Thanks for involving me in the seminar. I was honored to participate."

"I'm the one who should thank you, Emily Lattrell." He said her full name warmly. "This workshop was even more successful than I expected it to be. You sent my associates away with good, useful information." He nodded toward the plaque she was carrying. "And you obviously impressed members of the advertising federation, too. Congratulations."

"You're the one who offered me the challenge." Her statement was an honest one. She was smiling up at him as she spoke, and as he looked down at her, she reminded him of Clint's description of Lisa. She looked childlike—so dainty and small to him as she turned her petite elfin face in his direction. But she was an adult who knew her craft and had just conducted a successful workshop. She was like Lisa, part little girl and part woman. And as he watched her, Philip felt a strange feeling of protectiveness building within him. "Sometime next week I'll have my administrative assistant sit down and bang out an official thank-you note to you. But since I'm here right now and feeling on top of the world, I thought I'd come over here and shake your hand in person."

Philip extended his hand to her, and when he took her delicate fingers with the mauve-glossed nails into his own, he could already feel her pulling it away from him.

He wondered why she was being so formal. She had certainly been more relaxed when they were laughing about snorkelers and brides and men in jogging suits riding the Dallas city bus. He decided she was nervous. And he didn't want her to come away from his business seminar feeling unsure of herself. She had done a great job. He decided to keep her talking just a little while longer. "How's the city bus campaign coming along?"

"The same." He detected a hint of humor in her tone. "Lloyd and I are still in the 'compromising' phase." She shrugged, her eyes twinkling, and she reminded Philip of a little girl again. "We're the same place we were when you walked in on us the other day. But it's getting there."

"It's going to be a tremendous ad campaign once you and Lloyd finish hacking away at each other." Then Philip gazed down at her and grinned. And he asked her to lunch. He didn't exactly know why. He just knew she seemed natural and happy and honest, and he wanted to be with her a while longer. He didn't know when he would see her again. And just seeing the laughter in her eyes made him forget the pressures of putting on a seminar like this one. Emily was pleased with his invitation. "Thank you," she answered him softly. "I'd like that." *And I deserve it,* she reminded herself. She had done an excellent job at his seminar. But there was something more about his invitation, something about the way he was looking at her that made it hard for her to look away.

Emily waved goodbye to Lloyd and gathered her notes. Philip Manning motioned to her from the doorway and she followed him. They were almost out the door when a deep female voice called out his name from behind them.

Emily saw Philip's body become tense. He had obviously recognized the voice before he stopped and turned around to face the speaker.

"Hello, Morgan," he said coolly. He kept just enough control in his voice not to sound cold. His facial expression was neutral. Neither Emily nor the woman he called Morgan could have read any emotion there.

Philip had become so conditioned by Emily Lattrell's laughter during the past hour, so drawn by her smile, that seeing Morgan Brockner at the seminar was like a slap in the face. He hadn't issued her an invitation to this event. What was Morgan Brockner doing here at all? Morgan stood beside him now, her voice and her face oozing feigned gratitude, as she waved an invitation in the air. He hadn't sent it to her. Who had? Philip wondered.

"I'm impressed with your company," she told Philip slowly. "Very impressed."

It could have been yours, Philip wanted to say. But he didn't dare say it, not here, not in front of Emily. But then Morgan Brockner didn't need his company. She had one of her own.

He reached out and grasped Emily's elbow. He desperately wanted to get as far away from Morgan as possible, and the sooner, the better. Being anywhere near the woman reminded him of an old wound that hadn't healed—and she had been the cause. He was relieved, as he gripped Emily's arm, that he had someone here with him to hold on to. "I'd like you to meet Emily—Emily Lattrell, this is Morgan Brockner, president of Brockner Associates." His grin was a wry one when he turned to Emily. "Morgan is my biggest competitor here in Dallas. The material you wrote and discussed this morning was designed to give my company an edge over Brockner."

Emily studied Morgan Brockner for a moment before extending her hand. She thought it was odd that this woman should be here, attending business seminars at Philip's company.

Morgan Brockner's name was just as familiar to Emily as Philip's had been. Lloyd had tried to get the Brockner account a long time ago, when her business had been smaller, before Philip Manning had offered a retainer to the agency. Lloyd didn't believe in handling competing accounts.

"Hello, Morgan," Emily said as she extended her hand to the woman. "It's nice to meet you."

"I enjoyed your little presentation, honey. It was quite—" Morgan glanced back at Philip "—interesting." Morgan did not take her hand.

"Thank you." Emily nodded meekly as she folded her arm behind her.

Morgan was speaking to Philip now, and Emily felt as if she might as well have been invisible. "How is the Robertson deal coming along? You close on that two weeks from Wednesday, don't you?"

"Yes," Philip said stiffly, "we do." He was on his guard now. How did Morgan know about the Robertson contract? It was a commercial real estate sale that, at this point, was supposed to remain a confidential business transaction. And as he stared at the woman before him, he thought of everything he knew about her, and he was reminded that she never left anything to chance. She probably had his office bugged. He wouldn't put that past her. Morgan was someone Philip knew he could never trust. And the sad fact was, she seemed to enjoy reminding him of it.

As Emily watched the exchange between Philip Manning and this woman, she couldn't help but notice his reaction as the two of them talked. He had seemed to literally harden, as if his face had turned to stone the moment Morgan Brockner had called his name. And he hadn't let his guard down since then once. Something sharp and venomous hung in the air between them.

Philip broke the tension with a slight, controlled smile. "I'm sure you'll excuse us, Morgan."

"Certainly." Morgan flashed Emily an almost imperceptible smile. "I didn't mean to detain you."

Emily and Philip walked to his car in silence, and Philip held the door for her as Emily slid into the front seat of his charcoal gray Audi 5000-S. And as she studied the passing scenery, it was as if Philip was a million miles away, years ago in time, thinking about Morgan and how she had betrayed him.

Clint and Manderly had shared so much richness, so much texture, in their lives together, he reflected. For him, there had been only one woman a long, long time ago, who had made him think he could have that richness in his life, too. Morgan Brockner.

Once upon a time, he and Morgan had planned to share their businesses and their lives and live happily ever after. He had met her during his junior year at Texas A&M University in Dr. Magnuson's corporate management class. She had been everything she was now—polished, poised, treacherously beautiful. They had worked together on a group project for the class, and one night, when the three other members of the group had gone to pick up a pizza at the all-night place down the street, Philip had invited Morgan to a football game.

Looking back on it now, Philip realized he should have seen the warning signals even as their relationship began. Morgan had never seemed to laugh or to do anything silly. She had been intensely serious about her future. When he thought back on it now, he realized that they had never discussed his future, only hers. When he wanted to talk about his family or his fraternity brothers, she wanted to talk about the investment firm she was going to build. And one day in class, she had passed him a note that said simply: "I love you. Let's get married someday."

Philip had visibly paled there in corporate management class. He wasn't certain that he loved Morgan. She was always there for him and very beautiful, and he was the envy of all his fraternity brothers when she waltzed into a room on his arm. But he was uncertain about marrying her. He didn't want to lead her on, and he wasn't sure the things he was feeling for her could be classified as love. It all seemed so logical to him, the two of them together. Their relationship was something that had happened between them because of convenience and not because of passion or romance. And they had continued talking about building a business together as if they were talking about a marriage.

When the time came for the two of them to march confidently across the commencement platform with the other graduating business majors, Philip had decided to give committing himself a try. He wanted to see what it was like having her as a partner. He would start by asking her to become a partner in the real estate firm he was intent on building. Maybe later, they would be partners for life. His father had already agreed to finance the initial operation for him.

Morgan had accepted his offer on the spot. In fact, she hadn't seemed too terribly surprised. When she'd said yes, she had reminded him of an overzealous actress who had had her Oscar acceptance speech prepared for weeks. He realized later that he had hit upon the perfect analogy. An actress accepting an Oscar. He knew now that that day had been the first time he had almost seen through her.

Five months later, when the company's first major commercial deal had come through, Philip signed it over to Morgan. He had made the sale himself. The property consisted of three storefront offices near a shopping center, and the commission had been substantial. And Philip thought Morgan had been worried about money. He wasn't. He had his father's backing. He had enough capital to see him through three years at a loss, if need be. But Morgan needed something to live on. She had been out beating the streets without much luck for five months. Giving her this transaction was Philip's way of showing Morgan how he felt about their future together. He was willing to give them a chance. He left the contract on her desk with a note thanking her for sharing his successes. Thinking back on it now, Philip wondered if his note had been the last straw for her. Morgan had never wanted to share anyone's successes—she had wanted to generate her own.

The next morning when he had barged triumphantly into her office to see what she had to say to him, all her belongings were gone. The office was empty.

Morgan had run away with Philip's contract. For days, when he'd tried to call her, she hadn't answered her phone. And sometime during the next week when she had answered the phone, she had a new official title to place on her résumé. Morgan Brockner. Sole owner and president of Brockner Associates. She had taken the commission from the contract and had used it as capital to start a competing company.

For months Philip couldn't accept the fact that Morgan had seduced his trust, then betrayed it. But as the days went by, Brockner Associates grew with surprising dispatch. Morgan Brockner had used him. Everything they had shared together—the hopes, the goals—had been a farce. Morgan had picked him out from corporate management class for her own use just as easily and as meticulously as she had pulled a dress-for-success outfit from her closet. Everything she did was a means to an end.

It wasn't the fact that Morgan had betrayed their business partnership that still bothered Philip. It was the fact that she had betrayed his personal trust. He had opened himself up to her and had given her the very things that made him what he was—his dreams, his successes. When she left the office, Philip felt as if a part of him had been amputated. She had fooled him for two and a half years. He was never going to be fooled again. He had stumbled along, bitter, proud and sad, and he had survived by giving his soul to his company. It was ironic now. Morgan was probably the one major reason he had been so successful in building Manning Real Estate and Investment. He had decided to defeat her at her own game. He made certain that, whenever the sales figures came in at end of the fiscal year, Manning Real Estate and Investment was just a bit farther up the scale than Brockner Associates. His goal was to be better than she was—always. And gradually the bitterness he felt toward Morgan had subsided and changed into a determination to keep Manning Real Estate on top. His real estate investment firm was his family. He had built it from the ground up in much the same way he would have raised a child. And sometimes when he had trouble understanding Clint's deep pain and his fight to regain Manderly, Philip would picture himself and pretend something terrible had happened to his company and he would wonder if, like Clint, he would find strength enough to struggle and survive.

CHAPTER FOUR

THREE BROCHURES FOR Absolutely Moms, Abbie Carson's company, lay on the dashboard of Philip's car. Emily picked up one and leafed through it. Philip Manning hadn't spoken to her once since they had left the marketing seminar after meeting Morgan Brockner. They drove on a bit farther while she read the brochure, and at last Philip glanced over at her. Emily smiled at him, and when she did, the hardness in his face softened a bit. He turned his gaze back to the road, and then he nodded toward the pamphlet she still held in her hand. "Did you read that? Abbie Carson has quite a business."

"This is nice," Emily commented. She was always looking at brochures, analyzing them and getting ideas for her own work for clients. This one was handsomely done. "They've made nice ink and paper choices." She pondered whether she should say more. "Which company put this together for her?"

Philip glanced at her and grinned slightly, then once more he turned his attention back to the road. "Are your interests purely personal? Or might they be professional, as well?" he asked her pointedly.

Emily laughed. "Both, I suppose." She flipped through the brochure once again. "I was just wondering what the competition is putting together these days. I'm always curious.''

''That particular brochure was designed by a San Francisco agency. Abbie Carson keeps her corporate home office south of there in a town on the coast. Abbie is going to be in Dallas for a while, though. She's opening a branch office. She leased office space from me in Stemmons Towers.''

''Is that why you're carrying her brochures around?'' Emily asked. ''Or are you going to sign up with her to become an Absolutely Mom?'' It was an outrageous thing to say just then, when she just barely knew him, but she was desperate to bring some of the life back into his eyes. She cocked her head and gazed at him with a slightly unsteady grin. ''Or is she trying to find someone to mother you?''

Finally he laughed. The tension seemed to lift in the car. ''Yeah,'' he answered her. ''That's it. I was thinking about signing up. To be a mom.''

''You'd probably be a good one.'' Emily was grinning.

''Abbie Carson is going to need someone to update that brochure for her Dallas market,'' Philip said casually. ''I'll give her your name.''

''Thanks.'' Emily was always grateful for new business contacts. Philip turned the car to leave the highway. Then he glanced at Emily again. He was glad she had come. He needed someone to talk to, someone to take his mind off his unsettling encounter with Morgan. Even if they had just joked about Absolutely Moms and talked about nothing important, her conversation was still a nice diversion. And then, when the light turned green, Philip decided to explain to her why he really had the brochure in his car. There was something about Emily that seemed natural and soft, and he let himself feel drawn to her for a moment. He didn't know exactly what it was—maybe the fact she had remained silent most of the drive and hadn't attempted to force a conversation in the wake of his brooding, but he sensed that she was a good listener and a fair person. Quietly, with just a touch of resolve in his voice, he began to tell Emily about his brother and the kids. He told her about Amanda and the farm and the tragic results of his sister-in-law's operation. And then he paused. "That's why I'm trying to talk Clint into calling Abbie Carson. Those kids need somebody, and so does he. And someday maybe they'll have their mother back."

Emily watched as he spoke, and she saw Philip's firmly chiseled jaw seem to sag. Something sadly vulnerable washed across his face, and she was surprised at the melancholy look in his eyes. She suppressed an urge to reach across the car and hug him. She was tremendously touched that he had chosen to tell her about his family. There were times when she needed to tell someone about her family, too, but she simply couldn't. Her mother's alcoholism was something she kept hidden within her, something she shared with no one. And Emily found a strength in Philip, a strength that she didn't have, because he was able to talk about things that mattered to him.

"What happened the first time the children saw Amanda after she had gone into the coma?"

Philip was shaking his head. "Nothing. They haven't seen her since. Clint won't let them visit her."

"Why?" Emily was shocked.

"It's one of those confounded things he can't let go of." Philip unconsciously swept his fingers through his hair. "He wants the kids to think of Amanda the way she used to be. He doesn't want them to see her lying there looking frail and fragile. He's afraid they'll see her and begin to lose hope. Above all else, he doesn't want them to do that."

"He'd be surprised, I'll bet." Emily was staring out the window, letting her eyes follow the numerous skyscrapers as the car whizzed past them. "Kids have a knack for imagining things to be ten times worse than they really are." She remembered her own nightmares all too clearly. Her parents hadn't killed each other, after all. But there were times she still wondered how close they had actually come.

As they drove on into the city together, a telephone rang somewhere inside the car. Philip flipped open the leather armrest to reveal a mobile telephone, and he answered it on the second ring. "Hello? Sure," he said. "It's fine. Go ahead." There was a pause before he said, "Clint? What's up, bud?"

Emily watched as Philip's expression hardened once again. "No." Another pause. "That doesn't sound good. I know how she was feeling earlier. Do you think she would have gone on the field trip without your permission?" Philip cast a sideways glance at Emily. "That does make sense, though. No, it's fine. I'll get someone to cover for me this afternoon. In fact, I'm almost there already. Clint, stay calm. It won't be the worst." He stopped speaking for a moment and just listened and looked desolate. "It just won't be. We won't let it." Then he hung up the receiver.

"Lisa's missing," he said quietly without even turning to the woman who sat beside him in the car. "Clint's middle kid. I'm sorry. I don't know what to do. I could take you back."

"Let me call Lloyd." Emily gestured toward the telephone. "Maybe you could just drop me off somewhere." Emily couldn't conceal the worried look on her face. She had an important creative session with a client already scheduled for this afternoon. She hated for Philip to drive her back to North Dallas when he was anxious about his niece. And Emily was anxious about her, too. Philip had just spent fifteen minutes telling her about his brother and the children, and Emily felt as if she already knew them.

She dialed the agency's number quickly and was relieved when Lloyd's secretary put her call through to him immediately. "What's the status on the creative session this afternoon?" she asked.

"It's canceled," Lloyd told her. "Our client was called out of town unexpectedly. We rescheduled for next Wednesday at three."

"Is there anything else you need me for this afternoon?"

"As a matter of fact, no." Lloyd was smiling on his end of the line. "You've had enough challenges for one day. Why don't you just give yourself the afternoon off?"

"I will," she said quietly, and on his end, Lloyd wondered why Emily sounded so subdued. "Thanks."

She hung up the telephone, and her voice was somber when she made her offer. "I have the afternoon off. You can leave me at the bus station if you'd like and I can catch a bus home. But I'd rather go with you, though." She hesitated. It wasn't a bold thing she was doing. It was an honest idea, born of caring for a teenage girl she didn't know but who she guessed might be very much as she herself had once been. Emily had run away from home several times, too, because she had thought her mother didn't want her. But she didn't dare tell Philip that. She only wanted to go with him and to help. "Let me look for Lisa, too."

"Fine. Thank you. We can use all the help we can get." And then Philip fell silent as they drove on through Dallas and turned south into the country.

The North Texas blacklands spread out before them as Philip turned the car off the main road and headed over the rise on the Maypearl Road toward the farm. The Manning place was still a good three miles away when Philip pointed it out to her and Emily saw the homestead for the first time. It was backed up against the horizon, atop a hill, framed by the sheer richness of the green and black patches of soil rolling before them. There was something so open about it, and Emily felt as if it was a place where she could be truly free, at one with everything around her. Looking at rich farmland made Emily feel almost immortal. What a promise it offered. Living here, one would be aware that there would always be another season to come, another springtime, when the world would be greening, growing.

"It's beautiful out here." Emily sighed as she stared out across the horizon.

"I know," he replied. And then they both fell silent once more.

When Philip's car pulled across the front cattle guard, a man Emily knew must be his brother came out of the front door and the screen door banged behind him.

"I told you I was almost here," Philip called as he climbed out of the car. After he'd quickly introduced Emily, Philip asked, "How are you doing, bud?"

"I'm okay," he answered.

It surprised Emily how closely these two brothers resembled each other. Clint was an earthier version of Philip. He was shorter and stockier, but the lines on his face were all in the same places.

"Lisa never showed up at school this morning," Clint told them. "Somebody called me from the administrative offices. They're having problems with kids skipping school in the junior high. They wanted to make certain Lisa was home sick. By the time they called me, she had already been missing three hours."

"Did you call the police?" Philip asked.

"Yes. They won't do anything about it. They can't classify Lisa as a missing person until she's been gone for twenty-four hours. They haven't seen her at the bus station, so unless she's hitchhiking—which I don't think Lisa would do—she hasn't left town. The guy at the bus station promised to call if she showed up and tried to buy a ticket. It's hard to miss a sandy-blond, thirteen-year-old girl with green eyes wearing an aqua-and-yellow polo shirt and a pair of cropped jeans."

Emily did her best to hide a smile. Clint's description was such a typical one. There were probably a hundred girls in Waxahachie alone that fitted his description of his daughter. "Does Lisa have a group of friends she hangs around with? Are there parents you could check with? Maybe a group of girls has gone off together."

"I can't think of any. Since Amanda's operation Lisa has kept very much to herself. She used to have a group of four or five other girls she did things with, but that was many months ago. I wouldn't even know who to call now. She just stays up in her room listening to that stereo at top volume and we have our nightly quarrel. That's Lisa's social life."

Emily felt as if she would cry. "Your nightly quarrel last night," Philip interjected, "was about the school field trip to Austin. Am I right?"

Emily gazed across the rolling meadow that spanned the horizon behind the house. How clearly she remembered the desperation of yearning for a mother who might never be a mother again. Even now, the futility of that longing threatened to overtake her. And suddenly she remembered the places she used to go, the things she had once needed to do when she was almost overpowered by the circumstances life had dealt her. Emily wheeled toward the man who stood beside her. "I'd be willing to guess that Lisa's on this farm somewhere. She probably just needed to go off and spend some time alone. Clint, does Lisa have a place she goes when she wants solitary time? A place that's away from the house?"

Clint looked puzzled. "Not that I know of."

"My guess is that if we left her alone, she would be back at the house before dark. Since she could be in town somewhere, we'd better not wait to find out, though."

"I'll go into Waxahachie and see if anyone has seen her downtown or at the mall," Clint suggested.

"We'll stay here and comb the whole place together," Philip agreed as he glanced at the woman standing beside him. Just this morning he had been comparing Emily to a child and thinking how much she resembled Lisa. Now here she was, standing beside him with her back set against the world. She seemed so sturdy, so strong to Philip just then, and he wondered why she was taking this search so personally. Finding Lisa was obviously very important to her.

They began searching the farm in the barn, the tack room and the corral. After they had no luck there, they combed through the meadow and checked the cow pasture. And as Emily walked along beside Philip making suggestions, she suddenly felt her heart well up into her throat and she was horrified, for once again she thought she might cry. It was as if seeing this family in such an upheaval had set her own soul in turmoil, too. Nonetheless, she was glad he had included her in this search instead of dropping her off at the Dallas bus station on the way through town. "Philip." She said his name tentatively. It almost sounded like a question. She reached out and gingerly touched the crook of his arm. He stopped and turned toward her. "Thank you."

"For what?" He was bewildered.

"For bringing me out here today." There was something akin to shyness in her voice when she answered him. "I don't really belong in the middle of all this."

He was uncertain of what to say to her. Her statement was paradoxical. It was she who deserved his gratitude. Twice now today, she had taken her business time to help him.

Philip had no way of knowing that Emily was thanking him for the parts of him he had let her see this afternoon. She was thanking him for the conversation in the car about his family. Because of the crisis with Lisa, he had let her glimpse a part of him that she doubted other people ever saw—his concern for his brother, his love for his family. It made the little gold plaque with her name on it that she had won today seem like a sorry excuse for a lifeline. He had so much more than she did. He was surrounded by people who loved and respected him. He made a tremendous effort to worry about them, to care for them. She would have given almost anything if she could only have the courage to do the same.

They walked on then to a spot the Mannings called "the little place." It was connected by a trail to the main acreage of the farm, but it was surrounded by another man's cotton fields. It had been extra acreage that Amanda's grandparents had purchased during the Great Depression, Philip explained as he held up a rusty strand of barbed wire and motioned for Emily to step through. After Amanda and Clint had taken over the farm from her parents, Amanda's father had built a small cabin in a grove of pecan trees and had kept a few cows of his own grazing on the property.

"What's up this way?" Emily asked, pointing in the other direction.

"Just the trash dump. And several old fishing ponds the kids used to use. Come to think of it, there is another small barn and a corral up that way, too. It has a hayloft. We should probably check it out."

"You go on ahead," Emily urged him. "If it's okay with you, I'd like to look in the pecan grove."

"She won't be in the cabin, Emily." Philip gazed down at her. "That place has been locked up for months."

"I don't expect her to be in the house." Once more, Emily gazed back at the peaceful grove of trees. "There may be someplace else we've overlooked."

"Go ahead. Maybe you're right."

Philip left her then, and Emily was alone. From all around her came the early evening trilling of the cicadas and the melodic call of the meadowlarks. As her legs swished through the tall Texas native grasses, Emily felt as if she was alone in a world all her own. The peace seemed to envelop her. How Amanda's parents must have loved this place, she thought. They had loved it enough to pass it on to their daughter and, through her, to her children. How they must have enjoyed watching their grandchildren growing up strong and sturdy here.

Emily found herself wishing she had a place like this to bring children to someday. Motherhood suddenly seemed like everything to her, the joy of rosy cheeks, the pumping legs running across the grass, the sparkling clear eyes. What fulfillment it would be to see little fists full of this dirt. Emily closed her eyes and imagined herself and her own brood of children climbing the grape arbor and hanging upside down on the trellis.

Emily sensed someone watching her as she stood soaking up the peace of the place. And then she heard a muffled sound come from somewhere above her in the trees.

"Hello?" she called out as she gazed up into the leafy branches above her. She had a pretty good guess who was in that pecan tree. "Lisa? Is that you?"

There was no answer, but as Emily watched, the leaves began to move above her. The limbs of the tree were swaying and the leaves that had already turned brown from the first autumn frost were falling. Someone was descending from a high perch. She waited quietly by the tree, and finally her patience paid off. First there came a pair of aqua sailcloth espadrilles followed by the split hems of a pair of cropped jeans. Finally she had a clear view of huge melancholy green eyes staring out from a pale, grieving face. The girl crouched in a fork just above the trunk of the tree. The sight of her took Emily's breath away. She looked so delicate, so fragile, and she reminded Emily of a little bird who might flutter away at Emily's slightest movement. "Are you Lisa?"

As the girl nodded her answer, Emily thought she must be the most beautiful, tragic-looking teenager she had ever seen.

The two of them stared at each other. And it was Lisa who finally spoke first. "Yeah. I'm Lisa. Lisa Manning. Who are you?"

"I'm Emily." She shielded her eyes from the evening sun that was close to the horizon as she answered the girl's question. "I'm nobody too important. I had a seminar with your Uncle Philip this morning and we were going to eat lunch when your father called. He wanted your uncle to come help look for you. Everyone is very concerned that you're missing."

"Missing?" Lisa pronounced the word as if it were foreign to her. "Has he been looking for me since lunch? How did he...?"

"Someone from your school called."

"Oh, no," Lisa sighed. "Now I'm really going to get it. Daddy's going to kill me."

Emily smiled. "I doubt that." She paused. "Mind if I join you up there?"

"Up here?" Lisa's eyes widened. "In the tree?"

"Sure." Emily was laughing now. She hadn't meant to frighten or surprise Lisa. Her heart was just so much lighter now that she had found her. And it looked like fun to climb the tree. Emily reached up and grasped the lowest branch. She was instantly thankful for the pair of blue jeans she was wearing. Clint had let her borrow a pair of Amanda's Levis and a sweatshirt before she and Philip had started out on their search. She couldn't have done this in the suit and hose she had left back at the house.

As she swung herself on up into the fork of the trunk beside Lisa, Emily glanced back in the direction of the dump to see if she could find Philip. Maybe she was crazy to climb trees with Philip Manning's thirteen-year-old niece. Then she banished her doubts and followed her instincts. Lisa needed a friend right now, and Emily was willing to be one. She swung up higher.

"You climb trees," Lisa stated dryly. "I didn't know grown-ups climbed trees."

Emily couldn't help giggling. "Neither did I. This is the first time I've done this since I was eleven years old."

"Are you a counselor?" Lisa asked. "Dad said if I stepped out of line anymore, he was going to call a counselor and make me talk to her."

"No," she answered. "I'm not a counselor. I'm a writer." Emily gazed down at the pastoral scene spread below them. "I didn't know a place like this existed, particularly anywhere within a hundred miles of downtown Dallas. It's so quiet here."

"It is, isn't it." Lisa was more comfortable with her now, now that the teenager knew that she did climb trees and she wasn't a counselor. "This used to be..." Lisa struggled to finish her sentence and finally said, "My mother is very sick."

"I know about that," Emily reassured her. "Your uncle Philip told me about it." It was strange calling him Uncle Philip. She still felt as if she should be calling him Mr. Manning.

"This used to be Mom's favorite place on the whole farm." There was a restrained reverence in Lisa's voice. "She told me she used to climb this same tree when she was a little girl. And sometimes when everybody else was running around doing dumb stuff, Mom and I would pack a picnic lunch and we'd come down here and hide from everybody and talk."

A pang of regret shot through Emily. How wonderful it would have been to have had a relationship like that with her own mother. "You really miss her, don't you?"

Lisa nodded. "And I don't know if she'll ever be coming back."

Emily's heart went out to the girl. She felt the same way about her own mother. But she had given up on their relationship a long, long time ago. Lisa still had hope, and suddenly it seemed to Emily almost more painful that way. "I get the feeling you and your mom were best friends."

"We were." There were tears in Lisa's eyes now. "All my friends at school really liked her, too. They were really sorry when she went into a coma and couldn't come home from the hospital. Then they stopped talking to me about it. I guess they don't know what to say. I just wasn't in the mood to go to school today and face them all."

"Your mom must be very nice." Emily was trying hard to talk about Amanda in the present tense. She had almost said, Your mom must have been very nice.

"She wasn't grouchy and she didn't yell like a lot of my friends' moms. She liked to laugh. She told me once to remember that as long as you could find something to laugh about, you could face just about anything in the world that went wrong. Well, I try to find something to laugh about now, but I can't. Ever."

Emily was crouching on the limb listening, captivated.

"Once Mom let me have a birthday party here in the pecan grove," Lisa continued. "We all started singing these hilarious songs about boll weevils that Tracy learned in Texas history class. Then we started laughing so hard that Amy fell in the water trough for Granddaddy's cows. So we all went swimming in the fishing hole. Tracy's mom got really mad that my mom let us get our clothes wet without calling about us going swimming and getting all the other parents' permission and stuff. Tracy's mom wouldn't let her come over here again for a really long time. But Tracy still said it was the best birthday party she had ever been to."

"Are you and Tracy still friends?" Emily asked. The answer to that question was an important one.

"Not really." Lisa hung her head. "I guess it's a bummer, but we don't do much together anymore."

"Why not?" Emily swung back out of the tree with her arms and stared up at the white cumulus clouds that were marching across the sky. She was thinking of her own teenage years. She hadn't had many close friends, either. She didn't want the kids in her classes to know about her life at home, and it was hard for her to talk about the trivial things that the other girls talked about. It had just been hard for her to giggle over things that had seemed so unimportant.

"I don't know," Lisa said. "I just don't feel like being nice to people anymore. It's too much trouble. You have to be happy all the time to make people like you. It's just too hard."

"You know what your mother told you about laughing?" Emily asked finally after she had thought about Lisa's answer. "That's really important. Your mom knows what she's talking about. If I were you, I wouldn't be fake about it, but I would do my best to try to find honest things that made me laugh. Laughter is good. It does make you strong."

"That's why I come to this tree. Mom hasn't climbed it since she was little. But this is my laugh tree. Amy and I used to climb up here all the time and tell jokes. And we'd just talk about stuff and laugh. I come up here now to try to find something to laugh about. I figure if I could ever find anything to laugh about, like Mom said..." Her voice trailed off. "But I'm really trying."

"Your mother would want you to do more than just try. She would want you to find ways to really make it happen for yourself."

"Yeah, but it's not that easy." Lisa was still disheartened. "If it's so good to make things happen for yourself, why doesn't she just make herself wake up and come home?"

"I don't know," Emily answered honestly, "but I'll bet that she's trying."

There was a satisfied silence between them.

Finally Lisa spoke again. "You remind me a little bit of my mother."

"Why?" Emily was surprised and flattered. "Do I look like her?"

"No," Lisa shook her head quickly, "you don't. But you like to climb trees. Mom will like you. She used to laugh at people who thought grown-ups should be different from children. She said grown-ups were always working too hard to be grown-ups."

Just as Lisa finished her sentence, there came a very human growl from the base of the tree. "Gr-r-r. I am a big bear that climbs trees."

Emily grinned silently at Lisa. The voice sounded as if it belonged to Philip. He must have spotted the two of them when he had come walking back to the pecan grove, she guessed.

"I love to climb trees," Philip continued in his bear voice. "And I love to eat the things I find in them, particularly when I find little girls who have been skipping school all day long. Gr-r-r."

Lisa couldn't control her giggling anymore, and Emily was laughing outright, too. Suddenly they looked at each other and realized they were both happy despite the conversation they had just finished. "See," Emily whispered. "Your laugh tree does work. All you had to do was wait for some crazy bear to come along."

"Uncle Philip?" Lisa called down to him.

"Gr-r-r," came the reply. And then, with much shrieking and giggling, the two of them swung down to the lower branches and into the fork of the tree. Then they both jumped to the ground. Philip looked amazed. And it was Emily who laughed at him.

"I didn't know that girls climbed trees." There was a hint of teasing in his voice, but there was honest admiration, too.

"Yeah," Emily teased him back. "And I didn't know real estate barons could growl like bears, either."

"Okay." He gave his niece a jovial hug, but his eyes were on Emily. "You've got me there. Just don't tell anyone back in the city."

"I won't," she said with a chuckle. She held up three fingers and made the Girl Scout sign. "Scout's honor."

"Is that where they taught you to climb trees?" Philip was highly amused that he had found Emily Lattrell in a tree. "In the Girl Scouts?"

"No." She brushed her hands off on her jeans. "That's one of my few amazing talents that I actually taught myself."

CHAPTER FIVE

"I DON'T KNOW WHAT you said to Lisa," Philip told Emily after his niece had skipped on ahead of them toward the house, but whatever it was, it worked. I haven't seen her happy like this in a long time."

"I don't think it was anything I said to her." Emily stopped talking and turned toward him. "Your bear imitation is what really made her laugh. And she really needed this day of solitude. Souls, no matter if they're thirteen or three hundred, can be pretty intuitive about themselves. They know what they need to survive." Emily was gazing up at him and grinning. It was so easy to feel comfortable with him. He was happy and relaxed here with his brother's family.

The wind was blowing from behind them, and it seemed to gently push them across the pasture. Philip's hair was blowing to frame his face. He looked totally at ease and carefree. Three hours before, she could never have imagined him sauntering up to a tree and growling into it. Emily knew she was catching a glimpse of the man behind Philip Manning's professional mask. She was seeing him as if for the first time.

"I think she needed you." Philip couldn't resist touching her with his index finger right on the tip of her nose. It was the same gesture he would have used with one of Clint's children. He was so grateful to Emily for taking the time to come with him to the farm and to help him find Lisa. There were a hundred other things she might have done this afternoon. Philip knew it had been good for Lisa to have another female to talk to. And Emily had obviously used her best judgment in choosing her words to his niece. Lisa had responded to the things Emily had said. Another woman might have been less compassionate, less able to understand the teenager's grief.

"Maybe she did need me." Emily stared off into nothingness as she spoke. "Or maybe she just needed someone to climb trees with her. A monkey could have done that."

"Give yourself more credit than that, Emily. I don't think Amanda ever climbed trees with Lisa."

"She didn't. Lisa told me."

Philip stood and watched Emily silently for a moment. Then he grasped her hand. "Come with me." His words were so low that they were almost a whisper. She had shared an important part of herself with his niece this afternoon. Now he found himself wanting to show her something that was important to him, too.

As they walked into the twilight together, the sound of bawling cattle reverberated around them. "Over here." Philip led the way to the base of a lone pecan in the meadow where the native Texas grasses grew especially thick. And bedded down there, as if he were sleeping in a nest made just for him, was one tiny white-faced Hereford calf. "This is the farm nursery this fall," he explained in a hushed tone as he parted the grass to reveal the animal that was still too young to stand.

"He's beautiful." Emily scarcely dared to breathe for fear of frightening the animal, but when she spoke, he just looked at her. The calf was calm, and Emily had a long moment to examine the pink velvet muzzle and the forehead covered with fluffy furry curls that would never again be quite so white.

"There are two more over there on the other side of the tree. You can see them nosing around. This one," said Philip as he stroked the fuzzy forehead and then motioned to Emily to do the same, "hasn't gotten quite that far yet."

Emily's breath caught in her throat as she felt Philip move down closer beside her. For a moment, she didn't know why but she thought he was going to kiss her. He was so close and it would have seemed easy and natural to turn to him. But she didn't. Philip only inspected the calf a bit more closely by running his fingers along one tiny hoof. "This one is a good specimen."

"Are they all going to make as much noise as their mamas when they grow up?" She was desperate to say something, anything, that would break the sudden tension that hung in the air between them. The newfound kinship she was feeling with him suddenly frightened her. She had learned a long time ago that it was too painful to become attached to people. But she wanted to remember this feeling, too—the fear and the wishing.

"Oh, yes." Philip was chuckling. "That and then some. But isn't it a wonderful sound? It sounds just like Texas at dusk. Cicadas singing and mama cows bawling after their babies."

Philip took her hand and helped Emily pull herself up out of the damp grass. The mood between the two of them was one of quiet, peaceful satisfaction as they walked back toward the house and Emily felt cozily secure, as if she were snuggling into a warm blanket on a cold night. There was a part of Philip that she wanted to remember, a part of him that she was sharing wordlessly as they tromped along together through the Johnsongrass. She was drawn to the gentleness and compassion she sensed in this executive outdoorsman.

Philip drove her back to Dallas that night after taking her and Clint and the kids out for a sandwich at Tom's Bar-B-Q in Waxahachie. Over their meal, Emily had explained to Bethany that she was a writer, that she wrote advertising campaigns for clients and that she dreamed of writing children's books someday.

"What kind of children's books do you want to write?" Bethany asked eagerly. Philip knew by the way his youngest niece asked the question that she was honestly interested. And Philip was, too. But he wasn't surprised to learn Emily's secret ambition. She seemed very much like someone who would write children's books.

Emily focused on Bethany. "I have some ideas." Then she smiled demurely, but Philip thought he noticed a touch of pride in her expression, too. "My main character is a possum." He read something winsome in her eyes then, and he realized she was sharing something with his family that she hadn't shared with many others. "His name is Baby Sprout."

Then she stopped. Emily wasn't totally comfortable talking about the character. The little possum she had created in her mind and on paper was very much a part of her. There were traits she had given Baby Sprout and the other characters in her manuscript that came directly from her own experiences.

"Do you have a children's literature class at Waxahachie High School?" Emily asked Greg. Philip realized she had intentionally diverted attention away from herself.

"No." Greg shook his head. "We get to read fun things like *The Scarlet Letter* and *The Great Gatsby*." He screwed his mouth up in disgust.

Emily waggled a teasing finger at him. "Hang in there. I didn't care for *The Scarlet Letter*, either. But *The Great Gatsby* is a wonderful piece of literature. F. Scott Fitzgerald's characters are totally satiating. They are so strong that they control the events around them."

"And that's what really messes their lives up," Greg commented.

"You're right," Emily agreed. "Fitzgerald lived the sparkling life-style that he wrote about. And he observed what that did to the people who lived it with him. His characters are intriguing portraits of human nature."

Clint was standing to leave, and the rest of them followed suit. Emily shook his hand and then nodded at the children. "It was nice to meet y'all," she drawled. Then she waited for Philip to hold the door open for her, and she followed him out to the car.

"Sorry about that." She raised her gaze to meet his when he climbed into the front seat beside her.

"For what?"

"For launching into a long dissertation about F. Scott Fitzgerald."

If Philip had known her better, he would have teased her about being so unassuming about her talents. Her modesty was a part of her that was different from any other woman he had ever known. "You just brought him up because you didn't want to talk about yourself." *Why is she always so nervous and humble and formal with me?* he asked himself. Her manner set him off balance and it intrigued him. Philip was used to meeting people head-on, sparring with them, knowing where he stood with them. But Emily seemed to run forward eagerly toward him and then inexplicably to back away. He couldn't figure out why. "So tell me about your book," he suggested nonchalantly as they drove along.

"Why are you so interested in that?" She leaned forward and studied his face.

He watched the road as he spoke. "It sounds exciting." He frowned. He didn't know exactly what he should say. He wanted her to tell him something important about herself. He could sense that she hadn't intentionally been mysterious about her aspirations. She just hadn't wanted to talk about them. "I'd like to hear about it. Have you really written the stories?"

"I've written one." She sounded almost apologetic. "I haven't submitted it to a publisher."

"Why not?"

"I don't know. Maybe it needs more work. I'm not ready to send it out yet." Privately, Emily knew it didn't need more work. She had been over every word to make certain that it was perfect. But for some reason, she just couldn't let go of it yet.

"What does he look like?" Philip was having to coax every tiny bit of information out of her.

"He's a possum," she told him. "You must know what possums look like." She was surprised by him, surprised that he would even care about something like that.

Philip laughed. "We had possums wandering into our garage all the time when Clint and I were boys. We caught one once and named it Fang."

Emily threw her head back and laughed heartily, too. It was almost impossible to imagine Philip Manning naming anything Fang. Of course, before this evening it would also have been hard for her to picture him growling up into a tree like a bear, too. But she had just seen him do that.

"Possums are cute and cuddly with teeth that won't quit," Philip said.

"Ignore the teeth part," Emily said, shaking her head playfully. "A children's book publisher would never go for that."

"Okay." Philip screwed up his mouth and did his best to look serious. "Possums are fat and fuzzy. They are gray, sort of motley, with white faces and beady eyes."

"Very good," she replied with a laugh. "You've just described Baby Sprout."

Philip shook his head at her. She was dodging his questions again. He wanted her to describe Baby Sprout for him. Bringing her out of herself was becoming a challenge to him. He knew, because of the sincerity he could read in her eyes, that she was not intentionally being vague with him. But when he pulled his car into the driveway of Emily's apartment complex, he still didn't know very much about her. He only knew that she was joyous and spontaneous and different from Morgan in a myriad of ways. Important ways.

As he moved around the car to open the door for her, he didn't know exactly how to thank her. She had done so much for him today—at the business seminar, and at the farm with his family. He suddenly wished that they were both fifteen so that he could give her an innocent, uncomplicated kiss.

"The barbecue burger was delicious," she was telling him as he helped her out of the car. "That was much better than going out for lunch at some fancy restaurant downtown."

As she stood there before him on the marked pavement, Philip found that same comfortable welcome he had seen before in her eyes, the openness, the honesty, the refreshing girlishness. "Emily Lattrell..." Her name had been scarcely more than a whisper.

"Yes?"

He didn't dare say anything more than that. He was afraid he might say too much. He was just so grateful to her, and for some reason, he wanted to reach out to her and fold her into his arms. He was suddenly feeling anything but innocent. Without doing anything at all, he said the first thing that came to his mind. "Promise me you won't tell Lloyd Masterson about my bear imitation."

"No promises." She laughed and the sound of her laughter wafted into the air and seemed to linger. "That may be the one story that's too good to pass up."

He just looked at her. And he realized it was going to take every ounce of resolve he had to walk away from her without touching her.

"I had fun today," she told him quietly. Emily felt exhilarated by the day with Philip, by her success at his seminar, by their trip to the farm, by their lively conversation on the way home. Emily had never been brave enough to tell anyone about her Baby Sprout books before. She had done so today because she had seen it as a way to bring Bethany, Clint's younger daughter, into the conversation. Philip's obvious interest in her project didn't seem totally out of character to her now that she had seen how responsive he was to people and how animated he became around his brother's children.

"I'm glad," he said.

The two of them stood for a moment in the parking lot beside his car, neither knowing exactly what to say. Only twelve hours ago, the two of them had only been business acquaintances, and because his niece had disappeared, they had become friends. Friendships did not come easily to Emily. No one really knew her. Now, because Philip was a friend, he seemed even more like a newfound treasure to her. But she couldn't explain that to him. She wouldn't know where to begin without sounding like more than a friend.

"I'm fine," she told him. "You don't have to walk me up. That's my apartment there." She pointed to a balcony upstairs.

"I will, though." He touched her arm. She recognized it as the same reassuring gesture he had given her in Lloyd's boardroom when she had agreed to do the seminar for him. He followed her through the lobby and up the stairs and waited while she searched for her keys in her purse. They jangled in her hand when she turned to him.

"Thank you for today, Philip Manning." Her voice was low.

He grabbed her arm to keep her from turning away from him. "I'm the one who should be thanking you, Emily." He was so close to her that he was looking straight down at her. "But thanking you doesn't seem to be enough."

She threw her head back again and laughed. She couldn't help thinking that it was ironic, Philip's being so grateful. It had been such an honor for her to spend the day with him. It seemed like an eternity ago when she had wended her way through the crowd toward him at the seminar. He had seemed so much larger than life to her that morning, because of the things she knew about his career and his prominent status in the business community. Now he seemed more and less of the man she'd thought him to be. She had seen him as a human being against the backdrop of a place that he loved. And in a way, knowing him made her feel more confident about herself, about the fact that she was a human being with feelings and insecurities, too. Emily liked Philip. She admired him. It surprised her how at ease she felt with him, knowing how his reputation had intimidated her.

It was her laughter that spurred Philip on. She was so carefree about her laughter. It wasn't the programmed, ingratiating mirth he was used to hearing in his offices.

"Believe me, thanking me is enough." She smiled up at him and he felt the strangest feeling then, as if Emily had been sent to him by some discerning force to prove to him that his life was devoid of something very important, indeed. He was still unconsciously gripping her arm, as if by holding on to her he might be able to hold on to a trust that he had lost a long time before.

"Philip," she whispered. She didn't know him well, but she was concerned about the melancholy and the confusion she glimpsed in his eyes.

He bent toward her and cradled the back of her head against his palm. He only wanted to be gentle with her and to show her how thankful he was for the things she had done. Carefully, almost hesitantly, he brushed his lips across the top of her head.

Emily reached up and gripped his shoulders firmly, and her eyes were wide as she searched his face. His one gesture answered countless questions that she hadn't dared to ask. The day had been a special one for him, too. And the attraction she'd felt for him was mutual. She didn't say anything to him, but she didn't pull away. She only stood before him, bracing herself against him with her hands.

It had been years since Philip had allowed himself to feel the things he was feeling now. She smelled like the outdoors to him, like the native grasses and the pecan trees and the fresh country air from where they had just come. He pictured her in the tree again, up above him among the branches with Lisa, and this time it was his turn to chuckle.

"What is it?" she asked. And he almost didn't want to tell her, for fear he would frighten her.

"I was just thinking about you in that tree this afternoon," he said. And the indecision he was feeling registered in his voice. "I was thinking how very different you are from other women I've known."

"Because I climb trees?" She gave him an impish grin. She was feeling playful and girlish, and the texture of his linen shirt wrinkling beneath her hands threatened to make her dizzy. She found herself wanting to clutch the cloth between her fingers as if by grasping his clothing she could truly hold on to him, as well.

"Because of everything you did today," he told her earnestly. "Because you climbed a tree and because you cared enough to talk to Lisa." She smiled up at him then, and the reasons for his gratitude began to take shape in her mind. He was a man who cared deeply about his family. Clint and the children and the woman named Amanda were lucky to have him.

"It's easy to see how much you love them," she commented.

"They're everything I have," he told her. Somehow his confession surprised her. She had thought he would value other things in his life a great deal more.

"Don't forget your real estate company." She was in the mood to tease him and she did so now by addressing him formally. "Mr. Manning," she said to him, "I've heard about you and your business success during the past few years. I believe you could have anything in the world you wanted, if you would just set your mind to it. That's how your life has worked until now, hasn't it?"

"No." He was shaking his head at her sadly and looking down at her and thinking that the only thing in life he really wanted was to kiss her. "I don't always get everything I want."

She cocked her head at him and he saw a trace of amusement cross her features. She thought he was kidding. He wondered, as he watched her, if his life did seem that way to other people, if he did seem like a golden boy who could snap his fingers and make all his dreams come true.

"Emily." His voice was so low that she barely heard him. "My life isn't as uncomplicated or as magical as that."

"I don't believe you," she said solemnly. "You make success look so easy."

"It isn't easy." His eyes were locked on hers, and the ice blue color of them seemed to beckon to her, to pull her longings out of her heart. She moved closer to him and felt him against her, and she closed her eyes. He entranced her. Her other memories of the day dissipated. She only remembered him and the way he looked at her and the wonderful tingle that had surged through her when he had brushed his lips against her hair.

"I thought it was," she told him.

He didn't answer her. Instead he bent forward and cradled her against him with his arms. Then he took her face in his hands and tilted it toward him. She didn't say anything more. She only waited for him, wanting him, while he lowered his mouth to meet her parted lips with agonizing slowness.

When Philip kissed her, Emily reached her arms up to him and grasped his neck. The muscles beneath her fingers moved with the same exhilarating rhythm as his tongue as it traced the outline of her mouth and then probed farther to follow the contour of her teeth and tongue.

Emily was lost in the scent of him, the nearness of him. His kiss and embrace encompassed her and made her feel protected and warm, and she felt as if she were soaring above the world as he held her. He kissed her again and again while she clung to him, and finally, when she pulled herself away and looked up at him, everything she saw, his face, the shingle eaves above his head, looked beautiful.

"Philip Manning," she whispered against his lips. "What are we doing?"

He gazed down into her eyes, and before he answered, he kissed her once again on the tip of her nose. "Don't you know?" He didn't try to hide the playfulness in his voice. "I'm getting something that I've decided I want." He cocked his head and did his best to look mischievous, as if he was letting her in on a secret. "And I'm doing my best to make it look easy."

She grinned up at him, and for a moment, as she watched him, she imagined that this might work for them, that it would be easy to trust him, to love him, to be more than his friend. But she knew that was only imagination.

"I should go," he said quietly. "I've monopolized your entire day."

"It was wonderful," she said and he noticed that there was a certain sadness in her voice, as if she was already looking back on their time together as a distant memory. And Philip didn't quite know what he should say. He hardly knew her. But he had just kissed her on a whim, and he had felt her melt against him. And he didn't want to frighten her away or put her on the spot by asking to see her again.

He let go of her, and Emily put her key in the lock and opened her apartment door. She felt a great rush of aloneness and unsteadiness as he backed away from her, as if a protective barrier that had somehow eased up between herself and the world was now gone.

He made his way down the stairs as she went outside and stood on the balcony and watched him go. He climbed into the car and revved the engine. He put on his seat belt and paused to look up to find her. "Goodbye, Emily Lattrell," he called out to her.

"Goodbye." She waved at him as he drove off. And then she stood for a long time, feeling alone and unsatisfied in the darkness, staring down the street to the horizon where his car had disappeared, to where the streetlights cast a rose-colored hue on the asphalt below.

"THERE IS A WOMAN named Abbie Carson in the front office to see you, Ms Lattrell," Emily's secretary informed her over the intercom.

Emily recognized the name immediately. Abbie Carson was the owner of Absolutely Moms.

"Send her in," she instructed her secretary.

A gray-haired, jovial woman appeared in the doorway and moved to grip Emily's hand firmly in her own. "I apologize for not calling and making an appointment with you, but I'm frantic these days, getting my Dallas office put together. I'm always running around about ten miles from a telephone. We don't have ours installed yet."

Emily was instantly drawn to this woman. Abbie Carson radiated energy. "I saw one of your brochures a few days ago," she said, motioning to an office chair. "Please sit down."

Abbie moved to take a seat across the desk from Emily and handed her another copy of the brochure. "I need to redo this brochure," she said pointedly. The woman certainly didn't waste time with polite or trivial conversation, Emily thought. Every move, every word, was economical. It was obvious how this one woman had accomplished so much in one short lifetime. "Philip Manning said you were the person for the job. I'd like to target the copy for the local market. We've got tremendous potential in Texas."

"I agree." Emily pulled a notepad from the top drawer of her desk. "Mr. Manning told me a bit about your company. I'd like to hear about it in your own words, though." Emily's hand was trembling when she started to take notes. It had been three days since Philip Manning had kissed her and then had driven away. For three days, Emily had done her best to get him out of her mind. Their time together had been a quirk of fate, a tantalizing hint at something she knew she didn't dare long for. But sometime during the past three days, Philip Manning had recommended her work to this woman. Sometime during the time Emily had been trying to forget him, he had been discussing her with someone else. At first, just thinking of that made it hard for Emily to concentrate on the things Abbie was saying. But as the woman began to tell her story, it was such an impressive one that Emily could not help but become involved in it.

"My business started fourteen years ago when my husband died," Abbie told her. "I was in my forties with three grown children and no real goals for the future. An acquaintance whose wife had died begged me to move in with him and become an adopted mother to his two sons, aged eight and twelve. And the arrangement worked. My two new 'sons' and I had wonderful adventures every afternoon. We fished in the Potomac River, visited the Smithsonian Institute and spent days at the zoo. We did everything there was to do in Washington, D.C., where my first 'surrogate family' lived. And after we ran out of things to do in Washington, D.C., we went to New York and spent a day there riding everything that moved—the ferry, the subway, a taxi." There was a sparkle in Abbie's eyes as she spoke that seemed to come from loving children and doing childlike things. Emily could picture this woman dragging two little boys throughout a city, hailing cabs, catching trains, boarding boats. Emily had to grin. She was surprised Abbie and the boys hadn't figured out how to fly in an airplane and how to ride in a helicopter, too.

"After I'd spent one summer with those kids, their neighbors were all asking what I had done," Abbie said, laughing. Emily wanted to absorb the vitality that was sparkling in her eyes. "Everyone said my boys were so much happier with themselves, that they seemed so much more secure. That's when I began to realize that if two children could change so drastically with simple discipline and love, there must be many more families out there somewhere who needed a full-time, managerial, professional mother."

No wonder Philip Manning had been so impressed with Abbie Carson, Emily thought. The woman was so intent on her own cause, so certain of the work she was doing that Emily wanted to jump out of her chair and salute her. Abbie Carson was a diminutive, vivacious woman who was destined to lead a great many other women and children to happiness. She had taken something that could be termed "old-fashioned" and had turned it into something very, very new.

Abbie continued her story. During the next eight years, she had served as an "adopted mom" for five different families. And in each situation, she found a blessing on both ends.

"A natural mother has no salary, no time off and she also does the scrubbing, the vacuuming and the ironing. An Absolutely Mom cheers at Little League baseball games, goes to school plays and piano recitals and teaches kids how to bake cookies. She does the meal planning, the budgeting, buys clothes for the children, keeps things in order and is hired to be a problem solver, a manager, an organizer. She has the weekends off if she wants them, and she receives a paycheck. She is not a housekeeper. We have fathers who want our services so desperately that they'll spend the money on our service rather than a cleaning lady even if they must come home and do the scrubbing themselves on the weekends."

Abbie noticed a shadow seem to cross Emily's face. She was thinking of her own mother.

"I kept wondering if I was a freak for wanting this." Abbie leaned forward and placed her palms on Emily's desk with a small, victorious slap. "I wondered if I was the only woman in the world who recognized the joy and the challenges of being a mother. But I kept thinking about it and I became like a fire horse that heard the bell. I knew the time had come to spark other people's interest in my scheme. And it was easy. I had done it myself. I could honestly say that each day had been a special adventure, a special gift. And when the time came, it was easy for me to talk to other women about it. I was the one who had had all the fun. I was the one who had sat around in the firelight reading the children stories and loving them."

Absolutely Moms was a nonprofit corporation with offices in Arlington, Virginia, and Carmel and Palo

Alto, California, Abbie went on to explain. She worked now as the company administrator, constantly matching her mothers with families who needed them. To date, she had placed over two thousand mothers all around the world.

"Our major goal is to service motherless homes," Abbie explained. "Fifty percent of those homes need us because a mother has died and fifty percent because of divorce, separation or desertion."

When Abbie finished speaking, she noticed a faraway, intense expression in Emily's eyes. She smiled. She had seen that wistful expression in women's eyes plenty of times before. These professional women thought they had it all. But they didn't. Not by half. "Well?" she asked tentatively. "What about the brochure? Will you do it for me?"

"Of course," Emily answered softly. But even Abbie's question couldn't break her reverie. In her mind, she was far, far away... in a grassy pasture with baby calves and bawling mamas. She was thinking of Clint's children and wondering what a difference an Absolutely Mom would make for Clint and the Manning children. And she was wondering what a difference an Absolutely Mom could have made in her own life, for her father, for them all.

"Is it hard to find women to be your mothers, Abbie?" she asked.

"We have many women who want to be mothers, Emily." Abbie's voice was suddenly gentle. She had grown accustomed to redirecting lives and channeling women in the directions they needed to go. "There are many reasons to become an Absolutely Mom. Maybe a woman feels like something is missing in her life and maybe she wants to try to find it. Or maybe she wants to give to someone else what she herself could never have...or she has so much she wants to share some of it. There are a thousand different reasons why our mothers come to us." Abbie realized that they weren't simply talking about the brochure anymore. And she found herself thinking about her own career, her life, about the things she wished she could give.

"I've got four women placed right now who hold doctorates in various disciplines," she told Emily. "Some people say they're overqualified for this. But I say, if you love being a mother, you can't be overqualified. You pass all that you are on to the children. You share your creativity. You share your stimulation. You share your wealth of experience."

"I guess you have all the mothers you need."

"Oh, no." Abbie's laughter was like a gentle bell that tinkled throughout the room. "I told you we have lots of mothers. But we never have enough. It's much easier to find families who need them. I have a mile-long waiting list of families who need mothers."

Emily sighed. The thought of joining was enticing. Three days ago, she had been with children who desperately needed the services and the love that only a mother could offer. And Emily had lived a life that had been sadly devoid of that love, too.

Abbie was standing to leave and Emily stood, as well, to take her hand. "I'm honored to write your brochure for you. I believe in what you're doing more than I think I could ever make you understand."

But Abbie already did understand. She had made it her business to understand all her employees' reasons for believing in Absolutely Moms, and she could make an educated guess at Emily's. The young woman seemed forlorn when they talked about mothers, and Abbie figured that Emily had lost her own mother somewhere along the way.

"Here's my address." Abbie handed her a business card with her new Dallas address already printed on it. "The telephone number's on the card, but the service hasn't been hooked up yet. It will be in a few days, though. Call me when you have something for me to look at."

"I will." Emily smiled warmly. She hoped she and Abbie Carson could become friends. She felt strangely drawn to her. "When I get the copy done, maybe I'll just come over to your place. I'd love to see the Absolutely Mom offices."

"Good." Abbie grinned. "I'd like that." And then she was gone.

Emily sat in her desk chair for a long time thinking, wondering what type of women gave up everything they had, their careers and their homes, to become an Absolutely Mom. Talking to Abbie had moved her. Abbie was a woman who had openly followed her dreams without being afraid of where they might lead her. Emily found herself wishing she could do the same.

She rose from her chair and stretched and then went to her filing cabinet in the corner. She thumbed through her files for a moment. She had trouble finding the one she wanted, but finally the right one fell open before her and Emily pulled it out of the drawer. It was the Baby Sprout file.

She walked over and reverently laid it on her desk. The folder contained one of her greatest dreams. She had been working on this project off and on during her lunch hours for months. And one day when she could screw up the courage, she was going to submit it to a children's book publisher. Just talking to Abbie Carson and seeing how the woman had found the courage to start her life over again and make a victory out of it had made Emily want to start working on fulfilling her own dream again.

In Emily's manuscript, Baby Sprout the possum befriended a nine-year-old girl named Priscilla. Priscilla thought she should be allowed to grow up and become a princess. Together the two of them set out to prove to old Judge Wyland that Priscilla ought to be a princess and have a throne to perch on in the middle of the town square. The two of them are waylaid time after time because Priscilla's mother keeps asking her to fold the socks from the dryer.

It had all started as a funny, ironic tale in Emily's mind and it had remained there and taken shape until it had become something much more important. It had become the story of a young child who needed to find acceptance and love from the people who surrounded her. It had come to be her own mythical autobiography.

During her own school-age years, Emily had searched for the same acceptance that her imaginary character, Priscilla, searched for in Emily's Baby Sprout manuscript. Priscilla wanted to know that she was worthy of being a princess. Emily had wanted to know that she was worthy of being loved.

Three evenings ago, when Philip Manning had kissed her, Emily had become so lost in physical pleasure that she had almost forgotten the other things his embrace might mean to her. She was attracted to Philip for a great many reasons. He was handsome and kind and she had seen his compassion. Emily wondered, as she thought of him, just how easy it might be to let herself love him. But the word *love* conjured up painful images in her mind, memories of nights her father had waited up for her mother, the nights his diligence had been paid off by a swaggering wife who hurled insults and profanities at him with the same force that she would have hurled rocks.

Emily had wondered, a long time ago, why her parents' love had diminished. She blamed her mother and she blamed alcohol. She blamed her father sometimes, too. She didn't understand why he hadn't done something to help them all, to stand up for himself or to take better care of their mother.

Now that Emily had matured, she looked back on it all and thought how unfair she had been to both of them to blame them for those things. She would turn the accusations over in her mind until they rested on her. And that brought Emily back full circle to the guilt she had grown up with. It brought her back to a view of loving that made her feel sad and wary and ashamed.

Emily's greatest fear was that she might spend her life in a relationship as hopeless as the one her parents had shared. Never to become prematurely involved was a vow she had made a long time ago, when she was in high school. Although she'd had no steady boyfriends, she had dated in high school. Despite her unhappy home life, Emily had basically remained an optimist. She believed staunchly that she could be better than her parents had been, that she could, with foresight and the right choice of a mate, overcome things they had not been able to overcome. Somehow she knew she could walk into a relationship with the right man and could make it work because her eyes were open to the mistakes people made.

Then came the night of her first prom.

The dance had been lovely and the night had been balmy. Emily had come home early the next morning reeling from the sensations. She had told many childhood friends goodbye that night. The boy she had gone with had given her a wrist corsage made of roses and had kissed her, and it had been the first night Emily had really contemplated growing up and going away and falling in love.

Emily's father had been waiting up for her with a pot of coffee made when she arrived home, and it had been a bittersweet night for both father and daughter. Martin Lattrell had had to face the fact that his little girl was growing into a woman. And with great care he had told Emily about the prom night that he and her mother had shared, the flowers he had given her, the music she had requested from the band, the way they had driven to White Rock Lake and had walked together, hand in hand, until the sun had come up over the water. Emily's father had told her the story to show his daughter that he accepted her, that he understood the things she was feeling. He couldn't understand the terror he saw in her eyes when he talked about the prom and her mother and how much he had loved her then.

"I'm going to bed, Daddy." Emily had placed one cold hand on his shoulder. And then she had kissed him and had hurried upstairs because she didn't want her father to see her crying.

She had lain in bed for the remainder of her prom night, sobbing at first, and then staring up at the ceiling with dry eyes, thinking about the two of them, her mother and her father, and how easy falling in love must have seemed to them in the beginning, too.

Emily thought about her parents all night. She thought of how much she cared for them and of how they had failed each other and themselves as well as their children. She decided then that she would rather live her life alone than experience the disillusionment and the pain that her parents had struggled against during their years together.

It had been a time in her life when enforcing that decision had been possible. Emily was leaving Decatur for college in three months. At the University of Texas, a college with over 33,000 students, she had easily lost herself in the crowd and remained remote from everyone. She had not made close friends and she had not dated. She'd convinced herself that she wasn't missing anything. Her resolution had settled deeper inside her as the semesters had gone by until, at last, the comfortable numbness that Emily's decision brought her had become an anchor to her, something she knew she could hang on to throughout her life to keep her from feeling that horrible pain.

Three days ago, when Philip Manning had pulled her into his arms and kissed her, she had suddenly been helpless to fend off the confused emotions his touch had awakened in her. It had felt so right, so good, to be in his arms. She had felt protected and needed and beautiful. She had been able to tease Philip and to laugh with him. And for one afternoon, Emily had surrendered to the moment and allowed herself to feel something with a man.

Because of that, Emily's afternoon with Philip Manning would be a memory that she knew she would treasure long after the details of the marketing seminar had faded from her mind. She had thought of Philip a thousand times already, of the way he had stooped beside the calf in the pasture, of the way he had balanced Bethany on his knee, of the way he had looked up at her and Lisa as they had both climbed down from the pecan tree. Those events and the sensations they had given her were all that Emily dared let herself remember. She didn't let herself think of the thrill she had experienced when Philip Manning had held her in his arms and kissed her. No matter how she longed to feel that thrill again, Emily didn't dare let herself wish for more than their day together, for more than their memories.

PHILIP LEANED BACK in his studio chair and thought about an elongated nose. What did an elongated nose look like? How could he sketch a fuzzy elongated nose and make it engaging? Baby Sprout the possum had to have an elongated nose.

He made several short, light strokes with his ink pen and then he held up the sketch pad to study his work. He liked it.

Philip was drawing again. Here, in his studio on the second floor of his Walnut Hill condominium, was where he relaxed. This studio was a place that represented a part of himself that he kept effectively hidden from most people.

Philip knew the drawings he produced in this room would never win any major art awards, but he loved them because they were his release. He had great stacks of them piled around the room. Some were serious sketches of pastoral scenes he loved at the farm—windmills, cattle, the old house. Some of his drawings were silly and full of fantasy, sketches of funny nonsense animals or space people with tall antennae growing out of their heads.

No matter what the subject matter of his drawings, once completed they were all like secret friends to him. For they all served the same purpose. Working on them made him briefly forget the multimillion-dollar properties and the multitude of clients that waited for him each day when he walked into the Manning Commercial Real Estate and Investment offices.

This evening, Philip had started out drawing a pecan tree and a calf. That had been a mistake. Every time he pictured the tree, he thought of Emily Lattrell. Every time he pictured the calf, he thought of how Emily had looked, crouched in the Johnsongrass beside the newborn calf in the pasture. It was a game he had been unwittingly allowing himself to play for three days now, thinking of Emily by association. He played it when he talked to Lisa on the telephone, when he found *The Great Gatsby* on his bookshelf, when he glanced for the umpteenth time at the copy she had written for his brochure.

Thinking of Emily so often was making him crazy. So he decided to change his strategy. He decided to wallow in his thoughts, to do his best to think of her so much that he would get enough of her. He started out by taking his sketch pad and working on a drawing of the possum she had talked about, the possum in her book named Baby Sprout.

Then, after he had started working on the character, his idea had taken form. At the office that morning, Philip had prepared a list of associates and friends for his secretary to send thank-you notes to for their participation in his seminar. When he had jotted Emily Lattrell's name on that list, he had winced. The idea of all she had given that day so contrasted with the formality of the note Philip knew she would receive that it seemed grossly inappropriate to send it. He wanted to give Emily more than just a formal note of thanks.

He thought of all the tokens of appreciation he could send her. Flowers? A gift certificate to a restaurant? Stationery? Nothing seemed quite right until he had been in his studio the night before, pacing the floor, inexplicably thinking about Emily's fictional possum.

Suddenly he couldn't get the image of her face out of his mind. She had been so demure and dainty talking to him that day at the farm about her dreams, so unlike the cool professional she'd been earlier. It was hard for him to imagine a woman as feminine as Emily creating a possum as an imaginary character for a book. Philip had grown up thinking that girls didn't know a thing about possums and crawdads and fishing.

He did his best to remember everything Emily had told him about the possum, and as he stopped sketching, Philip was finally satisfied. Drawing something for her was like being close to her again.

He made several changes in his sketch as he worked. He eventually gave up on the elongated nose and made Baby Sprout's nose a tad squarer. He made the eyes less beady, drawing them larger and rounder instead. He made the white part of Baby Sprout's face fuzzy and soft.

Philip did his best to suggest the things he knew of Emily's personality—her spontaneity, her willingness to give—in the character. And by the time Philip had completed his sketch of Baby Sprout, he had become totally absorbed in the work he had done.

He propped Baby Sprout up on an easel and then strolled across the room before he turned and looked back at it. And, when he did, Philip was pleased. The little possum was perfect.

Not for a minute did he stop to wonder if it was a presumptuous gift to send her. Philip was accustomed to doing what others might call presumptuous things. Doing so was one reason he had been so successful in his business endeavors. He knew how to read people, and he sensed instinctively what was appropriate for each individual.

He tucked the pen-and-ink sketch inside his briefcase and carried it to a photography shop near the office to have it dry mounted. After it was mounted, he propped it up on a shelf beside his desk at the office, where he could look at it.

For an entire morning now, Philip couldn't concentrate on his work. He kept looking up at his possum sketch, grinning inanely. He felt as if he had created two new friends, a new friend named Baby Sprout and a new friend named Emily, and as he thought about it, he knew he couldn't have his secretary send the sketch to her. He wanted to see her himself, to show her what he had done, to watch her eyes light up when she recognized Baby Sprout. Oddly, the prospect of seeing her again scared him, and he didn't know what he would say to overcome his awkwardness because of their passionate kiss. He only knew he wanted to share Baby Sprout with her, and as he gazed out his office window at the traffic zooming past his office on the expressway below, he wondered if he could talk to her again, if he could touch her again, without falling for her, without wanting her, the way he had wanted Morgan so long ago.

Emily had the copy for Abbie Carson's brochure spread on her kitchen table Saturday morning when her doorbell rang. She went to the door with several papers in her hand and a pencil stuck behind her left ear. And Philip couldn't help but chuckle when she swung the door open and stared up at him.

"Hello," he said, grinning down at her.

Emily's heart shot into her throat when she saw him. She did her best to keep from feeling overwhelmed with happiness. She had tried so hard to forget him. And now here he was, chuckling at her, as if he knew he was tormenting her just by being there, just by appearing on her doorstep. "Philip." As she looked at him, she realized she was staring at him as if he were a space alien. She started to laugh, too.

"Maybe I should have called," he said apologetically. "Is this a bad time? Are you working, Emily?"

She nodded. "I'm working on Abbie Carson's brochure."

"Do you mind if I come in?"

Emily backed away from the door. "No." She shook her head earnestly. She was thoroughly and obviously flustered.

When Philip followed her into her apartment, he placed the large, rectangular package he had been carrying on the floor beside the sofa.

"How's your family?" she asked him. She sounded timid, as if she didn't know whether she had the right to ask about them or not.

"Much better. Clint wrote Lisa a note so she was excused from the classes she missed last week. He thought long and hard before doing that, but he decided she needed his support. He decided to give her permission to go on another field trip that's coming up in a few weeks. Lisa convinced him to talk to one of the mothers who's going as a chaperone. Clint has been convinced that these junior high field trips are nothing but one long party bus ride."

"I'm glad." She was honestly happy for all of them, especially Lisa. "It will probably be a little bit of that, too."

"I think that's okay, though, don't you?" Philip asked earnestly. "Lisa's a responsible girl."

"I do." Emily walked to the kitchen table and picked up the copy she had been working on. "Speaking of mothers, thank you for the referral. Abbie Carson came to my office this week. She's a special person." Emily hesitated again. She had so many personal questions to ask him, questions that, for some reason, she felt uncomfortable asking him now. She didn't want to pry. "Has Clint called her yet?"

"I don't think so. I decided not to push him."

"I wish he would call her," Emily said.

"I do, too," Philip agreed. He glanced curiously around the ultrafeminine room. He felt so big in her apartment, as if he didn't fit here, and he thought of sitting in one of her delicate wicker chairs, but he was afraid he might break through it.

Philip picked up the brown paper package and handed it to her. "I want you to have this."

Emily took it from him, all the while watching him, trying to figure out why he had come. "You didn't need to do this."

He grinned at her. "Yes, I did."

"What is it?" She didn't open it. She just pondered the boyish expression on his face.

"Go ahead. It's a present. Open it," he urged her impatiently.

"Yes, sir." She saluted him playfully. Then she ripped open the brown paper and pulled back the tissue. At first, she didn't realize what the sketch was supposed to be. She thought it was a picture he had bought for her. But when she saw the pen-and-ink drawing, she decided he had stumbled on a picture of a possum somewhere, and thinking of Baby Sprout, he had brought it to her.

She propped the drawing up on the coffee table and stepped away from it. "Thank you for the picture of the possum, Philip." She glanced at him from over her shoulder. She wondered if he thought she was odd because she had created a character that was a possum.

She kept looking at the drawing. There was something soft and whimsical about the creature. He looked vaguely familiar to her and she didn't want to seem silly, but Emily had the strangest feeling that she was looking into the face of an old friend. The possum in the picture he had brought her looked exactly as she imagined Baby Sprout would.

"You're going to think I'm crazy," she commented to Philip without turning toward him, "but this is a picture of Baby Sprout! Where did you find it?"

If Emily had been watching Philip, she would have seen his face fall. He was disappointed that she didn't realize he had drawn the possum. But, he reasoned, how was she supposed to know? She couldn't know he was an amateur artist. He had signed the sketch down by Baby Sprout's paw, but he had camouflaged his signature in the fur of the possum's leg. Unless he told her, Emily would probably never notice the name he had scrawled in the lower left-hand corner.

When he didn't answer her question, Emily turned toward him. "Where did you find this?" she asked again. The lilt of excitement in her voice told him she was delighted with his gift.

"Does it really look like Baby Sprout to you?" he asked her, beaming. "Is the nose right? It's a bit squarer than a real possum's nose. But it gives so much personality to his face, doesn't it?"

Emily studied the creature's nose thoughtfully before she answered him. "Yes. It's fine. It's perfect." She turned her eyes up toward his, and when he saw the elfin expression on her face, Philip felt his heart go out to her. "You know," she told him, "you'll probably think I'm crazy, but, Philip, it's uncanny how much like my Baby Sprout this possum really looks."

"Oh." Philip's voice was steady and humble. He didn't want to give himself away, not until she realized who had drawn the picture.

"The strange thing is..." Emily hesitated, pacing the floor. "I wasn't certain myself how Baby Sprout was supposed to look. I had an idea in my head of how other people were supposed to perceive him. But if someone had asked me to produce a picture or to describe the expressions on his face, I wouldn't have been able to do it."

"Is there anything about this drawing that you would change?" Philip asked her innocently.

"No." She considered the sketch again. "Probably not. Maybe his legs. I might make his hind legs shorter and fuller. Through here." She ran one finger down the possum's hind leg. When she did, she spied the signature, P. B. Manning, camouflaged in the fur.

"Here's the artist's signature!" Emily exclaimed. It seemed like a miracle that someone she didn't know had created a picture that fitted so perfectly with something she had only privately envisioned. Emily would have to find the artist and...

She stopped. The initials on the sketch nagged at her. "P. B. Manning." She froze with the picture in her hand and stared at him. *Philip Manning!*

"What's your middle name, Philip?" Her voice was quavering.

"Bradley," he told her.

In a flash, Emily realized what a gift it was that Philip had truly brought her. The sketch *was* a drawing of Baby Sprout. And he had drawn it for her. Tears came to her eyes. She felt for a moment as if Philip had taken her dream and had drawn it and made it real.

"You did this." It was a statement, not a question. There was no doubt in Emily's mind. She had seen his signature. And now she knew why the drawing was so appropriate, so nearly what she wanted. This wasn't a coincidence.

"Yes, I did," Philip said softly, looking deeply into her eyes.

Turning from him, Emily plopped on the sofa with the drawing in her hands. And Philip was surprised when he saw the tears coursing down her cheeks.

"Emily, don't. Please don't cry." He sat beside her on the sofa.

"It's okay." She turned her face up to his, and he felt terrible that she was distressed. Maybe she thought he had tricked her. But she was smiling at him through her tears. "I'm just an emotional person," she apologized. "I cry when I'm happy, too, Philip." She reached over and gingerly touched his knee. "This is the nicest thing that anyone has ever done for me. Thank you."

"You're welcome." Privately, he wondered if maybe he hadn't done something that was too personal. Maybe he had overstepped his bounds as an acquaintance, after all. He had given a face to something that was very, very important to her.

"How did you know how to draw him?"

"You told me." He wrinkled his forehead at her and his eyes were wide, and his expression made it seem as if her telling him had been very simple.

"I couldn't have." Emily was shaking her head. "I didn't know myself," she said, pointing to the sketch. "I couldn't have told you about these fuzzy gray ears. I couldn't have told you where his eyes should go or how his mouth should turn up on one side. You did that yourself."

"No." He held his hand up to her to stop her from the things she was saying. "You inspired it. I started with this elongated nose. Then I squared it. See. Here." He was pointing to his own work to emphasize the things he was saying. "When an artist works, he relies on things he feels inside to give his characters their depth and personality. It was exactly the same thing you were saying about F. Scott Fitzgerald when you were talking to Greg. I work that way, too. When

I designed Baby Sprout, I thought about who you are, Emily." He was talking with his hands and he faced her with his palms up, his fingers outstretched. "That's how I got this little guy. Maybe I figured out from hearing you talk to Bethany how you wanted him to look. You wanted him to be mischievous, so I gave him an impish mouth that curves up on one end. You wanted him to be curious and friendly, so I gave him this twitching nose."

"Tell me about his eyes." Emily sat on her hands and perched higher up beside him on the sofa. "How did you figure out how to draw his eyes?"

Philip looked at her, his expression playful. It was her eyes he saw then, gazing up at him expectantly from her round little-girl face. She looked so beautiful to him, so happy and expectant, that he wondered if, in trying to bring her such a special gift, he had brought her something she thought she didn't deserve and had never expected.

"I liked the eyes that way," he said simply. They reminded him of her eyes. "Sometimes you have to do things a certain way just because they seem right."

"That's how I write my advertising copy," Emily replied. She was still sitting on her hands and gazing at him. "See. I was right. You didn't create from the things I told you about my manuscript. You drew Baby Sprout because of the way you felt about him."

"Do you mind, Emily?" It was easy for her to see the concern in his eyes. "Maybe I shouldn't have drawn this. I didn't mean to detract from anything you've planned or created."

"No." She pulled one hand from beneath her and touched his arm to reassure him. Baby Sprout had sprung to life for her today. "No." The second time she negated his doubts it was for a stronger reason, not just because she wanted to reassure Philip, but because she felt that, in some way, Baby Sprout was better, that she knew him now, because Philip had worked on him, too.

"Do you know anything about illustrating children's books?" she asked him. "Do you know if publishers want to see artwork when a writer submits a story to them?"

"I'm not sure," he told her. He had never considered the topic before. "I suppose if you had an idea in mind, they would like to see it."

"When we submit a television commercial idea to a client, we have one of the artists at Petrie, Simms and Masterson do storyboards," Emily explained. "Would you submit storyboards with a manuscript?"

"Probably." Philip was nodding. He still didn't know what she was getting at.

"Maybe we could work out some sort of an arrangement." She had turned toward him now, and she was demure and yet businesslike when she made her suggestion. "Would you be willing to do some storyboards for Baby Sprout? If my book ever gets published, I want Baby Sprout to look exactly like this." She held Philip's work at arm's length and smiled.

"You would want me to do that?" He was pleased but the idea would take some getting used to. Philip had drawn Baby Sprout for Emily because he had sensed how important the character was to her and because he had wanted to give her a thank-you gift that was interesting and different. "Wouldn't you rather have a professional artist? It could make a difference between having your book published or not."

"Philip," she began, then paused to emphasize the importance of her words. "We've created something together now. Right now, it feels like I came up with Baby Sprout the possum and then you became involved and made him even better. I'm willing to share the limelight." She realized as she coaxed him that if she convinced him to do the artwork she would be obligated to submit her work to a publisher. But that was okay, she reasoned, because she was finally willing to commit to her dream, thanks to Philip.

"Emily," he said as he took her face in his hands. Philip couldn't say more. He was overcome by the fact that she liked his work so well, and that she trusted him enough to place a dream in his hands.

"We're going in the right direction with this," she told him. "I know it." Emily was accustomed to using her intuition when working with advertising accounts and she heeded her inner voice now.

Philip had the feeling, as he looked at her face, so close to his, that Emily was offering him a challenge that might redirect the course of his life. There were times when he felt as if he were two people. Sometimes he was the logical, calculating successful businessman. That part of himself was in direct conflict with his other side, the part that liked to sketch rickety windmills and to tell stories to Clint's kids and to stroll along across a fragrant, still pasture at the farm.

And here was Emily asking him to do something for her that was so much a part of that other side of him—create and sustain an imaginary possum. It sounded like a game to him, something he would only consider doing with the kids. And as he held his breath and closed his eyes and thought about the prospect of working closely with her, he felt very much the same way that she did. Because of their friendship and their ideas, they had given birth to something that was better than it could have been if each of them had tried it alone.

He turned to Emily then, and he grabbed her hand and pulled her up off of the sofa before he gave her his answer. And Emily was suddenly so excited that she didn't flinch or pull away when he swept her into his arms. "Let's collaborate," he said to her, and he planted a fatherly kiss on her nose. Suddenly, just as before, Emily felt stirred by him and enveloped by his closeness.

He looked down at her and felt as if an entirely new world was opening up for him. He couldn't resist telling her. "It sounds like so much more fun working on Baby Sprout than finalizing multimillion-dollar real estate sales."

She bit her lip and shook her head. "Sure, it's more fun. But you won't get rich from it. That's for certain."

"You never know," he commented wryly. "I want a contract. I want my share of the royalties, too."

"Oh?" She raised her eyebrows. "This could be a wonderful working relationship. Don't go getting greedy on me."

"I'll do my best." He winked at her. "I'm serious, though." His eyes were suddenly somber. "Doing things like this, being creative, thinking about people means so much more to me than just sitting in my office concocting deals."

"So why didn't you start out as a book illustrator or a social worker?" she asked. "Sounds to me like you jumped headfirst into an all-consuming business."

"I did," he told her. "It was what was expected of me, I suppose." *No, it was what Morgan expected of me,* Philip thought. His eyes narrowed. "Why are you asking anyhow? I did the same thing you've done."

"I know," she said, nodding. "I guess that's why I asked you the question." Emily couldn't help thinking of Abbie Carson, of the people-oriented business the woman had established, the business that counted its assets in love and discipline and children's futures rather than in dollars and cents.

"What is it?" Philip asked. He couldn't guess what she was thinking, but he knew her mind was someplace far away. "Are you very lonely sometimes, Emily?" He asked her quietly. "I am."

"Sometimes," she said, averting her eyes. "But that doesn't matter."

He held her face in his hands again, and for some reason, he looked different to Emily then, as if he had grown younger, as if he had grown carefree. He searched her face with his eyes as he smiled at her, and she wanted to cry out from the sheer sensation of his nearness. He was looking at her like a little boy who had just brought home his first bicycle.

"Philip," she said softly, and the tears came to her eyes again, this time because she knew she had to push him away.

He had his hands beneath her hair, on the back of her neck. And all Emily wanted to do was close her eyes and let him kiss her. But Emily couldn't let that happen. She couldn't let him reach out to her again. He had brought her the sketch of Baby Sprout and he had brought her his friendship, and she couldn't jeopardize the things they were sharing in the hope that they might find more. Touching this way, feeling this way, didn't last. Emily's parents had proved that to her. "No, Philip." Emily wedged her palms up between them. "Don't do this."

He pulled his hands back around on the side of her neck and stroked her skin there with his thumbs, and as he looked down at her, it was the first time that he consciously realized he was touching her. And it surprised him, as he studied her face, that he was holding her and running his fingers through her hair, and he wasn't thinking of Morgan at all. He could only think of Emily in his arms. She seemed so open to him, so alive. And as she pushed her arms up against his shoulders, he only wanted to protect her, to shield her from her loneliness.

"Don't push me away, Emily," he said, and the blue in his eyes turned to ice when it mixed with the resolve that welled up in them.

"I have to, Philip." She turned her face away from him and pressed it into his shoulder. It was too late though. Philip had already seen the fear in her eyes. "I have to, Philip."

"Why?" He gripped her by the shoulders and pushed her back so he could read the expression on her face. "What are you afraid of?"

"Nothing." She turned her face away from him again.

He cupped her head in his hands and turned her toward him a second time. "Don't tell me that." His voice was a low rumble in his throat. "Don't tell me it's nothing."

She saw the anger in his eyes and it frightened her, but it gave her more strength to stand up for what she believed was right. Anger was a familiar emotion to her. It was an emotion that, in her experience, went hand in hand with love. "Okay." Her voice was thick with conviction. "It's much more than that." She reached up and took his hands away from her face. She held them in her own while she spoke. "I don't want you to make me feel this way. I don't want you to hold me."

Philip pulled away from her. "What are you saying, Emily?"

She spun away from him, and when she did, she turned toward the drawing of Baby Sprout. It was propped up on the sofa, and now the creature looked as if it were jeering at her. She wheeled back toward Philip, and this time he saw the desperation in her eyes.

"Tell me, Emily. Tell me why." He could not hide the defeat in his voice. He had come with the hope of becoming something special to her. He had thought she was someone he could depend on. She reminded him of Morgan Brockner when she talked of the things she didn't want. And he felt betrayed because he had been with her before, and she had been so different.

She was shaking her head at him and backing away from him, and Philip had to fight for control to keep from shouting at her. "Talk to me. Please, Emily."

It was exactly the right thing for him to say to her. During the years she had lain upstairs in her bed and had listened to her parents venting their rage on each other, she had never heard either one of them say "Talk to me." The muscles in her face relaxed. "Philip," she said softly as she reached one hand out to him and tugged on his shirt sleeve. "I'm sorry. I withdrew from you. I didn't mean to shut you out. It's me. It's what you're doing to me."

"Are you afraid of this?" he asked. He didn't have to say more. She knew he was talking about the growing attraction, between them.

"Yes, I am."

"There's no need to be." It was funny. When Philip remembered Morgan Brockner's betrayal, it reminded him that there were reasons he should be afraid of these feelings, too. But Emily's fear automatically placed him in a reassuring role.

She looked up at him and saw the tenderness in his eyes, and she wanted more than anything to believe him. It seemed to her that the two of them had formed a wordless bond because he had been able to look at her and see Baby Sprout through her eyes. But even though he understood her in a way no one ever had, probably because of it, she stood the chance of giving in to feelings she wasn't ready to explore if she did let him touch her.

She let go of his sleeve and buried her face in her hands. She couldn't look at him. "I don't want to hurt you. I don't want to try to drag you into a relationship with me."

"Who said anything about a relationship?" It was his pride that was speaking now. Talking to Emily when she was like this, when she was so stubbornly unyielding, provoked feelings like those he had experienced trying to reason with Morgan. Only it had been different with Morgan. This conversation with Emily was infinitely more frustrating. Philip felt that with Morgan he had had a chance. But Emily wasn't giving an inch.

"Not me." She was furious now, with herself more than with him. "I don't want to need anybody, Philip. I don't want to rely on something that I know won't last."

He didn't know she was talking about the nature of love. He thought she believed him to be fickle, for some reason he was unaware of. "Don't, then," he told her gruffly. "Don't even try. What you feel when I touch you won't matter at all in the long run, will it?"

"No." Her voice was measured now and she spoke with no emotion. "It won't. Be my friend, Philip," she said, "but don't try to convince me I should be more than that to you."

"Maybe we shouldn't even try for friendship," he said sarcastically.

Philip turned away from her and stared at the funny, friendly little possum he had drawn for her. He didn't see the hurt in her eyes. He didn't know that for

Emily friendship was something she didn't place much faith in, either.

"I'm surprised," she said to him dryly. "I didn't think you would be cruel."

He went to the door and turned the knob before he wheeled back to face her. "I'm sorry, Emily," he told her. "I shouldn't have come."

She didn't answer him. She just stared at him as he stood with his fist clenched around the doorknob. At that moment, she wanted to scream at the feeling of almost tangible hopelessness she couldn't explain. She would have given anything if Philip had been willing to take her, just as she was, as his friend and nothing more.

But she knew, as she watched him walk away, that she had no right to expect that of him. He deserved so much more than she would ever be able to give him. That thought, when it came to her, was the one that gave Emily final resolve. She walked to the doorway and closed the door behind him. Then she picked up the portrait of Baby Sprout and stared at it in silence until she heard the sound of Philip's car roaring away from the parking lot below.

CHAPTER SIX

EMILY ARRIVED at Abbie Carson's office early. She did her best not to think about Philip and the things she had said to him while she waited in the front room of the Absolutely Moms office. One entire wall in the front room was covered with photographs—large ones, small ones, professional portraits and quick family snapshots. All were of children. Emily passed the time looking at them. The children were smiling and playing and posing, and there was something about the joy in their faces that made them all look similar, as if they were all cousins or sisters and brothers sharing in the same very special family. And in a way they were, thought Emily.

Her mind wandered back to something Abbie had told her during their first meeting, something about being a mother. "There are many reasons for becoming an Absolutely Mom. Maybe you feel like something is missing in your own life and maybe you want to try to find it. Or maybe you just want to give to someone else what you never could have...."

The idea of becoming an Absolutely Mom was diametrically opposed to the things Emily had once wanted—the golden plaques on the wall, the marketing seminars, the statistics. She had wanted all the status and glamour of success in advertising once. But now she knew there were other things she needed in her life besides money and professional recognition. The sketch of Baby Sprout that Philip had drawn for her kept tugging at her heart, reminding her of the dreams she had forgotten to follow. She wanted to be free of the fear that had pulled her away from Philip. She didn't want the superficiality of living for plaques and awards anymore. She wanted to truly live. And she thought she knew a place she could find out how to.

When Abbie walked into the room to greet her, Emily handed her the copy she had written for the Absolutely Moms brochure. "What do you think?" she asked breathlessly after Abbie had read over her work.

Abbie, smiling from ear to ear, was obviously pleased. "Now I know why Philip Manning recommended you, Emily. I love this. You've captured everything I wanted to say in these few paragraphs." Abbie stopped and looked at Emily for a moment as if she thought the younger woman might have something else to say.

Emily wondered if Abbie had already guessed what she was thinking of. Quickly she went over the billing that the agency would send for the brochure work. Next, she outlined the printing schedule. Then her face softened. "May I fill out an application to be an Absolutely Mom, Abbie?" Emily wondered if she sounded abrupt, as she often did when she was nervous. What if Abbie Carson didn't think she was qualified? She would feel like an utter fool.

But Abbie didn't discourage her. She did not ask, "Are you certain you want to do this?" the way anyone else would have. Abbie Carson had wondered about Emily ever since the morning she first met her in her office at Petrie, Simms and Masterson. There was something melancholy about Emily, something sad in her eyes, that made Abbie wonder if Emily was unhappy. Emily had asked Abbie about becoming an Absolutely Mom as if she was afraid that she might be unworthy of the position. Abbie wondered if the young woman approached all of life that way, as if she thought she should back away from it.

"Fill these papers out tonight, and I'll begin arranging things tomorrow," said Abbie as she handed Emily a packet of information. "Are you willing to move in with a family? I'll need you to do that."

Emily didn't hesitate. She wanted it desperately. It was all part of finally facing the prospect of having what she wanted most. "Yes."

Emily drove straight back to Petrie, Simms and Masterson to give Lloyd her two weeks' notice. And when she did, Lloyd was furious. He didn't understand why she was leaving. At first, he was certain she was becoming an Absolutely Mom out of spite, because he hadn't agreed to put the snorkeler and the bride in the city bus ads.

By three o'clock Lloyd had calmed down enough to talk to her. But when he asked her again why she had to leave, Emily didn't know how to tell him what it was that she longed for. She only knew that she wanted to share Abbie's vitality. She wanted to share a portion of her life with someone who needed her. "I have to resolve this for myself, Lloyd," she told him. "I don't need a professional career right now. I need something more."

EMILY KEPT HERSELF SANE during the next two weeks by sorting out her belongings and packing them away for storage. Shoes went into the "take" box. Pans and magazines went into the "Dad's basement" box. Eggs, vegetables and a half gallon of milk went into a container Emily was leaving with her neighbor. She finished packing at noon on Friday. Exhausted from the effort of packing and the emotional strain of changing her whole life on what now seemed like a whim, she went to bed. She slept until ten the next morning, rushed to breakfast and dress, and by lunchtime she heard a knock on her door. When Emily opened it, Abbie Carson was there, grinning. Abbie handed Emily three long-stemmed persimmon roses wrapped in green florist paper. "You have a family, Emily," she said quietly, her eyes shining. "You now are the adopted mother of three children. One for each rose."

Before Emily could take the roses, Abbie launched into a description of her new life. She would be living in a cabin that had its own small kitchen and a white wicker rocking chair and a porch for sunning on the south side of the house.

"Where is this place?" Emily asked, suddenly feeling like an expectant child. She hadn't felt this way since she'd been a little girl, playing house. And perhaps, she mused, that was what she was doing now. Abbie had certainly made it sound like the experience would be similar. "Is it near here?" Emily asked breathless. Then without waiting for an answer she said, "Tell me about the children."

"It's a good drive from here, down south in Ellis County near Waxahachie. You'll be living on a farm. The father's name is Clint Manning."

Abbie kept talking, but Emily didn't hear a word she was saying. Her blood had turned cold. All she could comprehend was the relentless pounding of her heart. The sound seemed to pulse up through her ears. The Mannings. Abbie had put her with the Mannings, to take Amanda's place with Philip's nieces and nephew.

I can't do it, Emily thought. *It's all been a mistake.* Clint Manning had no idea who he had just hired to take over as a mother in his household. Emily could only guess that Clint had finally called Abbie and that either Abbie had no idea the Waxahachie Mannings were related to the Philip Manning she knew in Dallas or else Abbie didn't think it was important that they were. She couldn't have known about the day that Emily had already spent on the farm.

Then, almost immediately, her panic disappeared. In fact, the more Emily thought about it, the more feasible the position at the Manning farm began to sound. There was nothing between her and Philip, anyway. They were only business acquaintances. And Emily decided she would love to accept the position on the farm in Waxahachie. She knew she would be living in the cabin in the pecan grove, and she could picture everything just the way it had been the day she had found Lisa in the tree.

Lisa. Lisa could be her biggest challenge and her greatest joy. The child needed a mother and a friend desperately.

As if on cue, Abbie pulled a manila folder from the satchel she was carrying. "The kids always help pick out their Absolutely Mom," Abbie said pointedly. Emily realized then that Abbie must know that Greg and Lisa and Bethany had seen her application and had selected her for a reason. The kids had asked for her!

The envelope Abbie handed her just said "To our new mom Emily from Lisa." Emily opened it and, when she did, she understood exactly why Lisa had sent it to her. It was a small poster with a colored photograph of a funny-looking furry monkey swinging through the broad waxy leaves of some exotic African tree. The caption below him read, "Find a place you like and go there."

Emily grinned up at Abbie. The gift was perfect. Of course she would go. She and Lisa were very much alike. They could spend hours talking about things and climbing trees. And maybe someday Emily could gather enough courage to tell Lisa about her own mother. And then there was Greg, lanky and friendly, and little Bethany who had been so interested in her stories about Baby Sprout. Emily found she didn't care about the adult Mannings anymore. Not Clint or Philip or Amanda. She only wanted to be with the children and give them what she could—her friendship and her love.

When Emily had wandered into the pecan grove with Philip three weeks before, she had peeked into the window of the camp house and she hadn't been intrigued by its furnishings at all. It was a typical one-room cabin with two metal beds at one end and a rustic kitchen at the other, with a two-sided wood stove in the middle of the room to separate the two areas.

Now, as she stood on the front porch with her suitcase in her hand, she realized that the cabin had been transformed. The kitchen was polished and spotless and there was a Kerr jar full of Texas flora that colored in the fall, pyracantha berries and yellow and red oak and maple leaves, sitting on the counter. It was such a simple, homey gesture that Emily couldn't help but be pleased. It was much nicer than an elaborate florist's arrangement or a growing potted plant to welcome her, and as Emily sniffed the wild weedy fragrance, she realized her priorities must already be changing, recalling the elaborate floral arrangements Lloyd always sent her after a particularly successful ad campaign.

The two metal beds had been replaced with one old-fashioned wrought-iron double bed, painted white and then antique gold on the tips and in the florets. It was covered with a peach-colored sheet and an exquisite cream hand-filleted cotton bedspread. There was a fat, obviously loved, white stuffed dog tied with a peach ribbon perched jauntily between the pillows.

"We didn't have any fancy furniture or anything," Lisa explained from the door where she stood. She had followed Emily around for the past forty-five minutes, ever since Emily and Abbie had arrived at the farm. "Bethany donated the dog. His name's Fluffy." She hesitated for a moment. "He's really her favorite animal, so you might want to give him back. She's got this huge animal collection in her room."

"I'll give him back with my thanks. It was sweet of her to lend him to me." Emily was touched by the way Lisa cared for her younger sister. She picked Fluffy up and gave him a hug. "But it's good to have him here as a welcome. I'll bring him back to the house tomorrow."

As Emily glanced once more around the cabin, she realized that at this moment she couldn't imagine herself in any other place in the world. She was as happy as she could remember, surrounded by soft colors and the sun outside and the rustling of the trees. She wondered how long she would be living there, how long she would be part of this family. For one moment, she let herself wish it might be forever. But the wish would never be fulfilled. For when Amanda came out of the coma, these children wouldn't need an Absolutely Mom around anymore. They would have their real mother back. And Emily wanted that for them almost as much as she wanted a family to call her own.

IT WAS AMAZING how fast things went back to normal at the Manning household after Abbie drove away and Emily settled in. She didn't do much the first few days she was there. In fact, she just sat in the main room of the big house by the fire working on a needlepoint and being available. She was disappointed that the kids didn't come to her immediately whenever they needed something, but she reminded herself to give them time to adjust. And soon enough she was rewarded.

She returned Fluffy to Bethany on the second day she was there, and Bethany shyly asked her if she would like to learn how to sign the manual alphabet. They started working together every evening after school was out, and Emily did her best to learn the letters.

Bethany and Emily practiced in the kitchen while they put together a recipe for sun sassafras tea and Emily spelled *sassafras* to Bethany without having to try twice. *Sassafras* had been an easy word to sign. It seemed as if *s* was about the only letter Emily had to know. Bethany had been excited and Emily had hugged her and she felt as if the two of them had made a breakthrough of sorts.

It was a quiet evening several days after Emily arrived when the two of them sat down in the family room in front of the huge white-manteled fireplace and Emily got brave enough to bring out the *"Baby Sprout and Priscilla"* manuscript. Then, carefully, so she wouldn't make many mistakes, Emily slowly read the story aloud to Bethany using the manual alphabet she had learned.

At the same time, Lisa, Greg and Clint were having a shouting match in the family room. Clint had been to visit Amanda before five that morning, and he was exhausted. He had come home to find that Greg had taken the Studebaker out of the garage and driven it to school. Lisa was involved because she was walking home with Tracy for the first time in many months, and Greg had given them both a ride back into town to the drugstore to buy a cherry Coke. And Clint was angry with them all.

"You are not old enough to drive that car," Clint said loudly from the family room. "It will be another seven months before you get your driver's license. Who do you think would have been responsible for your sister and her friend if you had had an accident?"

Greg didn't answer. He was learning about responsibility, and Greg didn't think it was fair of his father to place all the blame on him. He knew he had taken the car without permission. But Lisa had promised him she wouldn't tell if he only gave her and Tracy a ride. So he had been trapped by two thirteen-year-olds. And now Lisa wasn't saying anything. She was sitting on the sofa looking sad and sorry and innocent.

Clint looked out of the family room to Bethany and Emily at this point in the argument. He wanted to prevent both his older kids from using the car and the telephone and from going to the drugstore. He had in mind asking Lisa and Greg what they thought was fair before he doled out punishment, but he didn't think it was appropriate for Bethany to listen to the whining that was certain to take place. And he didn't want to scare Emily to death during her first week here. So he moved them into his study to continue the conference. They marched out in orderly file, looking collectively sheepish.

Emily and Bethany were all alone then, talking in hushed tones. Bethany was reading the manuscript aloud now, and Emily was giggling and doing her best to help Bethany pronounce *Priscilla*. They were sitting, heads together, laughing and reading, when Emily heard whistling outside and someone tromped up on the wooden porch.

"Anybody home?" The screen door swung open, and there stood Philip Manning at the door with an overnight bag on one arm.

Emily grabbed Bethany's arm without thinking. Now she felt silly, for Clint had told her that Philip wandered in and out whenever he pleased. She had been expecting to see him, but she wasn't prepared, all the same. Even though she'd mulled it over and over, she hadn't finished deciding exactly what she was going to say to him. She certainly hadn't imagined his wandering in after an hour's drive through Dallas traffic and just finding her sitting on the floor in his brother's home as if she had been there forever.

When Philip walked into the front room and saw Emily, he felt as if someone had pulled the rug out from under him. It was just like the day he had walked into Morgan's office and had found her belongings gone.

Philip had learned how to protect himself after Morgan. He had buried himself in his business, and he had grown a thick skin and had taught himself not to care about anyone outside his family. Morgan Brockner was not a threat to him any longer. But Emily Lattrell was. She was beautiful and joyous and sad sometimes, and Philip didn't know exactly how to deal with the attachment he felt to her in spite of himself. They had become friends and he had drawn her a picture of Baby Sprout and then she had pushed him away. Since then, Philip had made it a point to stay away from Petrie, Simms and Masterson. He had conducted his business with Lloyd Masterson over the telephone. He didn't intend to see Emily again. He was convinced, after the way she had treated him, that when she'd asked him to illustrate her Baby Sprout books she really hadn't meant it. She probably hadn't thought it through. She hadn't wanted Philip to touch her, but she had acted so impressed by his work and, in a way, that had been his attempt to touch her, too. He had tried to analyze the things she must have been feeling that evening. He had done his best to come up with a reason that she wouldn't let him reach out to her, but he was still confused about her reaction to him.

And now, here was Emily sitting on Clint's living room floor as if it belonged to her.

"Hello, Philip," she said quietly. The moment was an awkward one for both of them. Emily could have hit herself because her voice came out sounding so meek. She was desperately glad to see him, but she felt odd welcoming him into what had surely almost become his own home. She had a horrible feeling just then when she saw the look on his face, the feeling that she wasn't good enough for any of them, that she had nothing to give the children, that she should never have come. It was a flashback to her own childhood, into the hundreds of days when her mother had walked into the room and had looked down at her with dizzy distaste.

"What are you doing here?" he asked her and the neutral tone of his voice didn't even begin to hint at the turmoil he was feeling inside.

"She's our new adopted mom." Bethany piped up, saving Emily from a lengthy explanation. The nine-year-old tilted her head up at Emily and smiled at her. Emily was still holding her arm. "She's helping us until Mom gets well."

"This is quite a surprise," Philip said to Emily coldly. "I certainly didn't expect to see you here."

"I know." She answered, and as she did, she felt as if she was unintentionally playing a cruel joke on him just by being here.

Philip was furious with himself for the things he was feeling as Emily glared silently at him. He felt angry because she was here. But he was glad to see her, too. Walking into his brother's house and finding her was like turning back the clock to the first day they'd spent together. Emily seemed so reachable to him, so like a friend, and even though he had been avoiding her, just finding her here was a special sign to him, a sign of promise, as if God had seen fit to give him a second chance with her. Maybe now he could reach out to Emily to coax her into telling him what she was so afraid of. The way she backed away from him frustrated him and made him angry. But it was confusion that threatened to overtake him now, as he looked at her and considered his own feelings. He was furious with himself for being fool enough to want to see her when her rejection of him had been so clear.

"Where's my brother?" Philip asked. Emily wanted to shout at him. He had brought her here before and had played a nice game with her, but when it came to sharing what really mattered—his family—he couldn't do it. He made her feel the way her mother used to make her feel—guilty and sad and accountable for something she couldn't control.

"He's in his study with Lisa and Greg," she almost snapped, and even as she said the words, she was mad at herself for her tone of voice. She was feeling possessive and defensive, as if he was the outsider, not her. Philip pushed open Clint's study door and Emily heard the loud conversation inside halt.

Bethany sat on the sofa reading *Baby Sprout and Priscilla*, trying to understand the exchange between her uncle and Emily. "Are you unhappy?" Philip's youngest niece asked as Emily stood staring out at the night through the front bay window.

"Oh, Bethany—" Emily shook her head as she turned toward the girl. "—I'm fine. Just tired, I guess. I think I'd better go to bed."

"May I finish reading this?" Bethany indicated Emily's manuscript. "I like it."

"Thank you." Emily's smile was genuine. Bethany was the first person she had let read the entire manuscript. "Yes, you may."

Emily gathered her things and plodded across the dark meadow to her camp house in the pecan grove. She sat in the darkness for a long while, wondering about Philip, if he would talk Clint into sending her away, if this cabin would still be her home tomorrow.

The lights stayed on in the main house for a long time that night. Greg had been told not to drive the Studebaker around the farm, which Clint had let him do on occasion previously. Lisa couldn't talk on the telephone for a week. Clint hated to do that to her. He and Emily had talked just the day before about how pleased they were that Lisa was reaching out to her friends again. Lisa had been furious at him when he told her what he had decided, but she hadn't been half as angry as Philip was now, as he sat across the room from his brother, questioning Clint about Emily. The children had long since gone to their rooms, and Philip had practically pounced on his brother because he didn't understand what Emily Lattrell was doing there.

"Didn't you ask her?" Clint was taken aback. It had been a long time since he had seen his brother this angry. "I didn't know you knew her all that well. I would have talked to you about it, but it didn't seem necessary. Your friend Abbie Carson thought she would be right for the job."

"Great," Philip said. "Abbie Carson is in on this little joke, too."

"It isn't a joke, bud." Clint could remember only weeks before when Philip had practically begged him to call Absolutely Moms and hire someone. Now, ironically, he had done it and Philip was mad. "We all like Emily. And Lisa loves her. The two of them have become friends. And Lisa is making friends at school again because of her."

Philip softened a bit. "I'm glad for Lisa. What did Emily do? Just show up on your doorstep this week?"

"Give the woman some credit, Philip. She applied for the job. Abbie brought out information on several women she thought would be appropriate. We picked Emily."

Philip was silent.

Clint didn't know whether he should say what he was thinking now. Philip was likely to belt him. "You're attracted to her, aren't you? I haven't seen you act this way about anyone since you were working with Morgan Brockner."

Philip jumped out of the chair and stormed across the room toward his brother. "What if I am? What difference does it make?"

"You come in here like you're ready to belt somebody and you ask me that?" Clint asked pointedly. "It makes a big difference to me."

"I don't know what to think about Emily Lattrell," Philip said soberly. "I walk in here and find her sitting on the floor in the front room as if she owns the place. I feel like I'm flailing out at something, too. I can't seem to get away from her."

"She had excellent references." There was a sparkle in Clint's eyes. He couldn't resist teasing his brother just a bit. It had been a long time since he had seen Philip acting this way.

Philip saw the humor in his brother's eyes, and he softened a bit. "I didn't mean that, Clint," he said. "I'm glad she's here. I wanted the children to have someone special."

"Do you feel something for the woman?" Clint asked. He wanted to hear his brother admit it. Philip needed someone like Emily in his life. She was down-to-earth and joyous. And Clint had the feeling that just being with her would point Philip's life in the right direction. Clint knew that his brother would never admit he was lonely. But a multimillion-dollar corporation made a cold bedfellow.

"She won't let me feel anything for her," Philip said abruptly. He picked up a portrait of his brother's family from where it stood on the study file cabinet. He took it all in with a single glance—Manderly's grin, Clint's pride, the children's happy energy. Then he wheeled to face his brother. "This is crazy," he told Clint. "I hate feeling this confused."

"Is it Morgan?" Clint had to ask his brother that question. "Are you afraid to trust Emily because of what happened with Morgan?"

"No," Philip said vehemently. "That's what makes the whole thing so crazy. Emily Lattrell should scare me to death. But she doesn't. I see her and she backs away and I want to follow her. I needed to find a place where I could come and think clearly. Then I walk in and find her sitting on the living room floor. How am I supposed to react?"

"The kids are already pretty attached to her." Clint couldn't keep from smiling smugly. "You brought her out here and introduced her to them. When it came time for her to move in last week, they felt she was already a member of this family."

"Great." Philip shook his head at his brother. The sarcasm in his voice was obvious. "I'm glad I could play such an important role in helping your children adjust."

Clint smiled at his brother then, an honest smile, and Philip could see all the love in his eyes. "It's worth it, you know. Manderly and I have had hundreds of rough spots to climb over. But the joy of it all, the reassurance of loving someone and knowing they will never leave you..." Clint's voice trailed off. He was thinking, as he spoke, of the woman he loved lying silent in a hospital room. She hadn't left him. Clint had faith in his wife and he had faith in God. And Clint knew that if any outside force might bring Manderly back, his faith was strong enough to make it happen.

CHAPTER SEVEN

THE CABIN WAS COLD the next morning when Emily awoke, and something inside her was icy, too. She didn't know where she would go if Philip made her leave. She had already subleased her apartment for the next six months, and she didn't dare go back to Lloyd and tell him that she had failed.

She felt defeated this morning. In the past few days, she had given everything she had to give to Clint and the children. Seeing Philip last night and learning of his disapproval of her as a mother for his brother's family had been totally draining.

Emily walked to the main house to start cooking breakfast, and she was relieved to find everyone except Clint still asleep. It was Saturday and Clint hadn't yet gone to see Amanda. She was glad that at least on weekends he could get some extra rest.

Emily was mixing batter for apple raisin muffins when the telephone rang and she heard Clint answer it. He motioned for her. "The call's for you, Emily."

"Who is it?"

"They didn't say."

Emily took the call in his office, and when the woman on the other end of the line started talking, her voice sounded so feeble that Emily almost didn't recognize it. "Mother?"

"Yes." The voice was haunting. As Emily stood by Clint's desk, looking stricken and sad, Clint grabbed a folder of papers from the file cabinet and waved goodbye to her. He was going to visit his wife. Emily held on to his office chair for support. Her knuckles were white because her hands were clenched so tightly. "I stopped by your office to see you in Dallas the other day and you weren't there. They gave me this number. Where are you living, darling?"

"Here," Emily said, badly shaken. It had been a long time since she had talked to her mother, or wanted to. "On a farm. In Waxahachie." As Emily spoke, she didn't see Philip come down the stairs behind her and head for the kitchen. The telephone had awakened him, and he needed a cup of coffee. Once he was in the kitchen, Philip couldn't help but hear the things she was saying. Emily's voice was quiet, but it was shrill and quavery, too, and her words easily carried into the next room. "I'm working here."

"Lloyd Masterson tells me that you're baby-sitting children." The voice on the end of the line oozed polite displeasure. It was a tone of voice that Emily had grown accustomed to over the years. "And you've quit that wonderful position at the advertising agency. You know that's what we sent you to college for. You wanted to be a professional."

Emily flinched. Her mother had not sent her to college. Her father had. And Emily had helped him. The money she had earned during an internship with a local newspaper had gone to pay for books and part of her tuition each semester. "I still am a professional." It was all she could say right then. Tears were welling up in her eyes, and soon she would be trembling, too.

"I went by to see you so we could go to lunch together. But you weren't there." Emily was certain her mother was trying to rub salt in an old wound. But she couldn't have known her mother thought she was running away from her. It was hard for her now to see her daughter, to start things over, when she had never been there for her as a child.

"Where are you, Mother?" Emily asked. "The last time I talked to Daddy, he had no idea where you were."

"I live in Dallas," the woman said, and she did her best to make her voice sound pleasant. Emily had no way of knowing that on her end of the phone her mother was trembling, too. "I should call your father, I suppose." Then she added, "Does he know what you're doing?"

"Yes, Mother." Emily took a deep breath. "I'm proud of what I'm doing. Daddy promised he'd come out and visit the farm sometime to see it. I'm living here taking care of three children who don't have a mother. They've lost their mother." She didn't add *just as I lost mine*. For if she acknowledged the things she was thinking just then, she was certain that she would lose control and rage at her mother or simply start to cry. She couldn't do either. Not here. Not now.

"Why didn't they just hire a baby-sitter? I was proud of you when you were an advertising executive. I enjoyed talking about you to all my friends.

What am I going to tell them now? That you live on some man's farm and you're baby-sitting his kids?"

Emily couldn't endure the conversation much longer. The job with Clint and the kids was beginning to mean a great deal to her and her mother was belittling it. They hadn't talked to each other in months, and even now her mother couldn't do anything besides criticize her. Emily's heart ached. "I don't care what you tell them, Mother." But as her mother's disapproving voice droned on, Emily wondered if maybe she had made the wrong decision. Philip seemed to think so. And now so did her mother. "You've got to try to understand," she pleaded as if she wanted to convince herself as well as the woman on the other end of the telephone line. "I need this. I need to know I can love someone, that I can nurture others, that I can be a whole person, without having you and your alcoholic friends around to approve or disapprove." It was a cruel thing to say and Emily knew it. "Please, Mother, don't make me feel guilty for this, too."

"When have I ever made you feel guilty about anything?" Emily's mother honestly didn't know. The two had lived together for eighteen years and they didn't know each other at all.

Emily was getting brave, and she said something that had been swimming in her head ever since she had met Abbie Carson. "It's people who are important, Mother. Don't worry about things or reputations." One of the reasons her mother had turned to alcohol a long time ago was that she was concerned about her own reputation and the things she owned, but Emily had had no way of knowing that. "When it comes down to the bottom line, it's the people in your life who matter, not the awards you've won or your bank account or your professional image. People are all the same, Mother. And life is so much easier if you like them."

"You're being totally disrespectful." Emily's mother hadn't expected a lecture. There were muffled noises on the other end of the line, and Emily couldn't tell whether she was sobbing or just angry.

"I'm not being disrespectful. I'm telling you something you need to know." She could have added, because I love you, but she didn't. She wasn't certain whether she loved her mother. She didn't know if she was capable of it now. She had once, but that had been a long, long time ago. They had grown miles apart during the past years. It was the respect that had disappeared between them first, and with it had gone the love. But maybe she should try. She was about to say something else, to try to make amends once more, but she realized it was too late. Halfway through her next sentence, Emily heard a dial tone. Her mother had hung up on her. The moment had passed.

Emily stared down at the push buttons on the telephone until they became a blur. She listened to the dial tone change to a harsher tone as an immense wave of homesickness washed over her. Her knees buckled under her, and she sank to the floor like a broken toy. When Philip went to her, he found her sobbing with the telephone receiver still in her hand.

"Emily." His voice was gentle. He knew he had overheard something very private and very important. Whatever Emily's mother had said to her over the telephone had shattered her. He had no way to know that it hadn't just been today's call that had done it. It had been a lifetime of painful misunderstandings.

The tears streamed down Emily's face, and Philip couldn't help but compare her to a Raggedy Ann doll, with no makeup and flushed cheeks, dressed in blue jeans and a red plaid flannel shirt, looking totally broken. Philip was suddenly very, very sorry for the things he had said to Emily last night.

"You're here because of her, aren't you?" he asked. She nodded and Philip felt his heart go out to her when she spoke.

"I guess I just had to get away from all that."

"The fighting with your mother?"

"I haven't seen her in a long time, Philip," she explained. "Remember when I told you..." She paused. She was about to tell him something that had been very hard to tell anybody. The telephone call with her mother had broken down her reserve. "...that my mother had been sick once? She's an alcoholic, Philip. I haven't really had a mother, ever."

He didn't say anything. He sensed she needed to talk, and he was willing to be there for her.

"When I talked to Abbie and she told me about Absolutely Moms, it seemed like her ideas and this chance to be a mother for somebody might help me resolve some of the things I've been feeling all these years."

He stooped down beside her and she handed him the telephone receiver. He reached up and put it back on the phone for her. But he came back down to the floor and he sat cross-legged beside her to listen to her talk.

There was one tear hanging from the tip of her chin and Philip reached toward her and gently brushed it away. She was so sad, so wistful. He would have done anything to help her just then. He could hardly bear it as she smiled at him through her tears. "I guess I should be able to control those feelings. Her rejection shouldn't matter to me anymore, but it does." She wiped more tears away with the back of her hand.

"You know," said Philip, as he took one wisp of her hair that was stuck to the dampness of her cheek and stroked it back into place. "You told her the right things. You told her that it was people who counted, not jobs or images or awards." How different his own life might have been if he and Morgan had only been so wise. "Maybe someday she'll realize that." Philip was glad he had come downstairs when he had. Emily seemed so much more like a person he could understand now.

"I'm sorry, Philip." Emily started to get up off the floor, but he sat rooted to the spot. "I shouldn't have just come to your family like this. I should have called to let you know, at least. I'm certain that you and Clint and Abbie can find someone who will be a better adopted mom for the kids."

That was what Philip had thought last night. But now he wasn't so certain. Emily had a lot invested in being there. And it did seem fair to give her a chance. "If Amanda could see us all now, I know she would be pleased by the choices we've made. Clint told me last night how happy the kids were when they decided to adopt you. I had no right to be so hateful last night,'' he apologized. ''I hope you'll forgive me.'' Finally understanding why she had come, finally finding her, had touched something deep within him. Emily Lattrell had a lot to offer his nieces, his nephew and his brother. And they had a lot to offer her.

''I'd like to stay.'' Her eyes met his and held them. She wasn't sorry he had overheard her telephone conversation. She had held it all inside and had carried the burden alone for so long and her heart felt lighter, as if he was helping her carry some of it just because he knew about it, too. ''Thank you,'' she told him. ''And, yes, I forgive you.''

''What are you thanking me for?'' he asked.

''For telling me I said the right thing to Mother. I have a history of not saying the right things to her. The harder I try with her, the more I mess it up.'' Pouring out her heart to him felt wonderful.

''Stop trying so hard.'' He reached out and playfully struck a fist against her chin. ''Just be you,'' he said sincerely. He hated people who plotted every word and every movement as if they were blocking a play. Morgan had done that.

Emily seemed peaceful now and as he watched her he marveled that last night he had said such cruel things to her and this morning they were still friends.

''You know you can do it,'' he told her. ''You can be a wonderful mom to these children.'' He knew she needed encouragement right now. And he wanted her to know that he had decided to have faith in her. ''I told Clint a long time ago that someone would come along and would turn this family upside down. I just didn't know it would be you."

They heard Bethany coming downstairs, and Emily smiled at him as she dried her eyes and hurried to the kitchen to pour muffin batter into the tins.

"Jumping Jehosophat," Philip signed to Bethany when she came romping into the kitchen. "Good morning."

Emily's first Saturday on the Manning farm was a special one. Clint remained at the hospital most of the morning, but the rest of them strolled out into the pasture and spent the day meeting the cows. Greg was strangely quiet but he went with them, too, and Emily was honored to have so many people showing her around.

There was one particularly friendly cow that followed them across the pasture, and after following them a good while, the animal nosed Emily.

"That cow is Honey Snookems." Bethany held Emily's hand. Excited, she stopped walking and broke her grasp, to sign *Snookems* for her. "Her mama died when she was little so we had to feed her from a bottle, and now she follows us around."

"She's having her own calf this winter," Greg explained to Emily.

As the morning drew to a close, Greg went back to the house to watch a television show.

"He's certainly quiet today," Philip commented.

"He's just in a bad mood because Daddy told him last night that he can't use the car for a while." Bethany's eyes were somber. It sounded like the ultimate punishment to her. "Dad says he can't even work on the car. He's just bummed because he doesn't have anything to do."

"I think it's more than that," Emily said quietly, after Bethany had run on ahead.

Philip agreed with her. "He's not the kind of kid who rebels. He outgrew that in junior high school. I wonder what's eating away at him?"

"I think he needs to see his mother." Emily stared straight ahead at the meadow where they were walking. She had been here less than a week and she didn't know if she should offer her opinion. She felt comfortable around Philip, though, after this morning, and she decided to confide in him.

"Maybe so."

"What can I do? How can I say anything to Clint?" she asked him.

"You might have to wait a little while."

"I guess I will," she agreed with him. "I hate to come here and start giving my opinion when it isn't asked for." But she was right about Greg. It was time Clint let all the children visit their mother. He wasn't protecting them any longer. By keeping them from their mother, he was feeding their fears.

Lisa had gone back to the house earlier, and Emily and Philip were alone except for Bethany. She skipped back toward them from across the pasture, and together the three of them walked back to the house. Philip swung Bethany up onto his shoulders and he gave her a piggyback ride as she laughed and whooped and Emily walked quietly along beside them.

When they arrived back at the house, Clint was sitting in his easy chair trying to concentrate on the newspaper, but it was clear to Emily that he was exhausted. She knew immediately that it had been his visit with Amanda that had drained him so.

Emily cast a knowing glance at Philip as the three girls headed toward the kitchen to make pizza for lunch. Greg was upstairs in his room, and Emily knew just by watching him that Philip was concerned about both his nephew and his brother. A few minutes later, Philip came into the kitchen and offered to slice pepperoni. Emily waited until the girls had gone out to set the table before she said anything. "He's exhausted, isn't he?"

"I don't know how much longer he can keep this up." Philip's voice was low. "He's my baby brother. I hate to see him this way."

"You can't do anything for him, Philip." Emily took a handful of the pepperoni pieces and began laying them evenly on the pizza she was preparing. "You have to just love him, I guess. He'll draw the strength he needs from that. It's the only thing you can do. Someday things will change." Amanda could wake up tonight, Emily thought. Or she could be gone, too. Whatever the outcome, the situation couldn't be harder for anyone to deal with. Anything seemed better than this nagging uncertainty. "It would help if Clint would let the rest of the family share a part of the burden. He's a good father, but he's forgetting that two of his kids are almost adults."

Lisa and Bethany filed back into the room in search of paper napkins, and Philip watched all three working together in the kitchen. He had to smile at them, they looked so much like a family. He felt an almost insurmountable sense of protectiveness toward Emily.

Philip understood now why Lloyd Masterson had made her his protégée at the ad agency some six years ago. He must have looked at Emily and seen the sadness and the dreams in her eyes, and once having seen them, he must have wanted to make them all come true for her.

Philip recalled how he had found her on the floor that morning, crying, holding the telephone receiver and his heart in her hands. He had decided then that he would fight against her and for her, in order to reach out to her, to be her friend. And Philip was suddenly very, very thankful that Emily had come, that she had been willing to live with his family, that she had been willing to learn to love them all.

AFTER LUNCH, PHILIP PULLED a wooden case full of watercolors and a paintbrush from under his bed and he stayed in his porch room sketching the scene behind the house. He had a picturesque view of the blacklands with Clint's rachitic, homemade grape arbor in the foreground. This was one of Philip's favorite things, drawing on the farm, where the world around him was full of freedom and peace. He kept an extra set of paints here at all times. He knew himself well enough to know that he did his best work when he was inspired. And here, at the place where he had watched his nieces and nephew grow, where he had watched his brother build a love and a life, was where Philip often found himself the most moved to create, to sketch, to see.

"What are you doing all holed up in here by yourself?" came a timid voice from the doorway, and he turned to see Emily leaning against the jamb. He grinned at her as she stood there, looking so tentative, as if she wasn't certain she should be bothering him in the place that remained reserved for him. "Am I bothering you?"

"No." He shook his head vehemently. After lunch, Clint had hurried to Waxahachie to show several properties to a client. Lisa and Bethany had gone with him to have a soda and meet friends at the movie theater. His punishment lifted, Greg was in the garage working on the Studebaker. Philip had decided Emily probably wanted time to herself this afternoon, too, after her heartrending conversation with her mother this morning on the telephone. She had gone to her cabin to rest after the midday meal.

Philip was glad that she had come back to the house. He was worried about her and about the things her mother might have said to hurt her. There were so many things Philip understood now about Emily that he hadn't been able to understand before. He looked at her today and saw her in a different light. And he wondered if the feelings she ran away from, the things he knew she felt when he dared to touch her, might bring back some distorted memory of love as she had known it long ago.

Philip had wanted to ask Emily all day if that might be what she was afraid of, the feelings of distrust and of anger she must have felt toward the first people she had loved long ago. Philip felt as if she was a tiny, defenseless creature that the world had seen fit to place in his charge.

"Come in, Emily." He motioned to her.

"So this is where you stay when you spend your weekends on the farm?" She spun around and took in the details of the room. It was just as homey as her tiny cabin was, only without the extra feminine touches. The single bed in the corner had a massive hand-carved headboard made of oak, and it was covered with a patchwork quilt that sported squares of reds, blues and yellows.

"It's nice, isn't it?" he asked her. "This is my place. Manderly set it up for me a long time ago."

"Do you paint much when you come here?" She nodded her head toward the watercolor he was working on. He had just completed drawing in the grape arbor, and he was preparing to paint the hills a bright green where they spanned the horizon.

"All the time." He was making rapid strokes with his brush as he talked to her. "I keep this set around just in case I get inspired." He cocked his head and smiled across the room at her. "And that happens pretty often out here."

"You know you're shirking your job, don't you?" she asked him. He stared at her. Philip wasn't certain what Emily was talking about.

She was still leaning against the doorjamb with her arms crossed and grinning down at him. "I distinctly remember you promising me you would work on the storyboards for my book. I haven't seen you doing any Baby Sprout sketches lately."

She was teasing him and he knew it. But Philip couldn't help but hope it was more than that, too. He hoped she was forgiving him for overstepping his bounds with her before. He hadn't meant to be angry when she hadn't wanted him to touch her. But Emily had been so responsive in his arms. And he had been unable to comprehend the reasons she thought that she had to pull away. In a way, her fear had been the ingredient that had angered him the most. He was ashamed to admit it, but seeing the fright in her eyes had made him feel sorry for himself. It had made him sorry all over again for the way he had trusted Morgan.

"I didn't know if you wanted me to work on those anymore," he said to her.

Emily bit her lip and leaned her head back against the wall. She couldn't help but look a bit sad. "Philip, I'm sorry. I was very unfair."

"I wish you had told me then."

"That my mother is an alcoholic?" She walked into the room toward him. "Do you know what it's like admitting that to people?"

"I didn't understand how you could be so incredibly responsive one moment and so cold the next."

"Maybe I don't know, either." Her eyes were brimming with tears. "Maybe I still don't understand it."

"I would still love to draw your pictures for you, Emily." He picked up his sketchbook and leafed through it. "I took it as such a compliment that you wanted me to do them."

"It was a compliment," she told him. "When I was working for Lloyd Masterson at the advertising agency, I learned how hard it was to take an idea that you had conceived and turn it over to another person to interpret. I was never satisfied with the photographer's work, not because his work wasn't good, but because I had already pictured in my mind what I wanted and it was very hard to get away from that and turn it over to a professional artist."

He grinned at her. "That's one reason I chose not to become a professional artist. I don't handle frustration well."

Emily giggled and shook a teasing finger at him. "You can say that again."

He didn't answer. He just looked at her with a disgruntled expression. Then he couldn't resist grinning, too. "You are a frustrating woman."

"I still want you to do these storyboards for me." Emily pulled a copy of her manuscript from behind her back. "We can have a lawyer draw up some sort of contract, if you'd like. I'll give you a percentage of my first three million sales. How does that sound?"

"Let me take a look at that manuscript," he said as he moved toward her and took it out of her hand. "It sounds like a fair deal to me. We don't have to call a lawyer. You can just owe me half your book advance and five percent of the royalties."

"Hey," she teased him with a mischievous glint in her eye. "You sound like you know what you are talking about."

"Maybe I do," he said, winking at her. "Now..." He held out his hand toward the manuscript, and Emily handed it to him.

"As you read that, see if you come up with any mental pictures," she suggested.

Philip flipped the first page open and began to read. Emily turned and stared through the screen while he turned the pages. The winter wheat was just beginning to pierce the ground, and Emily marveled at the rich growth that was covering the land so late in the season. She did her best to think of anything except the man who was sitting in a chair beside the bed reading her story about a sad child and a little possum.

It had been a stretch for Emily to let Bethany read the book, but it had been such a natural thing to do because the child had been interested and the two of them had been working at making friends. Philip's reading the manuscript was a different story altogether. He was a grown-up who would read her work from a grown-up's perspective. And even though Emily's story was written for a child in the third or fourth grade, there was a deeper meaning to her work, a message, that was likely to speak to Philip, too. She worried that he might think she was silly or crazy or both.

Philip flipped over the last page, and Emily was surprised when he looked up and she saw admiration in his eyes. "Emily." He whispered her name and she didn't quite understand the respect in his voice. "You've got something here, little one. You send this thing in, and I'll bet it goes to the first publisher that looks at it."

Emily couldn't help but throw her head back and guffaw at the idea. "Most people only want their work to be published someday. You're sitting here telling me that the first publisher who looks at it is going to want it? Don't flatter me, Philip Manning."

"I'm not." He jumped out of the chair and went to her. He held her manuscript out and tapped it with his index finger. "Your writing is very visual, Emily. I can picture this... Where is it...?" He was thumbing through her work, trying to find a specific scene he thought he could illustrate well. When he found it, he sat in the chair again and pulled a drafting table out from the wall beside him. He flipped his sketch pad open to a clean page, and began to draw.

Emily stooped beside him to see what he was doing. She tried not to be amused by his excitement. His fingers were flying almost as fast as he was talking. "Find the scene in there where Baby Sprout first meets Priscilla," he said. "I think it's the third or fourth page." He was drawing an outline of a figure on his paper. "I need Priscilla's physical description." His pencil paused on the paper and he glanced up at Emily. "I guess you don't need to read it, though. You wrote it."

"Yep," she said proudly.

"Describe Priscilla to me," Philip instructed her.

"Okay, I'll try." It was hard at first. Emily quoted the lines from her work that said the nine-year-old girl had blond hair and that she was tall and willowy.

"Her eyes. What color are her eyes?"

"Brown," Emily answered.

"Like yours?" Philip looked down to where she was stooped below him and studied Emily's eyes.

"Darker than mine," Emily told him. "I want her to have dark eyes."

"Describe her face to me, Emily." Philip knew it had been sheer luck that he had drawn Baby Sprout so close to her expectations. He could have tried the same thing with Priscilla. But he wanted to be precise.

Emily squinted her eyes and did her best to picture Priscilla. "She has sort of a short turned-up nose," she told him at last. "And give her a mischievous glint in her eyes."

"No fair going back to eyes," he said with a laugh. "I've already decided on her eyes. Go to her mouth. What does Priscilla's mouth look like?"

Emily was ready for him this time. "I want a big, wide toothy grin. Like yours."

"Like mine? A wide toothy grin?" His pencil stopped briefly while he looked at her again.

"Well..." She was teasing him, and she couldn't keep from giggling at him. "Maybe her mouth shouldn't be quite as toothy and wide as yours is. I wouldn't want anyone to think she looked funny."

"Thanks, Emily."

"Does that tell you enough?" she asked, feigning innocence.

"Does this look like Priscilla?" He held a rough sketch at arm's length so they both could see.

"It does." Emily was openly admiring of his work. His drawings were just enough of a blend of caricature and realism to make his drawings engaging to children as well as attractive to adults.

"Now," Philip instructed her, "find the scene in there where Priscilla and Baby Sprout go to the old red sandstone courthouse to talk to old Judge Wyland. I like the part where she asks the judge if she can have a gold velvet throne to perch on in the middle of the town square."

"Here it is." Emily handed him her manuscript opened to the page he wanted.

"This part about the throne will make a nice illustration," Philip suggested. "Let's see." He threw his head back and thought aloud. "How do we portray the things Priscilla is thinking of?"

"Every Christmas, the people in this town decorate the town square for the holiday. Priscilla has this wild notion that if she has a throne in the town square, the townspeople will drape it with red, blue and green twinkly lights every time they decorate the rest of the place."

"Hmm." Philip was still staring at the ceiling and thinking. "That might work."

Emily watched him as he took his pencil in hand again and then drew the bottom half of a throne with twinkling lights on it. It was an avant-garde sort of drawing, with two chubby girlish legs that didn't quite touch the ground hanging down from the seat of the throne. Then, at the bottom of the page, he began to draw a close-up of Priscilla's face. She was smugly staring up at the base of the throne above her. Philip drew the sketch so the reader would know that she was only picturing the throne in a daydream above her head. Then he went ahead and worked on several more rough sketches to give her an idea of illustrations for various scenes he had in mind.

"These will work well," he said to her. "Is this what you had in mind?"

"Yes." She reached up and laid a tentative hand on his knee. "Maybe someday we'll both be rich and famous."

"Someday may not be all that far away." He laid his hand on hers.

He watched while Emily trailed her eyes down to his hand. Philip steeled himself for what he thought she would do next. He expected her to jerk her hand away. She didn't. Instead, she trailed her eyes back up and looked at him wistfully, full in the face.

"Don't feel like you owe me anything because of this, Emily." He thought it was best to be blatantly honest with her. He didn't want to think that she was staying there, so close beside him, just because she was thankful.

She turned her eyes up toward him and he saw the expression there that he hated, that eternal sadness, that hint of profound insecurity he had grown so familiar with since he had known her.

"I've been betrayed before by someone I cared about." He said the words flippantly, as if the fact held no importance to him now. "I know about the fears that you might harbor. I don't want you to feel you have to worry every time you come near me. I'm thrilled to do these tentative sketches for you. I would be overjoyed if a contract came through and I got to illustrate the entire book for you. I kissed you at your apartment because I'm attracted to you. But I drew you these pictures because I'm your friend."

"Thank you." She pulled her hand away from him and smiled up at him. The relief and the gratitude she felt because of the things he had said were almost tangible. In a way, his statement set her free to follow her own feelings. "I need a friend. I haven't had many of them, Philip."

"Is it hard for you to trust people?"

She thought about his question for a moment before she answered him. "I suppose so. I learned a long time ago that it just hurts too much to care about people."

"You do love your mother, don't you?"

"Yes," she told him. "But I don't think she ever loved me. I don't think she ever loved Daddy, either." Her mind traveled back to the conversation she had with her father on prom night. "Maybe she loved him once, before they got married. But I have to wonder what Daddy and Jim and I did to turn her against us. I look back on it now and I don't ever remember a time when Mother was happy. Except when she was drunk."

"Alcoholism is a disease." Philip watched her and thought about the joy that she found in the little things—things like baking muffins for the kids, climbing trees with Lisa, signing Baby Sprout to Bethany—and he thought how tragic it would be for her if she lived her life wondering what she had done to cause her mother's problems. "You can't hold yourself responsible for something that your mother chose to do."

"I don't know what I think anymore," she said to him.

"You've got to make a commitment to yourself to decide that you aren't responsible for your mother's life."

"Commitment," she said without trying to hide the ironic tone in her voice. "My mother and father made a commitment to each other once. I'd like to know what happened to that."

Her tone of voice and the distaste that crossed her face gave Philip a clue to what she must be feeling. "You grew up in a home that didn't contain much love." It was a statement, not a question.

"You make it sound so cold. It wasn't as bad as that. I loved my brother. And my father." She stared off into space. "I probably even loved my mother. I just didn't get to grow up watching my mother and father being in love with each other."

"Lots of kids don't."

"I know. I don't think love lasts in the world, Philip. I think you go to the high school prom and wear flowers and someday you marry the guy, and somewhere along the line, the richness and the joy of it all fizzles away."

"Emily." He walked toward her and then he stopped right near her. "Don't be that skeptical about life. Skepticism isn't a part of you."

"So maybe that's why the reality hit me so hard," she said dryly.

"How can you say that love never lasts?" He couldn't believe she felt that way. "Look around you. Look at Clint."

"I see Clint," she said quietly. "He's lost the only love he had, too."

"No." Philip felt his anger and frustration welling up inside him again. But he knew the last thing Emily needed was anger at this point. She had lived a life of that already. "When you see Clint, you see a man who has loved his wife almost since the moment he met her. They've had hard places in their lives to overcome. Most everybody does. They've had their financial troubles. They've brought up three kids together. They committed themselves to each other. And they've made it work, Emily. Look at all the happiness they've shared."

Emily didn't say anything more.

"Do you think he's been going to that hospital every night for the past year just because he felt he had to?"

"Maybe," she said.

"I would have given up hope by now," Philip said emphatically. "For God's sake, Emily. He's been talking to her and loving her and sharing things with her this entire time even though she can't respond. I would hazard a guess that it's pretty hard to remain dedicated to a sleeping body that never moves."

Emily looked away from him. He had driven his point home hard. And she was ashamed of herself for admitting that she thought Clint's commitment to his wife could ever be questioned. "I'm sorry, Philip. Perhaps it was unfair of me to mention your brother as a flippant example." She paused and looked back at him. "His Manderly is a very lucky woman, isn't she?"

He didn't say anything. They had come a long way together today.

She went to him and gingerly reached up one finger to touch his cheek. "Thank you for being my friend," she said softly.

LATE THAT NIGHT, after the children had gone to their rooms and Philip had driven back to Dallas, Emily sat on her bed in her cabin. She had talked to Philip about things she had never discussed with anyone before. She felt free tonight and light-hearted. Light-heartedness was almost foreign to her. And as she stared out the small cabin window toward the moon hanging high above her, Emily pretended that she could see into forever. Philip was her friend. Probably more than a friend, if she was honest with herself. She had revealed a deep part of herself to him today. And he hadn't backed away from her.

Emily pulled a cardboard box from under her bed and searched through it for her copy of *Writer's Market*, a book listing publishers that her father had given her for Christmas the previous year. She flipped it open to the section marked Children's Publishers. The page that marked the beginning of that section was tattered and dog-eared. She had turned to it hundreds of times before. But she had never been brave enough to send away her work.

Emily ran her finger down the list of names and addresses. She stopped two-thirds down one page at the listing for Hudson Publishing. The company was in New York City.

Emily scanned Hudson's list of editorial requirements. The company was seeking manuscripts approximately six thousand words long for elementary school-age children. *Baby Sprout and Priscilla* fit the requirements exactly.

Emily picked up the manuscript from the kitchen table. "Well," she muttered, expelling a sigh. "Here goes nothing." She slipped the manuscript into a manila folder.

It was taking every ounce of courage she possessed to do this. But Emily felt as if being with Philip that afternoon and talking to him after the ordeal with her mother had strengthened the courage within her. For only a moment, Emily felt lonely. It seemed like something very precious to her was inside the manila envelope. She flipped through Philip's drawings one more time and then she carefully slipped them inside the envelope, too. It was done. Baby Sprout was on his way.

This was something Emily knew she had to do. Submitting this manuscript was a reinforcement of something new she and Philip had found together. As she licked the envelope flap and pressed it shut, Emily felt a sudden surge of confidence. She was strong enough to follow this dream. And Philip Manning's friendship had been the catalyst that had spurred her on.

WHEN PHILIP DROVE up in front of his office and parked his car Monday morning, his mind was on Emily. He was thinking about his weekend, the home-baked muffins and strolling in and out among the cows with her and comparing life on the farm with where he was now—the corporate headquarters of Manning Commercial Real Estate and Investment, Inc.

This was one place where Philip knew he was in charge of things. The three secretaries said "Good morning" to him when he waltzed through the front office. His name was printed on all the stationery and also hung on a metal sign that could easily be read by the thousands of people who drove on the Lyndon B. Johnson Freeway every day. He could pick up a telephone and could easily clinch three separate real estate deals before lunchtime. This was his domain.

But today, for some reason, it had lost its glamour. He felt that he had come back to it with an entirely new perspective.

Brett Langford, one of his sales associates, met him at the elevator door when it opened on the seventh floor. "Philip, we have a conference scheduled in fifteen minutes. Bennett Huff wanted me to let you know. We've got some problem with the Robertson deal."

Philip frowned. What could possibly be wrong with Clyde Robertson's sale? Bennett Huff was the firm's corporate lawyer. Philip didn't like the sound of this at all.

Langford studied his employer carefully before saying anything more. Everyone in the office knew the reasons behind the intense competition between Philip's company and Brockner Associates. It was the sort of thing Philip had fought hard to keep private, but even after all these years, there was still talk. "Morgan Brockner is here with her attorney."

Philip clenched his fist around the handle of his briefcase, but the gesture went unnoticed by his employee. "Very well," he said simply, his tone measured. He had learned long ago to keep his anger with Morgan to himself.

He didn't hurry to the boardroom. That was what Morgan would want him to do. She was waiting for him to push open the door and begin growling at her. And he wouldn't oblige her. Instead, he spent the fifteen minutes in his office, going over the Robertson file, pacing the floor, trying to forget his anger. And when he walked into the boardroom and faced her twenty minutes later, Philip was totally composed.

"Well, Morgan." He was shaking her lawyer's hand, but he was addressing her. He didn't want this to last any longer than it had to. He wanted her out of his office. "What seems to be the problem?"

She smiled at the attorney beside her. "Johnson is handling this. He'll tell you."

Philip's legal counsel, the gray-haired man named Bennett Huff, was in the room, too, and Philip wondered why he looked worried.

"Gentlemen, sit down." The man named Johnson spoke in a booming voice. Everyone sat down except Philip, Bennett and Morgan. "We're here to question the legality of the real estate transaction that is scheduled to close this afternoon, the transaction between Clyde Robertson and Spencer Campbell."

Philip clenched his fists tighter. What would she think of next? This was absurd. She had known about the Robertson deal for weeks. Why had she waited until the day of closing to bring a complaint? She obviously wanted to catch him off guard.

As the man named Johnson continued to speak, it was as if he was talking about something else, somebody else, something that was foreign to all the Manning sales associates present in the room. The property was a twenty-five-story business complex that Philip had listed exclusively and had sold for just over $37 million. The commission alone was going to mean $3.7 million for the Manning corporate coffers. It had been quite a lucrative sale.

But now Johnson was accusing him of forging documents to make himself eligible to sell the property. He insisted that Brockner Associates had been given an exclusive contract to sell the office complex, which was located on North Dallas Parkway. And then Philip almost choked when he produced the papers to prove it.

Philip couldn't believe Morgan would stoop this low. Clyde Robertson would shed some light on this little misunderstanding, he thought, but the building owner was still battling traffic on the freeway trying to get here. The papers Johnson produced were perfect in every detail, right down to Clyde Robertson's signature. But Philip had been standing in the room when Clyde Robertson had signed the exclusive contract with his company. There was almost $4 million at stake in this deal, but there was something much more valuable in question, too. And that was Philip's reputation. It was worth a lot more than just $4 million to him.

Philip stared across the room at the woman whom he once had considered marrying, and she just sat there, her body rigid, her jaw set. It occurred to him as he looked at her that she was trying to ruin him. She had come to his seminar and she had seen his successes and she had decided it was time to run him into the ground once and for all. It didn't matter who he was to her anymore. He was her competition. And that's all that mattered.

"Morgan." He said the words quietly in front of all of them. "You are a fool."

"You're the fool, Philip." Her tone was just as measured as it had always been. "If you go through with the closing this afternoon, Brockner Associates is taking you to court. And I can assure you, it won't look nice in the papers."

This time, Philip let his anger control him. It was exactly what Morgan wanted. "Go ahead and take us to court, then. Your name will be spread across the papers just like mine will. And I don't think the general public will care who's the plaintiff and who's the defendant. That closing will take place this afternoon at three. It's my sale. I worked for it and I earned it, just like I worked for and earned my company. You can't take that away, Morgan. Go ahead and try."

"I will." She took her lawyer's arm and her eyes blazed as she turned to leave the room.

Philip went back to his office and sat at his desk for a long time, staring at the painting on the wall. It was one of his. The watercolor of the white wood farmhouse in Waxahachie as it used to be when Manderly was there, with geraniums in yellow pots and a cat on the front windowsill and a fiery Texas summer sunset in the background. It made him think of everything sad today—Manderly's coma and Greg's discontent and Emily's telephone call from her mother.

The farm was such a peaceful place in contrast to his office, but still, the people there had problems and sorrows, too. And as he thought about it, Philip tried to understand why God had created a world so full of cruel people and sadness.

CHAPTER EIGHT

EMILY WAS FALLING INTO a routine at the farm now, and she was beginning to feel as though she belonged there. She fixed breakfast for Clint every morning before the sun was even up, and she got the kids off to school and then, except for planning and shopping for meals, her time was very much her own until school was out. As the days passed, Emily started doing more with her free time, calling friends in Dallas and visiting Abbie and lunching with her father, who filled her in on the news of her brother and what he was doing in college at Texas A&M. She even stopped by the ad agency to chat with Lloyd one day, and when she did, he convinced her to start on a project for him.

He wanted her to write a short script for a narrated audio-visual presentation that a nonprofit Texas foundation had commissioned the agency to do. After Emily had seen the photographs she would be working with, she agreed to the project right away. And it was funny, it felt good to be writing again. It made her feel as if the parts of her life that were important to her were all meshing together perfectly. And the happier she was, the better she felt about herself, the happier Lisa and Bethany seemed to be, too.

Greg was the only one in the family she couldn't seem to reach. He spent hours in the garage working on the Studebaker, reupholstering the seats, finishing the work on the steering column, and then he played around with the rings and the engine block. The Studebaker had been his grandmother's car. Clint's mother had given it to him a long time ago. The car was a classic, a 1960 Lark VI, and Clint had been pleased that his son had taken such an interest in maintaining the vehicle. But Greg had cut himself off from everything else; he was scarcely ever in the house, and when midterm grades came out just before the holidays, Greg's had fallen sharply.

Emily didn't know where to turn. At first, she sought out Philip, and he was obviously concerned. But Philip acted oddly detached from them all and Emily wondered why. "I don't know what should be done, Emily," he told her one Saturday afternoon when he was visiting. "I'm not the father of a teenage son."

Emily was taken aback by his answer. She had decided they were going to be friends, and she had come to think so much of him not just as a man but as a person. The way he snapped at her disappointed her. "I'm not worried about teenagers, Philip," she told him sharply. "I'm worried about Greg. You've known him ever since he was born. I'm not so experienced either, you know."

As she spoke, Philip just stared off into space. He was so concerned about fighting Morgan Brockner these days that he didn't think of much else, and when he thought about Emily's words, he decided he should be ashamed of himself. It seemed as if the people in his life were pulling him in five or six directions at once, and though he felt ashamed for feeling this way, he had been wondering lately how much they all expected one man to handle. Morgan had filed suit against him exactly six weeks ago, and Philip was beginning to realize now that the nightmare she'd put into motion wasn't going away. Bennett Huff had already started on their defense, but Clyde Robertson, the man whom Philip made at least $15 million richer by the sale of his office complex, had decided not to testify in their defense. He told Bennett that he didn't want his name dragged through the mud, but Philip couldn't believe the man would be so cowardly. He began to wonder if the man might be one of Morgan's cohorts.

During the past six weeks, Philip had drawn further and further away from his family. Clint had noticed it, but Emily had really been the one who'd found it disturbing. She had just started telling him things about herself that were incredibly important to her, decided they were going to be friends and then he had shut her out. Secretly, Emily thought it might be because of the things she had told him. It had been glorious that day she had finally bared her soul to someone. She felt as though she had picked up a part of herself and handed it over to him. But now she decided she had done the wrong thing. She had shown him how much she needed somebody to need her, and now she was frightened that she had shown him too much. Maybe he didn't want to feel responsible for her pain in the way that truly intimate friendships required. It seemed as if when he looked at her, he looked right through her. She didn't realize he looked at everybody that way these days. Emily was certain his change in attitude was somehow her fault. She made herself remember that she had found a friend that day when she so desperately needed one and she made herself feel thankful for the experience, fleeting as it was. She tried to put him out of her mind and spent days, weeks, caring for her new adopted children, watching after Bethany and Lisa and Greg, and just quietly missing him.

It was Abbie who was turning out to be Emily's dearest friend now that she worked as an Absolutely Mom. Emily finally decided to ask Abbie for advice one afternoon when the grandmotherly, vital woman stopped by for a chat and a cup of hot spiced tea.

"I don't know what to do," Emily said to Abbie tearfully, after telling her boss about Greg's latest report card. "He's not just goofing off, Abbie. That's what his father thinks, but I think his problem goes much deeper than that."

"What do you think it might be?" Abbie was concerned, too.

"Maybe I'm way off base, but I think it's because his father won't acknowledge the fact that Greg is growing into an adult. Not letting him visit Amanda is only one symptom. Clint's doing that because he loves the kids and wants to protect them. The girls don't seem to mind, but Greg is going deeper and deeper into himself. I don't think he even feels he's a part of this family anymore."

Abbie set down her teacup. "Have you talked to Greg about it yet? If your feelings are well founded as far as Greg is concerned, then the two of you could go together and talk to his father. Or Greg could go alone. I believe that you two would be justified in doing that."

"Do you really?" Emily was shaking her head again. "I just don't want Clint to think I'm moving in and ganging up on him with his children."

"You're doing a fine job, Emily." Abbie got up from her chair and came around to hug her. "I think you're right. I think that somewhere along the line in your own life, you've learned to have a lot of insight into people's hearts. This family is very lucky to have you."

Emily beamed. It meant a lot to her, hearing Abbie's words. She often speculated about the other mothers Abbie placed. She wondered if they were happy, if they were successful, if they were learning to care for their adopted families the way she was learning to care for hers. It made Emily feel she measured up to all of them, knowing that Abbie was proud of her, hearing the things that Abbie had to say.

EMILY DIDN'T KNOW WHY she was so excited about Christmas this year. When she sat down and thought about it, the entire holiday season was going to be much different than it had been in previous years. Her brother whom she had lost touch with completely was skiing over the holidays with a group from the Corps of Cadets at A&M. Her father was spending his few days off with the family of a close friend who lived three hours away from Dallas where her brother attended school, Bryan/College Station. Her father had invited Emily to join him there, but she had declined. She knew he was planning a few restful days hunting on his colleague's deer lease near where he was staying and she would miss him, but she longed for an old-fashioned family celebration this year and Clint had invited her to take part in theirs.

Emily had spent weeks Christmas shopping for the Mannings. Finally, she had found the perfect gifts for each of them. For Bethany, she'd found a large stuffed purple cow that played "Home, Home on the Range" in a high tinkling melody that Emily knew Bethany would be able to hear. It was a perfect addition to Bethany's very loved collection of stuffed animals. People had turned to stare at her because she'd looked so joyous and excited as she'd hugged the bag next to her and left the store.

For Lisa, she bought a beautiful strand of silver beads. They were a bit extravagant but they would make the girl feel so special and so grown up that they were well worth the money. She wasn't sure what to buy Greg and finally settled on a navy blue Pendleton sweater.

Buying for Clint was more of a challenge than choosing for the children had been. After hours combing the racks in men's stores she'd decided on a handsome button-down shirt with maroon pinstripes worked into the weave. Emily knew it would match a suit he had been wearing to work lately.

Picking out a gift for Philip was by far the most difficult task, and Emily didn't exactly know why. She knew he would appreciate anything she chose. She had missed him so much during the past weeks. And it was ironic that she was missing something she had never really had before. She wanted to give him something that would make him understand her feelings. His friendship for her, even if it had lasted only briefly, had meant so much to her. Emily was excited that he was going to be with them on Christmas Eve. He was going to spend the night on the farm and so were Amanda's parents. Emily found herself wishing Philip would have a magical, wonderful Christmas, too, just the same as she was wishing it for the children.

There was a lovely Dior bathrobe in the window at a prominent men's store at the shopping mall, and Emily stopped by three times to look at it. It was maroon with soft wales of velour, and it brought to mind a thousand different images every time Emily touched it and thought of Philip. She finally decided it was much too personal a gift for her to give him and she picked out a sterling money clip and a matching business card case and had all three of his initials engraved on them. P.B.M., they both said with a flourish, to stand for Philip Bradley Manning, and Emily found herself fingering the letters over and over again that night before she wrapped his gift, thinking about the letters and his name and the man.

EMILY WALKED to the main house as the sky turned from purple to a dusty mauve on Christmas Eve morning. When Lisa and Bethany came downstairs two hours later, they found her in the kitchen, happily drawing faces on gingerbread men with powdered-sugar icing. Greg came down for breakfast, too, and he didn't say too much, but Emily thought it might be because the two girls jabbered on about presents and surprises during the entire meal. Neither she nor Greg had a chance to get a word in edgewise.

"Where's Dad?" he asked. Lisa and Bethany had left the table to look at the presents under the tree for the umpteenth time.

"I think he's at his office in town by now," Emily told him. "He left early this morning to go visit your mom. He's taking half the day off. He should be home by noon."

Greg turned his attention back to his scrambled eggs and bacon and his grapefruit and didn't say anything for a while. Emily walked over to the boy and laid her arm across his shoulders. She was wondering how she should begin asking him the questions she knew she had to ask. He was sitting at the breakfast table with his shoulders firmly set against the world, and it struck Emily that he looked old enough to be a man with the emotions of a man, too. He was keeping those emotions in a perilous check, but they were becoming evident in other obvious ways and Emily longed to do something to help him. "Greg," she said to him softly. "I know something's wrong. I'd like to talk to you about it. I'd like to help." But that's all she had the chance to say before the doorbell rang and she heard Bethany shriek "Grandmom! Granddaddy!" Emily knew that Amanda's parents had arrived.

The rest of the day was enjoyable and busy. Emily fixed lunch for the entire clan, and Amanda's mother helped while Clint and Amanda's father visited in the front room by the tree. Amanda's parents were a study in human resiliency, Emily decided. While their daughter lay comatose in a hospital bed, they were here with their grandchildren, laughing and whispering secrets and passing cookie tins filled with pecan-topped pralines and sugar cookies and two flavors of fudge.

Emily watched for Philip out the window all afternoon but he didn't arrive until five-thirty, when it was almost time for church. She ran to the front door to meet him. His arms were full of packages and he looked haggard, but he gave Emily a genuine smile when she greeted him. As she watched him placing the presents he had brought under the tree and hugging the kids, Emily thought he seemed happy. He looked tired, though, as if he had been worrying about something. There were huge dark circles beneath his eyes and Emily hurried to bring him a cup of hot spiced tea.

He was stretched out in the fat leather reclining armchair that sat closest to the fire when she returned, and when she handed him the cup of tea, he took it from her, took a sip and then smiled up at her with the first hint of animation she had seen in his eyes for weeks. "You're getting good at this mothering stuff, ma'am," he teased her. "I don't even live here, and the minute I walk in the room you're taking care of me, too."

His comment didn't fluster her. She came right back with one of her own. She was comfortable enough in her new role to do that now. "That's okay. It's obvious somebody needs to take care of you." She laughed at herself. "I sound like somebody's grandma, don't I?"

"Yeah," Philip said. He was glad he had come today. And he was trying to stop worrying about Morgan and his company, for at least this one day. He wanted to enjoy Christmas. "But you don't look like anybody's grandma, so you could probably get away with it."

"Thanks." She pouted playfully. Then she leaned closer to him and spoke softly so no one else in the room would hear her. She used the same tone of voice she had used earlier when she was talking to Greg at the breakfast table. "You know, Philip, one of these days you're going to have to tell me what's wrong at Manning Real Estate. You've been exhausted and worried during the past two months. And you act like your family is a million miles away. I didn't think you'd ever let your business do that to you."

He looked up at her, and his surprise showed all over his face. He thought he had been hiding it well. He had no idea anyone could tell something was bothering him. He had been brooding ever since Morgan had filed suit against him two months before. And things were getting worse now. The suit would be listed in the legal sections of both the *Dallas Morning News* and *The Dallas Times-Herald* the following Tuesday. The pretrial conference with the Dallas district judge was only seven weeks away. The conference would simply be a matter of meeting with Morgan one more time, of "cleaning matters up before you two go at it," as Bennett Huff had put it. Philip had been staggering under the weight of his private burden for the past months. He knew Morgan was serious about carrying out her threats, and yet he still prayed that she wouldn't. It wasn't that he thought she had a chance at beating him. It was just that he hated wasting time ripping apart something valuable because of the past. He would rather just get on with his life, hoping to find something positive in this experience and let go of the things that once had been.

Philip was going to have to tell his brother about the whole mess sometime during this holiday, and he was dreading that. The family name would be dragged through the mud in court, not just his own but Clint's, as well. And Philip could hardly bear to think of what this trial might do to his brother's new business successes, as well as his own.

He turned his gaze to Emily. Her eyes were wide, her face was open and honest, as if she were ready to absorb all the exhaustion from him. He took her hand then and searched her eyes, as if all the answers to his corporate problems might be found in that one face and in the wisps of blond hair that formed a fluffy halo around it.

He reached up and touched one of those wisps of her hair.

"It's Christmas Eve." Emily put her hand tentatively on his shoulder. He obviously needed a friend. Now it was her turn to be there for him. "Try to smile, okay?"

"Okay." He reached up and grasped her hand and grinned up at her. And when she grinned back, he felt a childlike excitement well up within him. It was Christmas and it suddenly seemed like her caring had set him free to enjoy the holiday.

It was almost time for the Christmas Eve service at a church downtown, and everyone was in a hurry to dress. The whole family was going to attend. Emily had brought her good clothes to the main house so she wouldn't have to run back to the camp house to dress. Lisa and Bethany let her share their bathroom to wash up before she slipped into her favorite holiday dress. It was a tailored red flannel shirtdress with a dropped waist and a full, flowing skirt, and it made her feel like a dancer as she swirled on stocking feet, the skirt billowing around her. She plopped down, laughing, on Lisa's bed, with both the girls beside her.

She was feeling exhilarated, and she guessed it was because she and Philip had talked. She felt they had renewed their friendship this evening, but the reason for her elation was something more than that. It was remarkable how he could make her feel just by being with her. She kissed Bethany on the nose and rumpled Lisa's hair. As she did, she realized that there was a sense of peace and quiet in the house, that hadn't been there the hour before. It was like this every Christmas Eve for her, just before church. It seemed as if the entire world was waiting, breathless, poised. Tomorrow, the gifts would be torn open and the paper burned in the fireplace and the football games would be blaring on the big television in the front room. But tonight, the world was waiting, as it had waited hundreds of years before, for all God's miracles to happen.

The church was already crowded when they arrived, but Clint found a pew in the center near the back where the Manning clan would fit. Greg seemed to be gravitating toward her tonight, as if the few words she'd spoken to him at breakfast had done some good, and Emily nodded at him as he stood aside to let her into the pew and then slid in on the end beside her.

The lights in the church dimmed then, and Emily was lost to the world as the spotlight came on in the sanctuary and there stood five tiny angels wearing white choir robes and tinsel-lined cardboard wings. The narrator began reading from the Book of Luke. "'For behold, I bring you good tidings of great joy, which shall be to all people. For unto you is born this day, in the city of David, a Savior, which is Christ the Lord.'"

The angels disappeared then and there were only shepherds in the scene, traveling long distances, following a star to a rickety stable not so different from the rickety stable that stood at one end of the corral in the pasture at home. There the shepherds found Mary and Joseph and the Christ Child while the children's choir in the balcony sang "Away in a Manger," a Christmas hymn.

The narrator continued speaking from the church balcony. "And so it was that this simple scene with these few players, a mother and a father and a babe, three kings and several bedraggled shepherds, changed the world."

The ushers handed out white candles to everyone, and as the choir walked with lighted candles up the aisle toward the altar, Emily lit her candle from Greg's and then turned to her right to light Philip's candle, too. She looked up at him as the light glimmered between them. Their eyes met, and tears of joy were shimmering on her cheeks. She cried every Christmas, and Philip thought then, as he watched her, that she was more beautiful that night than he had ever seen her before. There was something extra sparkling in her eyes tonight, not just excitement or joy of Christmas. It was something he had never seen there before, as if she had found her own private miracle—love and a sense of belonging.

Just standing beside her holding his candle and humming "Silent Night" was enough to satisfy Philip. It was enough to make him feel that he belonged, too. And it was enough to make him forget all about Morgan Brockner and Manning Real Estate and the lawsuit that threatened to ruin him and his brother.

THAT NIGHT AFTER CHURCH, the Manning family tackled the massive pile of presents that had accumulated beneath the Christmas tree in the front room. There were dozens of tiny packages for the girls from their grandparents—hair barrettes and posters and other trinkets. And Greg received a steering wheel cover for the Studebaker and an application for a personalized license plate.

When Philip opened the small box Emily had wrapped for him, he sat and fingered the money clip and the card case for a long while before he said anything. The kids had all jumped up and hugged Emily when they opened their gifts from her, and Clint had, too, but Philip didn't dare. He didn't want to touch her there in front of everyone. He was feeling very drawn to her. In fact, he felt closer to her every time he talked to her, and he was certain that if he hugged her he might never be able to let her go.

It was the first time he had admitted that to himself. Emily was drawing feelings out in him that he had long since buried. He had no idea why she had that ability when other women had tried and failed. It was probably the fact that he saw her here all the time, caring so much about the people whom he loved, too. There were parts of his life that those feelings drew open and exposed, and it scared Philip to death to think he might ever become that vulnerable again. So he didn't hug her. He just sat in his chair and nodded at her from across the room and held the engraved silver treasures in his palm until the metal was warm from his touch. And the entire night he sat thinking about Emily and how much he liked the gifts she had chosen for him, and he couldn't quite decide whether he treasured them so because of their individual beauty or because she had given them to him.

Emily was excited about the gifts she had received, too. There was a maroon-and-blue plaid flannel shirt from her brother and a lovely creme-colored angora sweater from Bethany and Lisa, a pink satin nightshirt with matching slippers and a bottle of expensive perfume from her father, and a lovely blue crocheted afghan from Amanda's parents.

Clint and Greg had gone in together and had picked out a set of writing pens with tiny roses engraved on each of them. "They're for your books," Clint said, laughing. "Bethany keeps reminding us that you're going to be a world famous children's author someday soon."

"Maybe I will be." Emily slipped one of the pens behind her ear and pulled all the hair to the top of her head with one hand in an attempt to look glamorous. "Just be nice to me now and, hey, someday when I'm rich and famous, I might remember to send you a Christmas card."

"My, but aren't you humble. Considerate, too." Philip was laughing with her now, too, as he spoke.

The last two gifts Emily opened were a box still wrapped in brown postal paper with a return address on it that she did not recognize and a small, round package wrapped in green cellophane that Philip said was from him. The brown paper box was addressed to her in a familiar spidery handwriting that brought back a rush of memories for Emily, some happy, some sad, all poignant. Emily struggled to remain composed as she tore open the wrapping. She hadn't expected to hear from her mother this Christmas.

"Who's that one from?" Bethany asked her. The girl didn't want to miss out on any of the exciting gifts.

"It's from my mother," Emily told everyone in the room meekly, and then she glanced at Philip. Only Philip knew how much her mother's gift really meant.

Inside the box was a green leather-bound book with blank pages. It was a journal for her poems and her thoughts and her Baby Sprout stories. Emily leafed through it briefly, and Clint made some flippant comment about the "resident rich and famous author." She quietly laid the book on her lap and Philip noticed that she acted as if she didn't want to touch it. Instead, she clung to the arm of the mahogany chair where she was sitting, and Philip had the thought that she was clinging to the chair with one clenched fist just as she was clutching on to the cozy world, the only place that she had found peace, here at the farm.

"Open that one," he urged her as he indicated the other present sitting on the chair arm beside her. And when she moved to do so, Philip watched her intently.

This was something he had found while he was downtown working with a client. He had purchased the gift almost a month ago. It had caught his eye in the window at Nieman-Marcus, and it was more than he should have spent, but something about it made him keep going back. He finally decided that it reminded him of the sparkle in Emily's eyes when she was laughing with the children. And so he had asked the saleslady to wrap it up for Emily for Christmas.

The gift had been sitting atop his bureau for the past three weeks. It was odd, but just coming home and gazing at that little package had been enough to preserve his sanity some days. He would come home from his office wondering if he could face another day of legal preparation for the trial, and then he would see the package and remember what was inside, and he would think of Emily and how she would look when she saw it, and of everything he knew that was vulnerable and delicate and good.

Emily tore open the paper and lifted the lid on the interesting round box. "Careful," he warned her once, and then he decided not to say anything more. He didn't want anyone else guessing that this was such a special gift. But when Emily pulled the tiny crystal duck out of its Styrofoam holder and held it, everyone in the room knew it was special. It was the most dainty thing that Emily had ever seen. The little duck was made of Austrian hand-cut crystal, and even the minute upturned tail feathers glowed in a hundred separate lights when Emily held it up and the teeny thing caught the colors and the reflected glow from the Christmas tree.

"Philip," she whispered, "this is lovely." It meant a lot to her, that they would all go to such trouble to accept her when they were celebrating a holiday that was most traditionally their own. But there was something about this little bird, something more, that spoke of life and all its shining facets, and it moved her that Philip Manning had given her such a precious gift. She went to hug him and bent beside him to circle his shoulders with her arms. And when she hugged him and said "Thank you" once more in his ear, she thought for one fleeting moment how good it felt to hold him. He smelled of warm spices and fresh-cut pine and all of Christmas, and she clung to him for a moment, just wishing to stay in his arms forever. She was surprised when he circled her waist and pulled her close to him. It was suddenly more than he could bear, having her so near and not daring to respond to her. "You're welcome," he told her quietly as all the family looked on. "Merry Christmas, Emily."

After they were finished opening their gifts, the family settled around the table in the brightly lit kitchen for a steaming cup of homemade hot chocolate. One by one, they tired and went to bed. It had been a full day for everyone. Amanda's parents were the first to bid everyone "Good night," and then Lisa and Bethany did the same.

Clint stayed at the table to visit with his brother, and then he disappeared, too. Greg found him later sitting in the family room staring at the presents that still waited beneath the tree. There was still a pile of them, wrapped in brightly colored paper, and no one knew exactly when they would be opened. They were all gifts for Amanda.

"Dad." Greg wrapped his arms around his father's chest as he stood behind Clint. "Why don't you take them to her?" Then Greg paused hopefully. "I could go with you."

"No, son," Clint told him patiently. "Would you kids mind too much if I went, though? It's Christmas Eve. Maybe I should stay here." Clint did his best to turn his head and hide the tears that were coursing down his cheeks. He had done well all day, hiding the loneliness and the desperation he felt because his wife wasn't here to share the holiday. "I need to be with her tonight."

"Go ahead, Dad," Greg urged him. "Go stay the night. We'll be okay. I can take care of anything that comes up. And Uncle Philip and Granddad are here, too."

Clint stood up and picked up one of the presents from under the tree. He hugged it to him as if just touching her gift would bring Amanda closer to him, closer to waking, closer to living. "I'll go, then." He rumpled Greg's hair. "Thanks, son."

Only Philip and Emily remained at the kitchen table after Clint drove away. Greg went out to the garage, and Philip was quiet for a moment before he spoke. He was stirring his hot chocolate for the umpteenth time and wondering if he should say anything. He wanted to; he wanted to bring back the closeness that the two of them were beginning to share. He decided he had hesitated long enough. "You didn't expect to receive that gift from your mother, did you?"

"No." She was stirring her hot chocolate, too. "I used to keep a journal when I was in junior high school. I'm surprised she even remembered." The hardness in her voice surprised Philip. He hadn't lived through the things she had lived through, but he would have expected Emily to have a forgiving spirit.

She saw his expression and interpreted it correctly. "I know. It's hard to understand if you haven't lived it. If you could only have been there the Christmases that she forgot, the time Dad had to hurry around town at four o'clock on Christmas Eve to find something, anything, so we kids would have gifts from her underneath the tree. And then came the Christmases when she wasn't even there. She was out drinking somewhere. She didn't care about us."

Philip looked Emily straight in the eye. "She cared about you this year." This was something he felt he had to say. It surprised him how she hung on to her bitterness from the past. Something about the hurt she had surrendered to had defeated her. It was Emily who had given up all hope, Emily who had slammed shut doors that should have been left ajar. "I think she still loves you. You just don't give her a chance."

Emily's voice was thick with conviction. "The part of her that loved me is gone. It's dead."

"I don't think you are giving that love a chance to come back to life. You're trying to find acceptance from other people when all you really need is acceptance from her."

"Look—" she stood up from the table so quickly that she almost upset her hot chocolate "—what suddenly makes you the expert, Philip?" She was furious with him, and he was sorry she couldn't accept the truth of what he was saying. "Let this alone." She grabbed her coat from the back of the porch door where it was hanging and hurried out into the night air.

That night, Emily lay in bed a long while thinking of the things that Philip had said and gazing up at the stars through the big picture window beside the bed. She admired Philip for what he was trying to do, his attempt to bring some semblance of a family back into her own life, but there was no way he could understand her feelings. She talked to him in generalizations about her mother's drinking problem because some of the specifics were too difficult for her to speak of, even to him. One of her worst memories was when she had been in junior high school. She'd been Lisa's age, and she had gone to a Christmas caroling party with several of her friends from school. They had caroled on several blocks and they had gone to sing at a retirement center, and then, one by one, they had gone to each of their own homes to sing for their parents. It had been one of the most heartbreaking things Emily had ever had to go through, not just because she was anxious about what would happen at her house when they arrived but seeing the other houses, the other families, the hot chocolate, the candy canes and gingerbread men—the love that other people shared that she knew nothing of.

By the time it was Emily's turn to take all of them to her house, she had decided she absolutely could not do it. She didn't want anyone to see her haggard father, her mother who was probably so drunk that she would go reeling off the front porch as they sang to her. She didn't want them to see that the dishes hadn't been washed for three days and the walls were filled with holes from the times her mother had kicked and screamed and had put her fist through the plaster. So Emily had found another house, as they were driving along, where the lights were all out and nobody was home, and she had told them all that it was her house. There wasn't anybody there, so there had been no reason to stop, she'd told her friends. After the party was over, the lady who had been driving them offered to take them all home. Then she drove Emily straight to the house that Emily had claimed was her own. She had gotten out of the car and had walked proudly up the driveway while her stomach churned and then she waited on the front porch until her ride had driven away. And then she had bundled up against the cold and had walked back down the driveway to her real home which was some two and a half miles away. And nobody at school had ever known the difference.

That feeling of desperate embarrassment was hard to explain to someone who had never felt it. Emily admired Philip for trying to talk to her about it. But he was mistaken if he thought she could just ignore the feelings that still bothered her. He might be right about her mother, though. It did seem as if she was trying to reach out to Emily. But it was going to take a lot more than just one leather-bound book to prove it to her. There were years of her childhood that still needed to be accounted for.

As Emily lay there, still wide awake, she heard a cow bawling in the distance. There was something different about the sound tonight. It was usually such a warm, reassuring, peaceful sound. Tonight it sounded frantic. Emily wondered if something was wrong with one of the cows. Surely, if there was, Clint would take care of it. Then she remembered that Clint was spending the night at the hospital with Amanda.

She lay there, tense, listening, and then she heard footsteps in the grass outside the cabin. She was up and throwing on her flannel robe before she heard the pounding on the camp house door. She flung open the door and saw Greg standing there. He was panting and frantic. "What's wrong?"

"It's Honey Snookems." He was breathing so hard that he could barely talk. "I...need you to help me." Emily ran into the bathroom and threw on a shirt and some jeans while Greg talked. "I was out walking. I was worried about Dad and mad at him and I heard Honey Snookems bawling. She's in this old corral, the one close to the cabin. I guess she felt safe there."

"Is she calving?"

"She's doing her best. I think the calf's hiplocked. We've got to help her or we're going to lose both of them. Uncle Philip was at the corral when I found her.

He had heard her bawling because he couldn't sleep. We've got to throw her... get her to lie down... or there's no way we can get to the calf and help her. Uncle Philip sent me to find you. Dad's still at the hospital."

"Can't your grandfather help?"

"There isn't time to go back to the main house and get him. We've got to throw her now."

Emily was out the door then, running toward the rickety fenced corral and stable, with Greg following right behind her. When they got to the stable, Philip was there trying to stroke Honey Snookems and calm her. "Oh, good, Emily," he said, then breathed a sigh of relief.

Honey Snookems was hunched up and frightened in the corner of the corral, and she wouldn't let any of them approach her. "I should have known something like this was about to happen." Greg spoke softly so he wouldn't spook her. "She was skittish all evening. I should have said something to Dad but I just wasn't thinking about cows tonight. It's too late now to even call the vet. He won't get here in time."

"Poor little mama," Emily crooned as she moved toward the animal that she had learned to love. "Poor little mama." Her voice was steady, but it did nothing to quiet the cow. Instead, the animal moved farther away from them and hunched in another corner. "Oh, Philip—" Emily spun to face him, "—tell us what to do. This is horrible. We've got to help her."

"I've delivered a calf or two with Clint." Philip's voice was quietly confident. He wanted to make Emily feel confident, too. They needed her to be calm. He gestured toward his nephew. "This is the guy who will tell us what needs to be done." He knew his brother had taught Greg well.

Greg took command of the situation. "Keep talking to her," he advised Emily. "She needs reassurance. She won't want anything to do with people right now but having someone she knows just talk to her may help her relax. We've got to get her to lie down. I can't do anything for her with her standing like this. I don't know how much more of this pain she can handle."

"We can't lose this cow, Greg," Emily almost whispered as she shook her head vehemently. "This family can't handle losing anything else."

Greg didn't hear her comment. He was already in the tack room of the old stable searching for supplies he could use.

"We can do it, Emily." Philip had heard what she said. "We have to." Without thinking, he gripped her by the shoulders and began to slowly knead her muscles with strong fingers. "You okay?"

"I'm fine." She leaned back against him and closed her eyes as the fear and the frustration she felt seemed to ebb away. "Come on, mama cow." She spoke to Honey again while she drew on Philip's strength. This time, Honey Snookems moved as if she was responding to Emily's voice. The animal moved toward Emily as if she had found a kindred spirit. Her forelegs began to bend beneath her.

"She's going down on her own." Philip scarcely dared to breathe for fear of frightening the animal into standing up again. But by the time Greg arrived back at the corral carrying chains, hooks and a rope, the cow was kneeling on all fours in the corner by the stable.

"Amen." Greg's sigh of thanks was full of relief. "She's down." Despite his worry, he turned and winked at Emily. "I guess you can go back to bed now. Uncle Philip and I don't need you anymore. That's why I came to get you, so you could pick her up and lay her on her side for me."

"Give me a break." Emily wagged a finger at him as she stroked Honey's fuzzy head with her other hand. "This cow probably weighs six hundred pounds. And that's when she's not expecting a calf."

"Pretty close," Greg admitted as he laughed and Emily laughed, too. Their laughter was a welcome relief, taking the edge off their tension. "I didn't particularly want to throw her myself, either."

Honey Snookems was mooing for all she was worth now, and Emily was certain the pathetic sound would wake the girls and Amanda's parents back at the main house. "Sit up by her head and keep talking to her the way you've been doing." It was strange how calm Greg was, Philip thought as he obeyed his nephew's instructions. Once again, he was thinking how much he admired the boy. He was thinking how strong Greg was, how much he could help his father if Clint would only let him. And Emily was thinking the same thing. Greg did dumb things occasionally to prove he was becoming an adult, but under pressure, he remained levelheaded and mature. He embodied the best of both his father and his uncle, Emily reflected.

"I've got to get up the birth canal some way and figure out which way the calf is lying. We'll wrap the chains around the calf's front legs and do our best to pull it out of there. That's when I'm going to need both of you." He glanced up at his uncle and Emily.

Greg worked gently with Honey Snookems and cooed soothingly to her. Finally, after what seemed like an eternity, he looked up and Emily sensed his discouragement. "Why does Dad have to be gone tonight? I'm the one who told him to go. I can't reach in far enough. There's nothing I can do."

"Let me try." Emily rose to her feet slowly to move up beside him. She didn't want to alarm Honey. "My arms may be longer than yours and more slender. I may be able to reach the calf."

"Okay." There was a touch of hope in Greg's voice now. Philip stooped down beside them as, gently, Greg guided Emily's arms where they needed to go.

"It's okay, mama. It's okay," she crooned. And as she stretched her arms to try to reach in to the baby, Philip got the feeling that everything in his life until now had been a fantasy, a mere shadow of the truth. He was a grown-up little boy playing grown-up games. All of it, his reputation, his business, his past, was diminished by comparison with this one moment, watching Emily fighting to save a new little life. He had been crazy to forget about his family here on the farm during the past two months. He had been desolate at the thought of losing his business. But maybe it wasn't as important as all that. Maybe he was missing out on something here, something special and important, by being so involved with things at the office.

Emily glanced across at Greg as he knelt beside her, and she realized that she was acting so calm and deliberate because Philip was with her. She wanted to prove something to him. As if somehow saving this calf would take some of her disappointment about life away, too. Being around Philip made Emily want to be deserving of him. It made Emily want to overcome the negative emotions that had been controlling her for so long. "There." Her voice was triumphant. She could feel the calf.

"Take this chain and hook it around the calf's forehocks," Greg instructed her. "It's a little confusing. I've done this once before and I'm almost certain the head is up this direction. I can tell by feeling here." He pushed his hand against Honey's hind section.

"Okay." Emily nodded. She took the chains he handed her along with some rope and she carefully worked the rope up inside Honey's belly. She could feel something there, some hint of life, the spindly legs, the wet fur. She thought at first she couldn't detect movement. But then she thought she felt some slight movement. Emily didn't know if the calf should be moving at this point. She would be glad when this part of the delivery was over. Her arms were beginning to ache unbearably.

"You're doing fine." Philip was behind her now, pushing against her shoulders. His firm pressure gave her the extra endurance she needed. He could see how hard she had been straining to reach up inside the animal.

"There. I've got it," she told both of them finally. "I can't tell exactly where it is, but I know I've got it hooked somewhere between the front and back legs."

"That will have to be good enough." Greg was standing beside them. "We've got to get that calf out quickly." He picked the ends of the chains up out of the dust and began to tug them. Nothing happened. He strained against the chains and then, slowly, the tiny forehocks began to slide out of the birth canal. Greg motioned once more to Philip and Emily. "I need you both. Emily, can you reach up again and direct the calf's head? Uncle Philip, I need you to help me pull."

Emily obeyed him without question. The calf's head was further down now and easier to reach. Without realizing what she was doing, she was talking to the calf, begging it to be okay, begging it to be born so its mother would live, too. "Come on," she said over and over again. "Come on, baby critter. You can handle this."

Philip locked his arms around his nephew's waist and eased back until Greg's weight was centered against him. Then together they pulled.

The calf's head was born easily but, after that, their progress came to a grinding halt. "I was afraid of this," Greg groaned. "She's hiplocked. And there's nothing else we can do except what we've been doing."

Emily helped pull then, too, from between Greg and Philip. She locked her arms around Greg's shoulders and Philip locked his arms around her waist, and for long, excruciating minutes nothing happened. Honey Snookems was quiet now. She was exhausted, on the verge of giving up, and Emily wanted to scream. It all seemed so hopeless. She turned to Philip and he glimpsed the resignation in her eyes. "I can't stand much more of this."

Just as she spoke, the calf began to budge again, and with a good second effort, the hind legs came out with a great sucking sound and the calf was born.

Honey Snookems nosed the tiny form and bawled at it. But the calf did not respond. Instead, the tiny body remained still.

"We didn't make it." Emily just stood there staring at the unmoving tiny carcass on the ground. She felt so numb with disbelief that she couldn't cry.

Greg didn't make a sound. Instead, his legs buckled beneath him, and he collapsed beside the calf. Emily couldn't feel anything except Philip's arms still locked desperately around her waist. She turned to face him, and he took her head in his hand and guided it gently to his shoulder and there it remained. Philip wanted to comfort both Emily and Greg but there was nothing he could say. He did the only thing he could do—he brushed his lips in a light desperate kiss atop her head. When he did, she seemed to melt against him. Then, as if his movement had sparked something within her once again, she pulled away and turned toward Greg. She only knew that she had to comfort this young man who had experienced yet another loss. "Greg," she said softly as she moved toward him and gripped his arm. "Greg. I'm sorry."

There were streaks of dust and tears and sweat running down his face as he shook his head at her. "I should have known it would end this way when she started having trouble." He managed a brave, halfhearted smile. "We gave it a fierce try, though, didn't we?"

"Yeah," Philip said from behind her. "We did." Emily turned toward Philip again, and she glimpsed a familiar melancholy expression in his eyes. She realized then that his arms were still around her. It was as if he needed something to hold on to just as desperately as she did, and Emily stood next to him, thanking him with her eyes for being there. It had been a long night for all of them.

Finally, Philip pulled his gaze away from Emily's. "Where can I find a shovel?" he asked his nephew. "I want to bury this calf before the sun comes up. This is going to be hard enough as it is. Lisa and Bethany have been so excited about Honey Snookems's calf." He caressed Honey's nose when he passed her, going to look for the tool he needed. "I'm glad we saved this mama cow." He looked sad again as he spoke again. "We could have easily lost them both, you know."

"You dumb old cow," Greg bellowed at Honey Snookems just a little too loudly. "You always were the one to get yourself into messes." Tears were coursing down his cheeks.

Philip came back with a shovel and propped it up against the corral fence before he went to his nephew and wrapped his arms around Greg's shoulders. "Birthing that cow was a brave thing, Greg. No matter what the outcome, I'm proud of you. I know your father will be, too."

Greg spun around to face his uncle. "He won't be proud. He doesn't trust me. He doesn't think I'm mature enough to handle any responsibility. He'll think I screwed this up. He'll think it's my fault that Honey's calf died."

"But Honey didn't die, Greg." Emily moved up beside them and gripped Greg's arm. As the boy spoke, she had begun to realize that the boy's distress went much deeper than just bereavement over a calf that hadn't survived. The pain went clear down to Greg's soul. His father was keeping him from his mother's bedside out of a sense of love, no matter how misdirected that move might be. And Greg couldn't interpret it that way. "You're laying the blame on yourself. For the calf. For your mother. For the pressure your father is under."

Greg looked up at her.

Philip had to walk away to keep from shouting at her. He could tell by Greg's face that she was interpreting Greg's thoughts correctly. Of course she was. It was easy for her. The subjects she was discussing were dear to her heart. She could just as easily have been talking about herself.

"Don't blame yourself for something that you're not responsible for," Emily continued. "Personally, I think you should be allowed to visit Amanda at the hospital. I'd be willing to go with you and talk to your father about it, if you want me to. But no matter what he says to you or whether he lets you go see her, just remember all the many capabilities you have."

When Philip walked away from them, he turned toward Honey. She had moved away from the calf and she was not bawling, but she was hunched up again just the way she had been when they had first found her. "Emily!" he cried out. "Greg! Get over here. This crazy cow is having another calf."

Greg was beside the animal immediately with Emily right behind him, and this time, Honey Snookems had a much easier time of it. Philip stood with his arms around Emily's shoulders, bracing her against him in the early-morning moonlight. Greg delivered the second calf himself. "Dumb cow," he crooned over and over again as he guided the calf's head down the birth canal with his hands. "Crazy, dumb cow. Twins. I can't believe this."

When the second calf was born, Honey nosed it and it moved immediately. It was all wet fur and gangly legs. The tears streamed down Greg's face. Emily laughed and Philip applauded when Honey Snookems stood and then nosed persistently until the tiny calf stood, too, and nursed.

CHAPTER NINE

IT WAS THREE in the morning by the time Philip walked Emily back to the camp house. The stars shone like pinpoints into forever as the two of them walked along toward Emily's adopted home. It was Christmas morning, and all was right with the world. They had shared so much during the past hours that it seemed good and true and right to be together, walking homeward through the night, absorbing the silence.

"Hey!" Philip broke the spell first as he pointed to a flashing red light crossing the sky. It could have been anything, a meteor or a star or an airplane. "I'll bet that's Santa Claus. I'll bet his night has been almost as long as ours has."

"Yeah." Emily peered into the sky in the direction he was pointing. "I'll bet it has. I wonder if he's stopped at our house yet. With all the excitement Honey put us through, I forgot that Santa was supposed to stop by tonight." She grinned at him and then her smile turned to concern. "You still look exhausted, Philip." She could see the lines under his eyes even in the moonlight. "This restful holiday with the family hasn't done you much good."

He chuckled and it was a warm sound, a sound that seemed to ripple out into the night and bind the two of them closer together.

Emily spoke again. "I'm going to call Mother tomorrow." She hesitated when she realized how late it was. "Today... a little later, after the sun comes up. I think I can get her number from information. I have the return address on the package she sent."

"What are you going to say to her?" They were outside the cabin now, and Philip turned and studied her expression. Maybe the things he had said earlier had done some good.

"Whatever comes to mind, I guess. Thanks for the Christmas gift. Thanks for remembering me. Stuff like that." Almost anything was going to be very hard for her to say.

"I think you'll be glad you did it."

"I'll have to trust you on that." She laughed.

"Are you tired?" he asked. For a moment, he didn't know exactly what else to say to her.

"Tired but not sleepy," she answered honestly. "I can't wait until the sun comes up on that new little calf. I want to get a closer look at him. And Bethany and Lisa are going to think that little guy is their best Christmas present of all."

"You're right." As Philip looked down at her, there was something in her face, that same openness she always showed him, coupled with the fatigue from the past few hours, that made him long for her. She was beautiful and fragile and so different from Morgan. She wasn't just a feisty ad copywriter or a confused, sad woman who was taking care of the kids to prove something to herself. She was his Emily. He realized suddenly how much he cared for her and respected her. She had done quite a job helping to deliver that calf tonight. And suddenly he found himself wanting her, too.

"Philip?" Her eyes were filled with questions as she reached up and gingerly touched his cheek. "What are you thinking?"

When he didn't answer, she sensed that he was troubled. She speculated that he was thinking about her. "I'm glad you came to spend Christmas with us," she said softly.

"Where else would I go?" He was surprised at her comment. She talked as if she was used to having her family spread out all over Dallas during the holidays. He had always spent Christmas with Clint and Amanda and the kids. He could think of no other place he would rather be during the holidays than with his family.

"I don't know." She was laughing now, teasing him. "Maybe you'd be off viewing some exotic investment property in the south of France. Or you'd go to a ski resort. That's a popular spot this time of year. But then..." she was looking at him intently again, "...you aren't like that really, are you?"

"I'm not."

Emily had half a mind to ask him what he was like. She saw him with his brother and the kids, and he seemed so relaxed and happy. At those times she found herself very drawn to him. But lately one minute he was her confidant and the next he was somebody else—a professional totally wrapped up in his career and his company, someone who stayed distant and determined. Sometimes she feared that one day something inside him would snap and he would be back with them all for a while. She wasn't always certain what to expect from him. But she didn't tell him that. So she talked about the newborn calf. It was much safer. "I learned a lot about birthing babies," she teased.

There was admiration in his eyes when he looked at her. "You did wonderfully out there tonight."

She turned away from him and gazed up at the stars. "When the second calf was born, I was thinking what a wonderful sign of renewal it was. To Greg. To me." She faced him again. "I guess after our talk tonight, I started feeling I was the one who needed to be forgiven for something. I'll always wonder why Mother didn't love me as much as she loved her drinking. But maybe I'm wrong to resent her for it. Maybe it's time I began to forgive her."

"And maybe it's time you started to forgive yourself," Philip said cautiously.

He could see the haunting doubt on her face when she turned it up toward him. "I'm not a very strong person, am I?"

A consuming tenderness welled up in Philip. As he looked at her, he remembered a hundred other times in his life when he had been watching an associate or a friend have to learn something without his assistance. Watching Emily learning to trust was like watching a child learning to walk. He wanted to reach out and grasp her each time he saw her lose her confidence. But he couldn't do that for her, not when he cared this much about her. He knew he had to let go and let her profit from her mistakes one by one. "Think back to the things you told Greg tonight in the corral," Philip reminded her. "You told him to stop blaming himself for something that had never been his fault. You told him to recognize his own capabilities as a person."

There was something in her eyes then, some small spark that Philip guessed might be hope. "Those are the same things I should have been saying to myself all along, aren't they?" she asked.

"Yes, they are," he replied.

Emily turned away from him and gazed up into the night sky. There were a billion stars blazing overhead and, at that moment, she felt that each one of them was shining for her. When she finally spoke, her voice sounded very small. "I sent my Baby Sprout manuscript to a children's publisher not long ago." Philip was the first person she had told. It still scared her, thinking that her manuscript might be sitting on a desk somewhere, waiting for acceptance. She grinned up at him. It made her feel better about it, knowing that they were in this together. "I sent your storyboards in, too."

Philip's eyes widened. He knew what submitting the manuscript meant to her. He picked her up and spun her around; then he set her back on the ground in front of him. "What a Christmas Eve this has been," he almost shouted.

Emily grinned. "It's Christmas morning now." The sky was just beginning to glow a faint apricot against the eastern horizon. It was almost sunup. "Come on in the cabin and I'll fix you a cup of coffee, Mr. Manning.'' She pulled the screen door open and he followed her inside.

He sat down at the little kitchen table and watched her while she rummaged through the cabinets to find things she needed—the battered aluminum coffeepot, a spoon, the matches, a can of coffee. She stopped and stretched, and he went to her.

"Are you sore?" He ran his palms up her shoulder blades in a gentle motion.

"No." She laid her head back against his chest. "I'm just stiff." She loved the way he smelled as she leaned against him, of leather and sweat and dust. She loved having him here in her cabin.

Philip used one finger to stroke her dust-covered hair back behind her ear and then he whispered to her, "You were wonderful with Greg tonight."

"Thanks." She craned her neck back farther and looked up at his face. "And you were wonderful with that cow."

"Give yourself some credit," Philip told her. "We would have lost the second calf and Honey Snookems, too, if you hadn't been willing to reach up inside and do something a lot of women would have been too squeamish to try."

"Oh, I was just brilliant, wasn't I?" She wheeled around and faced him playfully. But when she looked up at him, Emily sobered. She had expected him to tease her, too, but there was something dark and haunting in his eyes. "Philip?" she asked. "What is it? What's wrong?"

He hesitated before he answered her. But he decided that it was time for them both to be truthful. "I'm so proud of you," he told her. "You're giving so much to this family." He stared up at the ceiling for a moment and then he looked back at Emily. "But I am a man, Emily. I need you to begin giving to me, too."

It was a combination of everything that had happened on the farm tonight, the family Christmas celebration, Honey Snookems's second calf, Greg's discontent, that made Philip finally voice the things he had wanted to tell her for weeks. Emily's caring had cemented fragmented parts inside him. Being around her seemed to mesh all the parts of his life together... his concern for his company... his love for his family... his disillusionment at the past and his hopes for his future. Emily tied everything together for him.

"I don't know what you mean." There was fear in her eyes when she said it.

"Yes, you do."

Her eyes were great huge pools when she turned them up at him. "Does it have to be this way?" She was trembling. Philip had to swallow the urge to reach out to her and to tell her he wanted to protect her. But both of them were past that point now. She didn't need him to protect her any longer.

"Emily." He reached out to her and gripped her shoulders so forcefully that his fingers bruised her through the plaid flannel shirt she was wearing. "Look at us. Look where we are in our lives together. Think of how far we have come."

"Have we changed together?" she asked. She reached out to him and cupped his face in her hands. "I know I've grown here. I know I've come to trust you. But is it something that we could have done without each other? This changing?"

"No," he told her frankly. "It isn't." Having Emily in his life was beginning to mean everything to Philip. For the first time, he felt like a whole person. He laughed at the irony of it all. People in Dallas thought he was omnipotent. But it had only taken this petite woman and a few sketches of a grinning possum to turn his life topsy-turvy. "You make me feel like a little boy, Emily. As if I'm discovering life all over again. You make me proud of the little things. Of the nights I spend delivering calves. Of the days I spend drawing or with my family." He was still chuckling.

"Good." She grinned smugly up at him. "It's about time somebody put you in your place. You act entirely too uppity at times." Then, gingerly, she stood on tiptoe and kissed his nose. "That's the part of you I like the very best, Philip Manning. The part of you that makes you act and feel like a little boy." It had been the part of him that had growled at her and Lisa like a playful bear so long ago as they sat hiding in the branches of a pecan tree. It was the part of him that made her feel safe enough to do what she knew it had come time to do now. She reached up with one finger and traced the outline of his ear. When he lowered his head to her, she let her lips trail around the outline of his ear, too. "You're right, Philip Manning." Her voice was filled with certainty. "It is time for both of us to start giving." Emily's lips trailed from his ear down his jawline to his neck. When she kissed him, Philip drew back his head and sighed. "Kiss me, Philip," she whispered. And he would have, except Emily's lips found his first.

The power of her kissing him and the longing he felt for her almost knocked him over. All this time, the two of them had been just quietly there for each other, like two good friends. And now it seemed as if a dam had broken within him because she trusted him. She was finally willing to reach out to him. It was something Philip wanted to savor, the very richness of wanting her this way. He let go of her shoulders and ran his fingers through her hair. Then he took both of his hands and crumpled her curls up inside them. He was lost in the feel and the smell of her, and he knew by her body's response that Emily wanted him as badly as he wanted her.

She pulled away from him, and when she did, he ran one tentative finger over her face. He outlined her brows, her nose and then his finger stopped on her lips. "Oh, little one," he said breathlessly. He had in mind to tell her she was beautiful. But when he looked at her, he wanted to kiss her. The two of them had spent months talking, jousting with their fears. Now it seemed as if the strength the two of them shared made everything else secondary. They had delivered a calf together tonight in the darkness. And they had started a new beginning in their two lives, as well.

His finger still rested on her lip, and he watched her as she raised her hand to his and held it there while she kissed his fingers, one by one. Then with a contented sigh, he raised his other hand to hers and pulled her toward him. She came to him willingly, and this time, when Philip saw the shining assurance in her eyes, he was overwhelmed.

"This is okay," she whispered. "I don't care if love might not last. We have tonight, don't we?"

"We have this morning," Philip said without remorse. "The sun is almost up."

When she smiled at him this time, it was a smile that he had not seen on her face before. She had a small, strong expression on her lips. She was pursing them together and the corners turned up slightly at each end of her mouth. She looked quietly contented. It was a smile that told him all he needed to know.

He ran one hand down the side of her face and then he cupped it beneath her chin. And this time, when he kissed her, he was in no hurry. He had nothing left to prove to her. He probed the inside of her mouth with his tongue, then trailed kisses across her jaw, down the pulsing vein on her neck.

Emily felt a fire slowly kindling inside her, a longing for him that warmed her and filled her and made her forget years of insecurity and sadness. He was all she needed now.

Emily opened herself to him and she was, at last, everything that she could be for him.

Philip did not make love to her that Christmas morning. He was so used to caring for her, to guiding her gently down paths he thought she would do well to tread. He guided her gently now, and he waited for her while she explored the things she was feeling. Slowly, he unbuttoned her flannel shirt and slipped his fingers across the silk of her skin. He eased the shirt off her shoulders and then he massaged them again. Her muscles there were still stiff. She reached out to him again and again, and as he caressed her, the discomfort eased from her body.

As the sky to the east brightened from a deep purple to a soft apricot, she lay in his arms, totally at peace.

"This is what it's supposed to feel like, isn't it?" Emily asked, giving him a contented half smile. She was lying beside him on the quilt that covered the bed. He had started a fire in the wood stove earlier, and it was crackling as it filled the cabin with warmth.

"Yes," he told her. "It is."

She grinned up at him. "Think the kids will notice you didn't spend the night in the main house?"

He couldn't help but look sheepish. "Probably," he admitted. "But the way people come and go around here, I'll bet you nobody will ask."

He was right about that. Greg had been up all night long with the calf. No doubt he would be sleeping late this morning. Clint had spent the night with Manderly at the hospital. And the kids were used to Emily's wandering in and out of the house at various times of the day.

"Philip?" Her eyes were serious now.

"What, little one?"

She reached up and tousled his hair. "I want to thank you."

"You're welcome, ma'am," he teased her. Then his eyes turned somber when he looked at her. "It's been a special Christmas, hasn't it?"

"Yes," she answered quietly, and he loved the confident glow that he saw in her eyes. "It has."

Later, the two of them walked hand-in-hand toward the main house and as they neared the corral by the house, Emily recognized the familiar bawling coming from the stable. But this time, she heard laughter there, too. Bethany and Lisa had already discovered Honey Snookems's new calf.

"What's going on in here?" Philip called as they neared the barn.

"Come look at the new calf," Lisa urged them.

"We named her something really special," Bethany chimed in. "We're going to call her Baby Sprout."

Philip scooped his youngest niece up in his arms. "Where did you two come up with such a poetic name?" he asked. "And so original, too." He winked at Emily.

"I think it's perfect." Emily said, grinning from ear to ear. Bethany and Lisa giggled when Philip stuck his tongue out at her.

Emily couldn't resist giggling, too, as all five of them headed back toward the house.

Manderly's mother was in the kitchen when Emily arrived. The house smelled of Danish cinnamon rolls that the woman had covered with orange glaze. Emily sliced the venison sausage, a treat Clint provided every Christmas morning from his hunting trips, and the girls helped her in the kitchen. The aroma of the meat wafted through as the sausage sizzled on the stove.

As the venison cooked, Emily found the chance to slip away and join Philip on the porch.

He was already bent over a canvas with newspapers and paints spread out all around him. He was so engrossed in his work that he didn't hear her approaching. Gazing into the distance, Philip was trying to recreate with his brush the colors he'd seen in the morning sky.

"Hi." Emily spoke softly so she wouldn't startle him.

He turned to her with one arm and looped it around her legs in a motion for her to sit beside him.

"I can't stay," she explained, touching his shoulder gently. "I have to put the eggs on."

He turned from his work and grinned up at her, a haphazard, cocky sort of smile that made him look like a little boy instead of a man in his thirties. "You're wonderful, you know," he told her.

"So are you." She gazed lovingly at him for a moment, at his nose, at his lips, at the faraway expression in his eyes as he gazed over the horizon. "What are you painting?"

He held the rough sketch up so she could see it. She could make out the pencil outline of a mother cow nursing her newborn calf. He had already painted in the deep crimsons of the sunrise. "I'm going to title it *Christmas Morning*." Then he tugged her arm playfully. "Tell me you don't think it's too sentimental."

She laughed. "I'm not going to tell you anything of the sort. It is *very* sentimental." Emily hesitated, keeping him in suspense for a moment. "But," she continued, "I guess that's okay. I love it."

"Breakfast is ready!" Lisa called out.

"Oops." Emily grinned at Philip sheepishly. "Sounds like somebody else got stuck doing the eggs."

"That's okay," Philip whispered mischievously. "You had a rough night. You deserve a break this morning."

"Thanks loads." She reached out to him and tousled his hair before he could stand up beside her.

The entire family assembled around the dining room table while Lisa poured coffee. And even Greg was grinning when he came downstairs.

Clint reached out to his son and hugged him. "I'm very proud of you, son," he said, his eyes shining.

"Thanks, Dad."

Clint had arrived home shortly after sunup. He had slept in Amanda's room at the hospital almost all night. There was something about him this Christmas morning—an extra sense of hopefulness that made him seem more like his former self to his family.

"How is she, Dad?" Lisa was the first one brave enough to ask, and Clint surprised everyone when he glanced up from his plate.

"She's doing much better, Lisa."

Amanda's parents both stared at their son-in-law. Clint saw their expressions and answered their unasked questions. "She's gaining weight. She gained twelve ounces in the past week." Amanda survived on the intravenous glucose and proteins the doctors poured into her body. The fact that her body was finally accepting that nourishment was a major victory.

But that was only the beginning of Clint's story. Last night late, he had spent his time with her reading her their Christmas cards. He had brought the entire stack from the top of the spinet piano in the family room, and he had gone through them all, talking about the verses and describing the photographs and naming old friends. There were oodles of kids all over the country that Clint had never met, with names like Samantha and Eric and Lisa Jo, who meant something to them because he and Amanda had once been friends with their parents. He read to her about their accomplishments, their band trips and their National Merit Scholarships. He spoke to her about their own kids, Bethany and Lisa and Greg, and he listed the things they had accomplished and talked to her about the things that made him proud of them.

He'd been talking about all three children—first, about Greg driving the Studebaker and studying for exams and next about how Bethany teased her brother sometimes, when he'd looked up and, centimeter by centimeter, in an obviously deliberate movement, Manderly had placed her hand on his. Actually, it had been an almost imperceptible movement, one that could easily have been explained away by a reflex, but Clint had too much faith. He knew it was something more than that, her not waking up but touching him, and this time even the doctors had been impressed. She'd been kept under close observation throughout the night but no more movement had been noted. Finally, Clint had fallen asleep on a cot beside her, and carolers had sung outside in the hallway while Manderly had lain sleeping silently but breathing strongly and steadily.

"Hey, bud. What do we need to talk about?" Clint asked Philip late that morning while Emily and Amanda's mother worked in the kitchen basting the Christmas turkey. Clint saw Philip's face fall when he asked. His question had visibly pulled Philip back from his private brooding to reality. "If you'd rather talk later, we can." Clint wondered what could be so wrong that the mere mention of it could physically jolt his brother. Philip was usually not so transparent.

"It's fine," Philip assured him. "You're not going to want to hear this, though."

"Sounds like I'd better."

Philip followed his brother into his study and told Clint about Morgan Brockner and the allegations she had brought against his company, as well as the lawsuit she had filed. And as he spoke, Philip was in the corporate world once more, the world where dollars represented his worth and deals represented his family, and for the first time in twenty-four hours, he totally forgot about Emily.

"I can't believe Morgan would pull a stunt like this, Philip." Clint was concerned about the problem now, too, not so much for the family name but for his brother's sake. "She's outdone herself this time, hasn't she?"

"Morgan Brockner outdoes herself every time. That's her style. She plans her moves like a major Hollywood production and then pulls the punches. Below the belt. But not so low that the news media might miss them."

"What's the scheduling on this thing?" Clint asked. "How long do we have to work on a case?"

Philip counted back on one hand. "She filed two months ago. The legal listing will appear sometime this week. The pretrial conference is in seven weeks. That sets the trial for the end of April or the first of May."

"What is the amount of the suit?" Clint could not believe what this woman was about to do to his brother. He wanted to throttle her.

"More than ten million. The commission we earned on the sale of the Robertson property plus personal damages."

"That is incredible—" Clint was shaking his head "—just incredible."

"Bennett Huff has been working around the clock on the litigation. The case hits the newspapers here in three days. I'm hoping most of our clients will stick by us when the press gets hold of this thing." He reached his fist across the desk and brought it down hard. "This shouldn't have to be your problem, Clint. It's Manning Real Estate and Investment she wants." *And my head on a silver platter.* He thought the words but he didn't say them. Instead he offered, "I'm certain your name's going to be involved."

"What if it is?" Clint clapped his brother on the back. "If I lose clients over it, I know it's because those clients weren't the ones I wanted to represent, anyway. We'll fight her with everything we've got." Clint was furious. He couldn't believe his brother had waited so long to tell him about their problem. It had obviously taken a while for the reality of the situation to hit Philip, too. What made Morgan Brockner think she could carry off a coup of this magnitude? A few carefully forged documents? A client she perhaps had paid off not to testify for them? How long would all this last? Neither of them could guess. The woman couldn't handle competition of any kind. For all Clint knew, Morgan Brockner would professionally stalk his brother for as many years as he kept his company.

EMILY WAS DIALING a number on the telephone in the main room when Clint and Philip came out of Clint's study. She had used the return address on the Christmas gift her mother had sent to trace her mother's new number. Just as Philip walked up behind her, the call went through. Emily grabbed Philip's hand as he walked by her and made him stay with her. As she talked, there was a tremor in her voice. Philip ached for her as he stood by and listened.

"Mother?"

"Emily?" The voice on the other end was so shrill and sharp that Philip could hear it from where he stood beside her. "Emily, is that you?"

"It's me."

"Is something wrong?"

"No, Mother. I just wanted to call. I got the green book you sent. We opened presents last night here on the farm. I just wanted you to know how happy I was—" she paused, searching for the right words "—that you thought of me."

There was silence on Emily's end of the line and silence on her mother's end, as well. It was uncomfortable for both of them, each wondering who was going to say something next.

Finally Emily couldn't stand the silence between them any longer. "I'm sorry I didn't send you anything. I thought about it, but I didn't know where you were." It was a weak excuse but as good as any.

"That's okay, honey." Her mother's voice was softer now. "Christmas isn't an 'I give you...you give me' proposition. I've been thinking of you lately and hoping you were doing well. I decided since you aren't writing at the agency any longer, you might find time to pursue some creative work of your own."

Philip was surprised at how animated Emily's features became at this point in the conversation. "I am." She didn't tell her she had submitted a manuscript to a publisher. "Mother... are you having a nice Christmas? Good. I'm glad. Let me tell you about mine."

The conversation went on from there. Emily talked about their Christmas on the farm and about the baby calf she'd helped bring into the world. Her brother had called the house last night, and she told her mother about that, too. "He's skiing up at Jackson Hole," she told her, and Philip was relieved. It sounded as if she didn't need him, as if this was turning out to be a normal conversation. "He and five guys from the corps are sharing a condo at Teton Village. He says the snow's great."

Emily's face darkened after a moment, and Philip realized the phone call must be coming to an end. "I'll let you go, Mother. I hope you have a Merry Christmas." There was a pause. "Mother." Emily's voice was quavering again. "Mother, I love you."

When Emily turned to Philip after she'd hung up the phone, she was shaking. "I did it, didn't I?" She gave him a halfhearted grin. And then he saw the tears begin to pool in her eyes. "Hold me, Philip." Her voice was thick as she stumbled toward him. "Please, just hold me."

When he reached out to her, Philip felt as if he might enfold her spirit, her courage, her self-esteem as he clasped his arms around her shoulders. And the only thing he could think of was how much he loved her as he gently rocked her back and forth while she cried.

CHAPTER TEN

PHILIP STARED AT THE PAPERS he held. Here it was, with his name printed in bold type at the top of the page. It was real. This trial was going to happen.

"Morgan Brockner/Brockner Associates, Plaintiff, vs. Philip Bradley Manning/Manning Commercial Real Estate and Investment, Inc., Defendant, for contract infringement, compensatory damages in the amount of $3.7 million and personal damages for undue suffering and loss of reputation in the amount of $7 million more." If the judgment went in her favor, Philip would have to scrape the bottom of the barrel for a while to pay off the settlement. But he wasn't planning on losing to her, and if he did, the important part of his company, the building, the associates, the clients, would remain intact. It was his reputation he stood to lose. But he didn't plan on putting that in jeopardy, either.

He was glad the pretrial consultation was over. He had been dreading it since before Christmas. And now he had another month's reprieve until the trial began. The trial had been moved up several weeks, and Philip didn't know whether it was by luck or by design. He was ready to get the farce over with. He speculated that Morgan was, too.

The pretrial conference had been simple. Bennett Huff had done his best to talk him into settling out of court. But Philip wouldn't hear of it. It might save him time that way and it might save him money in the long run, but he refused to take the easy way out with Morgan. He wanted to fight her, and if all of America wanted to stand at the bullpen and watch, then that was okay with him, too. Besides, it seemed to Philip that settling out of court might just as well be an admission of guilt. Huff asserted that if the board of directors would agree to it, settling out of court would keep the drama of the trial out of the newspapers. But Philip knew better. They weren't dealing with a predictable opponent here. They were dealing with Morgan Brockner. Philip was certain that if he settled out of court, Morgan would find a way to get news of the settlement into the headlines, too.

And so they had gone about the business of finalizing the specifics of the trial before they "went at it," as Bennett Huff had once phrased it. They sat at separate tables with an army of attorneys and met with District Judge Keslow Wilson to work out the details. Philip wasn't surprised at all when Morgan requested a jury trial. In a civil matter like this one, despite the phenomenal amount of money involved, the case could have been tried by the judge. It would have saved them at least a week of jury selection at the onset of the trial. But Morgan wouldn't hear of it. She had to have a jury, and Philip suspected it was because she wanted as many people involved in this trial as possible. The average layman was much more interested in what a jury decided than what a judge set forth. And because Morgan requested it, even though he didn't want it, the Brockner vs. Manning trial would be a trial by jury. Philip had thrown his hands up at her when he'd left the room. *Let her do what she wants to do,* he'd thought. *She'll find out in the end that it's all been a waste of her valuable time.* He would see to that.

When he went back to his office, Philip was exhausted. He and Bennett Huff had been going over papers and talking to witnesses and analyzing all the facts themselves until Philip felt that every time he sat down in his chair he was making a calculated movement. He stared at the watercolor on the wall and thought of the farm and of how far away he felt from all the people there. He had only been able to make it to the farm twice since Christmas because of this trial—once on New Year's Day for a family celebration and once at the end of February to celebrate Bethany's birthday. It had been a wonderful party for her. Emily had planned it, and there had been kids and balloons and pizzas all over the place. Eight girls from Bethany's fourth-grade class had slept over on a Friday night and Philip had found it hard, with all the ruckus going on, to talk to anybody. And so he had watched Emily admiringly all evening long as she prepared her fifth pepperoni-and-mushroom pizza and poured what was perhaps the fiftieth paper cup full of orange soda.

Philip had seen how tired she'd been and then he had remembered some of the parties his mom had hostessed for him and he'd realized that giving a birthday party for a child took a lot of love and a great amount of patience. And then he'd remembered Emily's telling him once that she had never been brave enough to invite any of her friends to her house to spend the night. Emily was giving the girl one of the things she'd always wanted and had never had, a slumber party. With bubbly, giggly girls who played records and whispered secrets about boys and ate all night long.

Philip had always loved visiting the farm but now that he knew Emily was there, he liked it even more. The house seemed alive again, the way it had been before Amanda's illness. The girls laughed freely again and his brother was less subdued, more prone to giving his opinion and, like his daughters, to laughing. Even Greg seemed contented. Emily Lattrell had worked miracles with his family. And it was fun now just to call the farm, just hoping she would answer, so he could hear the sunshine in her voice and think of all the things he was feeling for her.

Philip was worried about the trial, though, and what Emily would think when she found out about his relationship with Morgan Brockner. He was certain that the competition between the two companies would be emphasized in the local media. Philip knew how Morgan worked. He expected certain details of their romantic relationship to be splashed across the front pages of Texas newspapers and the *Wall Street Journal*, as well. Philip wasn't being pretentious. He knew it could be just as dangerous to underestimate this trial's impact on the business community as it could be to overestimate it.

One thing Philip was certain of: he did not want to underestimate the impact this trial would have on Emily. She had been so fragile and forlorn when she had come to the farm.

She had learned how to trust him. Philip was afraid if she took the trial testimony seriously, she might question that trust. He hated Morgan for potentially souring his relationship with Emily even more than he hated her for the risk that suit posed to his company.

So Philip decided he should talk to Emily about the trial before the fact. He was desperate to see her, anyway. Since she had submitted his storyboards and her manuscript to Hudson Publishing, the two of them had not worked together. Philip missed their time together.

He called her at the farm, hoping he could set a time to talk to her. "Emily?"

"It's me," she said in her singsong voice, and he couldn't help but grin because he was so glad to hear her speak.

"Do you have any time this afternoon? I'd like to see you. I might even feed you lunch."

"That would be nice," she said, laughing. "Actually, I do have some time today. I might be able to fit you into my busy schedule."

He made arrangements to meet her at a Mexican restaurant called Santa Fe Annie's in an hour.

As she entered the lobby and followed the waiter, he watched as she glided in and out among the tables, until she reached him. She looked exquisite to him, so vulnerable and natural and soft. She was wearing an ivory silk blouse with billowing sleeves, an angora fawn-colored skirt with a long angora V-neck sweater, half fawn and half ivory, with a braid of the two colors straight down the middle to her hip. The outfit suited her perfectly. It wasn't showy, just quietly sophisticated. She looked like somebody important, and Philip felt wonderful warm sensations as she came up beside him and hugged him.

"Thanks for inviting me to lunch, sir," Emily said as she sat down. She kissed him playfully on the nose when he rose and pulled out her chair for her.

They ordered their lunch and munched on tortilla chips and hot chili salsa. Philip leaned across the table and tentatively touched her hand.

"Philip? What's wrong?" He was acting strangely. She knew something was troubling him.

"I'm being sued." He said the words abruptly, as if the very sound was distasteful to him.

"Why?" Her eyes were huge. "Philip, who would do such a thing?"

"Morgan Brockner," he said simply. "She's suing me and my company for contract infringement."

"Why would she do that? What could she possibly stand to gain from it?"

When Philip explained the extent of the suit, Emily gasped. "It's been going on a long time, Emily," he told her.

"Why would she do something like this? Why would she expend so much energy trying to ruin your reputation?"

Philip told her the rest of the story then, not with all the details, but he included the things he thought she should know. He told her he had cared for Morgan in college and about the way she had utterly betrayed him.

After he'd finished talking, Emily stared at her plate without speaking for a long time. She tried to imagine how he must have felt, having someone he cared about leave him. It had remained impossible for him to put his animosity aside. Morgan Brockner was always competing with him to remind him of it. Emily considered everything that he had told her and everything she knew him to be. Philip sat across the table from her looking like a wistful boy who was being punished in a way he didn't deserve.

He paid for their lunch and they strolled out into the late winter sunshine together. She turned to him once more, just as he was opening the car door for her, so she could get in and drive away. But before she did, she had to ask him one question. Knowing the answer suddenly meant everything to her. "Were you in love with her, Philip?"

He thought about his answer for a moment before he shook his head. "No," he told her. "I wasn't, I guess I was in love with who I once thought she was. But I never loved Morgan Brockner."

"Have you ever loved anyone else?"

He knew what she was asking him. She wanted to know how badly his relationship with Morgan Brockner had scarred him. "No," he answered her slowly. "I was never able to fall in love." Then he looked at her and his eyes seemed to bore great holes through her. "Until now."

"Philip." She placed her hand on top of his on her car door handle and held it there. "Don't. Not here.

Not now. I don't know what to say." She wanted to tell him what she was feeling. It seemed only fair to her. Philip deserved a woman to love him, to care for him for a long, long time. There were days now when Emily longed to be in love with him. But she couldn't admit it to him, not yet, not until she knew she could commit herself to him forever.

He looked down at her sadly. "I didn't want to drag you through this. I didn't want you involved. There's going to be lots of publicity. And it isn't going to be pleasant."

"I'll go through it with you," Emily said as she touched his shoulder and searched his face with her eyes. "Why didn't you tell me about this a long time ago?"

"I didn't want to talk about it." It had been extremely difficult talking about the trial and it had been excruciating talking about his relationship with Morgan.

"That's not a good excuse." She was half teasing and half serious.

"Does that make a difference to you? Knowing about Morgan?" He hoped that it didn't. He didn't want her to change her mind about him or to think any less of him because he hadn't told her about Morgan before. And he wondered if she'd think he was a fool because he had once desired a woman who wanted his company instead of him.

In fact, knowing those things about Philip did make Emily feel different about him. She was comparing herself to him, knowing that he had lost an important part of himself, too, when Morgan had left him and his company to start building her own.

Philip had every reason to be afraid of another relationship with a woman. But he had reached out to her nonetheless and had been her friend. And all the times she had thought he didn't understand her loss, he had. In a way, he had been through it, too.

"You're braver than I am." She was staring straight out into the parking lot, but she wasn't seeing the cars or the Texas sun or the asphalt. She was recalling a night at Christmas, a tiny calf in the corner of a corral and luxuriating in the memory of a caress that had suddenly taken on a much deeper meaning for her.

"Not really," he said wryly. He knew what she meant. "I think I just decided you were worth any risk. And it's about time that you decided that, too."

"Mr. Manning." She wanted to laugh and cry at the same time. "You are crazy."

"No," he told her. "I'm not."

When she saw the love in his face, Emily felt as if she was interpreting her own self-worth through Philip's eyes. She was going to be okay. He was giving her a great gift. She stood on tiptoe and kissed him lightly on the cheek. "I'd like to come to part of the trial," she told him. "But I don't know if I can get away from the kids."

"You don't need to worry about being there." He smiled at her. "It's not going to be all that much fun."

"That's not why I want to be there," Emily said as she stood on tiptoe again and held him with her arms stretched up around his neck. Then she kissed him full on the lips.

"Hmm," he raised his eyebrows. "I should tell you my sad sob stories more often. That was nice."

"Go ahead," she teased him. "Be my guest. I'm all ears."

Philip reached around to encompass Emily's back. He pulled her to him. He lowered his head to hers and brushed his lips across her forehead. "Oh, little one," he whispered. "I'm so afraid that I'll lose the company. Or that I'll lose you."

"It's going to be okay, Philip." Her words were scarcely more than a murmur against his cheek. "You've done nothing wrong. It's crazy of you to even think of losing Manning Real Estate." Emily closed her eyes and leaned against him. She wished she could have added, "It's even crazier of you to think that you might lose me. It was something she wanted desperately right now, to look at him and to know that she was that committed to him.

THE JURY SELECTION in the Brockner vs. Manning trial took exactly one week. The jurors streamed through the room and Bennett Huff questioned them. Philip couldn't keep from thinking, as he observed their stoic faces, that these people held his future in their hands. He was curious about them. He wondered about their families and their children and about what they had eaten for dinner at home the night before. That made it easier on him, thinking of them as if they were real people instead of players in a drama that threatened the future of everything he stood for.

At 1:45 p.m. on Friday, the jury selection was complete. Morgan's attorneys and Bennett Huff were satisfied. One of the women worked in the infants' department at Dillard's. One of the men laid telephone lines for Southwestern Bell. The jurors were ordinary people, all of them.

At 9:00 a.m. the following Monday, the trial testimony began. Philip sat silently at the defendant's table with Bennett Huff at his side, waiting for the inevitable—the parade of players, lies, unwitting pawns that had to be present for this farce to take place.

Farce was a strong word for Philip to use. But it fitted the situation. Philip marveled that a district judge the caliber of Keslow Wilson would let a case like this one go this far. Philip had seen the man in court before and knew him to be an honest, just judge.

When Morgan entered the room at precisely 9:00 a.m., Philip decided that his choice of the word *farce* had been a good one. Morgan looked beautiful. She looked innocent and pretty and pure, and for a moment he stared at her blatantly from across the room. And she stared back.

Morgan was wearing her hair down on her shoulders in a style he hadn't seen her wear since college. It had been curled on the ends, professionally he suspected. He couldn't help thinking that it wasn't the way Emily curled hers, by rolling it on heat rollers and then sitting out against the trunk of the pecan tree in the backyard reading a book until her hair set. Or chasing the girls all around the big house and tickling them and giggling and carousing until, one by one, the curlers fell out on the floor. He had stepped on one once, one day when he had driven to the farm to see his family. And to see her.

Philip shook his head to clear his mind of thoughts of Emily. He couldn't help it, though, because Morgan reminded him of Emily this morning. She was wearing a winter-white wool suit with a gray, blue and cream flounce of a bow at her neck. Her sling-back pumps were taupe with tiny strips of gray leather woven into them. And there was a mere hint of a gold chain wrapped around each ankle. Her hair was swept back from her temples with delicate gold combs. And she was wearing gloves.

She smiled at him once to break the stare, and then she marched to the front of the room to sit beside her lawyers. And when she spoke to one of them, she reached over and laid a small gloved hand on his elbow.

It was hard for Philip to keep from jumping up and shouting at her. She reminded him of a heroine in a Danielle Steel novel dressed like that, looking dainty and desperate and sad, and Philip wanted to slap her for playing with their lives. When he looked at her and analyzed the things he saw there, it seemed as if Morgan was cheapening all the things about Emily that he held so dear—her vulnerability, her delicate beauty, her overwhelming innocence. And he understood now why Bennett Huff had instructed him not to get angry with her in front of the judge or the press or the jury. He would come across as the big, bad wolf pouncing on little Red Riding Hood. He knew, as he watched her, that was exactly what she wanted. She was baiting him.

Now that he knew Emily, Philip could see things he hadn't seen before when he dared to meet Morgan's eyes. There was a covered darkness in them, and he couldn't read anything there except a small light of anticipation. He realized she was struggling to remain in character

As if Bennett Huff could read his mind, Philip's attorney turned his head down to the table and acted as if he was examining his papers once more. "That woman is going to foul up one of these days," he whispered to his client. "There's too much malice in her to be able to cover it very long. We'll be patient. She's putting on a good act but she's a viper inside Keslow will sense that, too. And one day, the big, bad wolf in her is going to spring out from behind the innocent disguise and bare its ugly teeth."

Philip grinned at Bennett's choice of fairy tales. He had been thinking of that one, too. "Let's just hope it's while the jury is in the room," he commented.

"Yes." Bennett Huff nodded his head in agreement. "Let's do."

CHAPTER ELEVEN

PHILIP WAS EXHAUSTED. If there was anything he'd come to despise it was sitting in one place for eight hours listening to testimony about his character. If he had to hear one more person tell the court what an outstanding businessman he was, he thought he was going to slug someone.

It was an emotional and physical release for him when Bennett Huff called him, at last, to take the witness stand on his own behalf. He was certain this part would be easy. But he was wrong. Morgan Brockner knew him well enough to hurt him. She knew his weaknesses. She had spent long hours with her attorneys, briefing them, and Philip was horrified when they began firing questions at him. They asked him about the financing his father had put out for his company. They asked him about pranks he had played on fraternity brothers in college. At the end of the morning, Philip felt that the only question they hadn't asked him was his shoe size.

By noon, Morgan's lawyers had painted him as an overeager businessman who was anxious to make a fast buck by doing away with his competitors. Philip could only hope that the testimony the jury heard was so contradictory that the jurors would be totally confused. That seemed like his only hope.

That, and the testimony of Clyde Robertson.

When Robertson took the stand and began telling his story, Philip wanted to jump up out of his chair and scream at the man. He lied. Blatantly. Clyde Robertson told the jury he had signed a contract with Morgan Brockner instead of Manning Commercial Real Estate and Investment, Inc. When Bennett Huff showed Clyde a copy of the contract he had signed with Manning, Clyde sadly shook his head. "I didn't sign that one," he said hesitantly. "That one must be a forgery."

As Philip considered the millions he had made for this man in his office complex transaction, he had to wonder what hold Morgan Brockner had over him. He wondered if she had paid him. But it would have had to have been an incredible sum of money to override the profits that Philip had earned him. Clyde Robertson was testifying under oath in a courtroom that he had signed a contract with her to sell his office complex. Philip was furious enough to remain stoic throughout Clyde's entire testimony. He felt as if he'd turned to stone. He couldn't move and he couldn't rationalize. If he did, he was going to hit something.

When it came Bennett Huff's turn to cross-examine the man, Philip knew his attorney was fighting for control, too. "May I ask you, Mr. Robertson, why you went ahead and accepted a $37 million sale from Philip Manning when you say you signed an exclusive contract with Morgan Brockner?"

For a split second, Clyde Robertson squirmed in his seat. Then he answered Huff's question with a question. "Wouldn't you do the same thing? Would you turn down a $37 million contract when somebody offered it to you out of the blue? Of course I couldn't turn it down."

The trial continued for the remainder of the afternoon while Philip sat in a daze. Clyde Robertson's testimony made him look like a crook of the worst order.

That night, when he climbed into his car and headed home, Philip was exhausted from mentally fighting Morgan. Her lies had crushed him. He was certain he would lose the trial and possibly his company. Morgan Brockner was beating him again.

As Philip pulled his car into the parking place beside his condominium in Dallas, he thought of the stairs he had to climb and he didn't think he was strong enough to go inside. That was what it felt like to be without hope. He sat in the car for a while with his head propped on the steering wheel. Everything about him seemed to whirl. And in his head, all he could see were rolling blacklands and newborn calves and Emily walking by his side.

Philip straightened his back and turned the key in the ignition. He knew now where he was going. He would drive to the farm tonight. He needed to be around the people who gave him strength. All of them. Especially Emily.

When he pulled across the cattle guard forty-five minutes later, Philip felt like a great burden had been lifted from his shoulders. He was home. He swung his suit jacket back over his shoulder and went to the door.

When Emily saw him standing there in the doorway, she wanted to cry out. He looked like a different man to her. There were great dark circles under his eyes and he looked ten years older. As she looked at him, it was the first time that Emily hated Morgan, too.

"What happened, bud?" Clint asked.

Philip sat on the sofa then and told them the entire story. Emily was distraught when she realized that Philip's career in real estate could be over. It wasn't fair. He had worked so hard for what he had. She had never seen him this discouraged, and there was absolutely nothing she could do.

She glanced across the room at Clint. He was watching both of them with a frown on his face. Emily knew what she had to do. "Philip." She touched his arm. "Can we go to the camp house? I need to talk to you. Alone."

He nodded at her, and silently she took his hand and led him outside, away from the children.

"You can't let this happen." Her voice was quiet, but it was firm. She knew he needed bolstering right now. Emily decided that she was going to be strong enough for both of them. She was not going to let him lose everything he had worked for. It was too important to him.

"I have no other choice," he said bitterly.

"Mr. Manning," she said to him as they walked across the pasture, "as I see it, you have several choices. You, sir, have obviously taken the dumbest one. You have decided to lose hope."

He turned and stared at her and said nothing.

"Now," she said to him, "when are you going to start fighting back?"

"I have nothing to fight back with."

"Yes," she told him. "You do. Clyde Robertson's testimony was very important to you, wasn't it?"

"It was the strongest testimony we thought we had," he admitted. "Bennett was planning to build his entire defense on that."

"Maybe I have too much faith in human nature these days." She couldn't keep from grinning up at him. It seemed like an absurd thing to do at the moment. But Emily couldn't help it. For some reason, she had started to be optimistic about everything lately. "Go talk to Clyde, Philip. Find out what Morgan has on him."

"I could be convicted for contempt of court," he said dryly. "That's the last thing I need right now."

"The last thing you need right now is to lose your company. Talk to him, Philip," she urged him. "Let him see you face-to-face so he'll know what he's doing to you." They had come to the camp house now, and together they went inside. "If you can somehow find out the hold that Morgan has on him, figure some way around it, maybe the man will change his testimony when he takes the stand again tomorrow."

Philip's expression softened for the first time in the past twelve hours. "You're right, little one." He looked at her standing beside him, and he was surprised at how strong he felt suddenly. "I don't have much else to lose."

"Go tonight," she urged him. "Don't give Morgan any more time to get to him."

This time, it was Philip's turn to grin. "You're beginning to understand how that woman works."

"Sure I understand her, Philip," she told him. "But it's much more than that, too." She was thinking how much she cared about him. And she was thinking how good it felt to be strong for him.

He grasped her shoulders. "You're always giving so much. I'm the lucky one. I am glad you care for me."

"No." She held up one hand and stopped him. "I can't be bitter about my past anymore, Philip," she told him. "Actually, there are times I can thankful for it. Because it brought me to you."

"Oh, Emily," he whispered down at her, and she could scarcely bear seeing the boyish joy that shone from his face. All his discouragement about the trial was gone. It didn't seem to matter to him any longer.

Philip hugged Emily to him. She reached up and took his face in her hands. She kissed his lips and his eyelids and his nose. And he closed his eyes and surrendered to her loving.

"Let's go inside," she suggested, leading him by the hand into the camp house.

"Emily," Philip said, hesitating, "I'm afraid of how much I need you tonight. Maybe I should just say good-night."

"No," she said, smiling. "Come inside. I'm not afraid." Then she stood on tiptoe so she could reach his neck to kiss it. Then she added softly. "I never will be again."

When they entered her room Philip took her shoulders in his hands and pulled her to him. She felt encompassed with peace and shelter next to him, feeling the warmth of him through his clothes. And when he kissed her, it was a deep soul-searching caress that spread that warmth to her very core.

"Philip." She said his name once, as he kissed her. It came out as just a breath brushed against his lips. She took his hair in her hands and ran her fingers through it before she pulled his face down to meet her own. This time it was her turn, and when she kissed him, all the fire and the strength he had found in her poured up out of her kiss and into his heart.

"Oh, little one," he told her. "I love you so." He opened his eyes and looked at her and the pure, honest hope he found in her face made him almost melancholy, he wanted so to please her. He bent again and kissed her face in a hundred different places, on her eyelids, her forehead, her cheeks. He couldn't pull her close enough. He was desperate to belong to her.

"Come with me, Philip," she whispered up into his ear as she kissed it. And then she kissed his neck and her lips found his mouth again. She took him by the hand and led him to her bed.

She seemed different to him somehow, not just because she cared about him, but because she was stronger, more confident. "Oh, Emily," he whispered to her. "I love you so much." He knew she was ready to hear that now, ready for the things he had to say to her, ready for the things he had to give her.

And when Emily heard his words this time, when she heard him say that he loved her, it was different. She accepted his love now. Her eyes sparkled with intense emotion. It was such a miracle to her, having Philip love her and being able to love him in return. In a way, she had him to thank for that, too. He had taught her so much about herself. That thought conjured up a thousand different images once again of how much she needed him now, of how much she wanted him.

And then, as if Philip didn't think his words said enough to her, he told her again. "I've loved you for a long, long time, Emily."

She reached up and kissed his neck, and he pulled away from her for a moment. He turned his attention to building a fire in the wood stove as she watched him. They were alone now, each wanting to give so much to the other.

At last, after the fire was crackling in the stove, he turned toward her once again. He searched her face with his eyes. "Emily?" he asked her quietly. "Does our closeness frighten you? Is this what you want?"

She knew exactly what he was asking her. Wordlessly, she began to caress him.

"Little one." He pulled her hand away from his body. "Are you certain? Are you ready for this?"

"It's time for the giving," she whispered up to him as she grasped both his hands in her own. "Being with you is a part of who I am now."

Philip kicked his shoes off and stretched out on the delicate hand-filleted bedspread. And it struck him then that he didn't feel awkward around her dainty, feminine things any longer. Her lacy things only made him feel more masculine, more the man she needed. And she was so true to him now, so strong but still so delicate that Philip felt he was handling the most precious treasure in the world when, at last, he pulled her down on top of him.

She rained kisses down on his face as her hair fell around her face. And when, slowly, Philip reached up and began to peel off the clothes she was wearing, the fuzzy angora peach sweater and the pearls and the linen skirt and then, finally, her silken underthings, he felt as if he was unwrapping a fragile, precious gift that had been hidden away somewhere unattainable.

He knew how much she trusted him now, and she knew how much he was willing to risk. And they were both awed by their feelings, the loving, the sharing.

As Philip touched her in the places she needed to be touched, she arched herself up toward him and reached for him and Philip felt as if he was taking an angel in his arms.

All Emily needed to do was to please him. Philip lowered his head time and time again to show her, to teach her the things he knew that eventually she would need, too. And, finally, when he lay back spent against the pillow and Emily slept cradled in the crook of his arm, Philip looked down at her and thought he might weep because he had been so blessed, because he was overwhelmed by the new generosity of her giving.

PHILIP LAY AWAKE for a long time that evening watching Emily sleeping in his arms. Then, when he felt the rhythmn of her breathing slow and deepen, he nestled her back against the blankets and covered her. He hated to leave her just now. It was like ripping a part of himself away. But there was something else that he knew he had to do tonight. He owed it to her. And he owed it to himself.

Philip slipped back into his clothes and walked back across the pasture to his Audi. He flipped the key in the ignition and turned his car toward Dallas. And as he zoomed north on I-35, he said a silent prayer of thanks for Emily. It was uncanny how caring for her seemed to always point his life in the right direction.

When he walked up to Clyde Robertson's front door and knocked on it twenty minutes later, Clyde's wife, Marsha, answered. And Philip decided she looked frightened when she saw him.

"I came to straighten out a problem, Marsha." He said it loud enough that the others in the house could hear him, too. She was holding the door against him. But Philip didn't care if she didn't invite him in. He would wait on the front porch all night if he had to.

"Let him in," Philip heard Clyde say to his wife.

Marsha swung the door open, and Philip walked into the Robertsons' front foyer. It was late, but he could see all Clyde's kids still awake in the family room. They were sitting in a row on the sofa eating popcorn and watching a rented movie on their video cassette recorder.

Clyde was ashen when he turned to his former real estate agent. "Marsha," he commanded his wife without turning to her, "get the kids in the other room."

"It's okay, Clyde." Philip saw the fear in the man's eyes and hurried to reassure him. "I'm here to talk. I just came to find out what's going on."

Clyde Robertson glanced back over his shoulder. "Could we talk somewhere else?"

"No," Philip said firmly. "We're going to talk right here. Right now. I don't care who hears this."

"Maybe I do."

There was a guarded look in Clyde's eyes, and Philip knew immediately that the man was preparing to cover something.

"Why did you come all the way back from some exotic vacation paradise to testify against me, Robertson?" Philip's tone was coarse. Clyde's answers mattered too much now for him to be careful. He might have done the wrong thing in coming here. But he didn't think so. It was time for all of them to face reality.

"I can't talk about it, Philip." There was genuine concern in the man's eyes. "I'm sorry."

"Don't be sorry, Clyde. Be honest. Why did you come back from the Virgin Islands? Why did you tell those lies in court? You were under oath, for God's sake. Why did you have to lie?" Again Philip studied the man's face. He was almost certain the man's recent behavior had something to do with Morgan Brockner. "What is she paying you to testify against me?"

Robertson's eyes widened. "She isn't paying me anything." Neither man needed to mention her name. They both knew who they were talking about.

"Okay." Philip decided to trust him. Maybe that would have a positive effect. "So she isn't paying you anything. I know how Morgan Brockner works, Clyde. I also know that you and I have had a pretty fantastic client-agent relationship. What does she have on you? Why is she making you do this?"

This time the man's face crumpled, and Philip knew he was getting close to the truth.

"No," Clyde said, but he didn't sound quite certain of his answer.

"Clyde." Philip was pleading now. "Give me more credit than this. Give yourself more credit. Don't let her destroy your integrity. I can promise you, you'll be sorry. Once you let her beat you once, she won't back off until she's beaten you into the ground."

Clyde looked confused and sad.

"Come on, Clyde," Philip continued. "I made you a hefty profit on that business complex sale. At least tell me what I've done to deserve to lose everything."

Clyde Robertson motioned toward the den and Philip followed him. Robertson sat on the sofa and looked up at his former agent. He was clearly a broken man. "Okay." He was staring at the floor. "I'll tell you. I'll tell you where she's got me."

"Where?"

"The office complex. When I built it, I used substandard steel beams on the foundation. I wasn't trying to rip anybody off. It was the only thing I could do at the time. But after that building sold, she sent some inspector out there and he documented the whole thing for her. She's got all these papers now that prove my building practices aren't what they should be. But they are. I'm an honest man. I made one wrong choice. Now she has the ammunition to ruin me."

Philip's comment was a dry one. "You learn not to make wrong choices when you work around Morgan Brockner."

"If Morgan releases that information about that building, I could have every lawsuit in the books slapped on me. I can't risk it, Philip."

"Oh, yes you can." Philip grasped the man by the shoulders. He was genuinely sorry for him. "You may lose face in the business community but you won't lose your own self-esteem. So you made one mistake. So what? If you let Morgan hold that over your head now, I guarantee she'll hold it over your head for as long as she lives. If you stand up in court and tell the truth tomorrow, tell Keslow Wilson about the things she threatened you with, everything will fall into place."

"But those steel beams aren't a figment of Morgan's imagination," Clyde said. He was frantic. He didn't know where to turn. "If this comes out—"

"If it doesn't come out, you're going to regret it for the rest of your life," Philip interrupted him. "Think about your kids. What if they find out what you've done? Do you think they'll respect you?"

"Do you think they'll respect me if it comes out in the press that one of my buildings might not pass code inspections because of my own negligence?"

"They'll respect you for telling the truth, Clyde." Philip turned to go. He had done everything he could.

AT EIGHT-THIRTY THE NEXT MORNING, Emily was ready to leave for Dallas District Court. She had talked to Clint and gotten permission from him to let the kids fend for themselves today. They were certainly capable of doing that. And Emily was desperate to be in court with Philip. She knew how much he needed her now.

Emily drove her own car to the Dallas courthouse. After she parked, she had a few minutes before the proceedings began. She strolled across the street and sat on a bench beside the old red sandstone Dallas county courthouse. The place had long since been made into a museum with a Texas historical marker on the front door. The old building was not unlike the Ellis County courthouse that remained in use in the town square in Waxahachie. Both buildings had been built in the mid 1890s.

It was ironic, Emily thought, that life and history had so much planned for Dallas, and this beautiful friendly old building had been outgrown a long, long time ago. Emily looked up at the old clock tower and thought of the matching one in Waxahachie that was still in use. There, the clock still bonged out the hour for the entire town to hear. The Ellis county courthouse was still full of typing secretaries and huffing politicians stomping around on creaky floors.

It was the old building Emily gravitated to now. It was as if the past was pulling at her. But it was the pull of the past that gave Emily hope for victory in her future. She turned away from the broken-down clock on the Dallas county clock tower and checked her wristwatch. It was time to go in. She picked her purse up off the grass and hurried across the street to the new building that housed the courts.

When she walked into the courtroom, she could tell Philip was prepared for a good fight. His chin was firm and his head was high and his back was set squarely against the rows of reporters watching the proceedings behind him.

There was one available seat in the row directly behind Philip, and Emily moved to take it. Philip heard her footsteps behind him, but he didn't dare turn around. But as he recognized the familiar scent of her perfume, he knew she was there behind him, supporting him.

She brushed one of her hands lightly across the back of his suit coat so the judge couldn't see.

Judge Keslow Wilson called Clyde Robertson to the stand once again. Unobtrusively, Emily slipped one of her hands forward and held on to the back of Philip's elbow while Clyde Robertson began to speak.

And this time when Morgan's attorneys began to question Clyde Robertson, the man told the truth. He told the judge and the jury that he had been mistaken, that he had signed an exclusive contract with Manning to sell his property. Morgan's attorneys saw what was happening and they finished questioning the man almost immediately. But Bennett Huff had come prepared. He questioned Clyde carefully and Clyde continued his story. And then, in the middle of his testimony, Keslow Wilson stopped the proceedings.

"Are you aware," he asked Robertson, "that you were testifying under oath yesterday? Why have you changed your story?"

Morgan Brockner shot up out of her seat. And when Philip saw her face, he wanted to applaud. Her demeanor had totally changed. She was no longer the demure businesswoman she had tried to portray. If she could have bared her teeth like a cornered animal just then, Philip decided that she would have. "Don't do this, Robertson," she hissed.

Keslow Wilson banged his gavel against the judge's bench.

But Morgan had lost control. "You know what's going to happen to you if you back down on this story now, Robertson. You've got it coming to you now."

"I suggest you sit down, Ms Brockner." Keslow Wilson's face was hard and unmoving.

"I suggest we take this man off the witness stand," she shrieked at the judge. "He's lying now. He's ruining everything."

"Ruining everything for whom?" Keslow Wilson asked. "For you?" The judge turned back to Clyde Robertson. "What's going on here? Why are you telling a different story today? What is this woman threatening you with?"

Morgan jumped from her chair again, but this time one of her attorneys grabbed her arm and wrenched her back down beside them.

Keslow Wilson was still talking to Clyde Robertson. "Is Morgan Brockner blackmailing you, Mr. Robertson?"

Morgan's face went white. She glanced at her attorneys. Then she turned to glare at Philip.

"Tell us what's going on, Mr. Robertson," Keslow Wilson insisted. And Bennett Huff guided the man while he told the entire story. When Clyde Robertson told the court how Morgan had threatened him, several of the jurors looked shocked. But Keslow Wilson didn't. And Philip speculated that the judge must have guessed what Morgan's involvement was in the case all along. Morgan was furious. She was sitting on her side of the courtroom glaring at Philip and Emily. She reminded Philip of a wild animal preparing to pounce. But it was too late for Morgan. She was finished. Several reporters had already rushed from the courtroom to call in their stories. And Emily was certain this story would hit the *Wall Street Journal*.

The public would finally catch a glimpse of the real Morgan Brockner. But better than that, so would the jury. And from what they had seen, Philip didn't think they were likely to rule in her favor. But defeating Morgan didn't really matter to Philip any longer. He wanted to shout for the sheer joy of everything he was feeling. Emily was here for him now. And it didn't seem to matter now whether he kept Manning Commercial Real Estate and Investment. Because now he had something so much better. Now he had Emily. The person he wanted to be strong and successful for was standing right behind him.

Keslow Wilson called a recess at 4:45 p.m., and then his gavel fell. Philip stood silent and still for one moment before he wheeled to face the woman behind him. Emily was there beside him the next moment, holding her arms out to him. She looked up at him, not even trying to hide the tears that were coursing down her cheeks. The battle hadn't been won yet. But it would be. Emily was sure of it.

Philip swept her into his arms and clasped her to him, and suddenly she was laughing and crying at the same time. And so was Philip. There were reporters peeking in, watching them, taking pictures. But Philip and Emily didn't care. A whole new world was beginning for them.

"Philip?" Emily reached up and touched his cheek softly. "I love you." The words she said to him now were words that even last night she had not been capable of saying.

They had shared so much the night before, Philip thought. And Emily was his life now. Philip put one arm around her tiny waist and guided his Emily out of the courtroom door, past Morgan, past the reporters, past the crowds.

CHAPTER TWELVE

GREG CAME DOWN for breakfast shortly after Emily had left for the courthouse. He poured himself some cereal and sat and watched it sink into the milk in his bowl while he considered the things he was planning to do. Emily was going to be in Dallas with Uncle Philip all day. His father was tied up showing executive homes to a potential client from Waco. And Greg knew his sisters wouldn't tell on him. He decided it was time to put Plan B into action.

He would have gotten away without any problems at all if Bethany hadn't come downstairs for breakfast to find him searching through their dad's desk for the Studebaker keys.

"What are you doing?" she asked.

"Nothing important," he told her briskly. "Leave me alone."

"If you drive the Studebaker off of the farm, Dad's going to kill you."

"I don't care," he told her. "I'm going to see Mother."

Finally he turned to her and explained to his youngest sister what he was doing. Bethany reasoned that Greg trusted her enough to tell her plainly about something that was vitally important to him. And she decided her brother was probably doing a good thing.

Greg and Emily had talked to Greg's father together just after the holidays, begging him to let the children see their mother. But Clint had stood by his decision not to let Greg or his sisters visit Manderly. Greg had done his best to abide by that decision. But he couldn't do that anymore, no matter how hard he tried. His father was wrong. And he felt bad for sneaking out this way. He hoped Emily would forgive him. She had tried to help him, after all, and now she was the one he was taking advantage of. His father would be furious with her, he knew.

He drove the Studebaker away from the house slowly, out past the front cattle guard, and then he turned it south on the main road and headed toward town. It was almost noon when he pulled up and parked opposite the double glass doors that served as the visitor's entrance to W. C. Tenery Community Hospital.

Greg surveyed the parking lot before he climbed out of the front seat and locked the Studebaker door. If his father arrived during this next hour and discovered what he had done, Greg knew he would probably be grounded for the rest of his life. But he didn't see a familiar car anywhere in the parking lot and he was satisfied he was safe, so he strolled into the hospital, feeling conspicuous, as if everyone there in the hallway knew who he was and why he was there. He stopped at the information desk on the first floor and asked for directions to his mother's room. He half expected the nurses' aide behind the desk to tell him that he couldn't go in. But the girl just smiled at him. She looked younger than he was, and he thought maybe he recognized her from school. She pointed the way down the hallway to the stairs. He followed her directions and climbed the stairs and turned to his left and there it was just as she had said it would be, a hospital room with the door standing slightly ajar and a small card slipped into a metal frame that read: Amanda Manning.

Greg longed to burst through that door and pounce on his mother's bed and hug her just the same way he used to when he was a small boy. He had imagined this moment for months. His dad was mistaken. Manderly wouldn't be sleeping when Greg arrived. She would be sitting there, waiting for him to bound in, just the same way she had always done before, a hundred or so times, a hundred days when he had come home from school and had found her waiting for him.

"Mother?" He pushed open the door and went in.

The first thing that struck him when he walked in and saw her was how tired she looked, and he felt as if he should tiptoe toward her. Even his own breathing sounded labored and heavy and loud in the room. He moved toward the bed, and he wanted to take her hand in his, but he didn't dare. He didn't know what touching her might do to her. Greg wondered if she could feel him there whether she might try to respond. "Mom," Greg said softly. His own voice sounded awkward and out of place in her silent room. "How've you been?"

He didn't wait for her to answer. He knew she couldn't. He just kept talking about everything he could think of. He wanted to tell her something, anything, that would make the still form that looked like a wax image of his mother react. As he talked, he wondered what he would do if, by some miracle, she *did* move or reach for him while he talked.

"Dad doesn't exactly know I'm here," he said to her. "We're off school for the spring break. Emily—that's the lady who lives in the camp house and keeps an eye on us—well, she had to run all these errands, so I brought the Studebaker and came on here. You should see the Studebaker, Mom. That chrome polish you bought took all the water spots off the steering wheel." Then he laughed. He had almost forgotten for a moment that she couldn't hear him. "Bethany borrowed some to use on her bike, but she got so much on the fenders that it took her a whole roll of paper towels to get it off. It's still smeared on there, but she rides around thinking she's hot stuff, anyway." His voice softened. He was talking about everything that came to his mind without censoring himself the way he had for months now. "I'm sorry I haven't come by to see you sooner. Dad didn't ever want us to come. I guess he figured if he let me come, he'd have to let Bethany come, too, and seeing you like this would scare her to death. I've really wanted to spend time with you. Dad's tried to be strong for all of us. And he's done a real good job of it, too. But he really gets tired a lot lately. It seems as if he gets mad at Lisa about something new every night. But I think Lisa understands why he isn't very patient with her. Plus, you know her, a dumb girl who's always running around doing dumb stuff. You know how much we love you, Mom. I can't wait until you come home again. Oh, and Honey Snookems's calf is getting so big..."

Greg's voice droned on until finally, after about an hour, it faded off into silence. He sat quietly then and memorized the room where his mother had lived during the past year.

It isn't easy to make a clinical hospital room look homey, but Clint had done his best. There were touches of the Manning family and the farm everywhere Greg looked. There was a poster that read, "Find a place you like and go there" just like the poster Lisa had given Emily. There was a hand-stitched calico pillow sewn in the shape of a sheep sitting in an old rocking chair in the corner. Greg had never seen the pillow before, but the rocker was one that had been up in the attic at the farm for ages. There was a stereo in the corner, too, one that Greg had never seen, and a bucket of *Wall Street Journal*s, assorted magazines and a tattered spy novel with the front cover torn off. Greg realized that his father must be doing most of his reading aloud here early in the mornings. There was a mobile of calico hearts, navy blue ones and peach ones and plum ones, hanging over Manderly's bed, where she could see them if she opened her eyes. There was a calico tablecloth to match the pillow with ruffled eyelet trim draped over the bedside table and an oak-framed portrait of all of them together that had been taken two summers ago. The family had been having a picnic in the pecan grove and everyone was smiling, their arms around one another.

There were three wooden buckets in the windows overflowing with geraniums, and Greg guessed correctly that his father had been buying freshly blooming ones every month from the greenhouse in Waxahachie. There were personal, everyday things all around the room, too, things that belonged to his mother, things Greg realized he hadn't missed from the house—a lipstick, a white heart-shaped box of dusting powder, a pink toothbrush and a bottle of her favorite perfume.

Looking around the room like this, with his mother so still and silent in the bed, was eerie. It was as if he was experiencing the depth of his father's love for his mother for the first time. Visiting this room was like visiting a shrine that Clint had single-handedly built for Manderly. Greg began to comprehend why his father had been so protective of her in this state and why he'd kept his children on the farm. Everything at home was overflowing with life...the growing things...the laughter and the arguments around the kitchen table at dinner...the kittens that were born wild and grew in the hayloft in the barn. When he'd heard about this hospital room from his father, it had been so easy for Greg to imagine it that way, too, with sunlight streaming in the windows and his mother sleeping. But something much heavier than sleep hung in the room, something that had grown stronger and sadder with the passage of time. Life outside the hospital went on without his mother. Even the portrait of their family on the bedside table was already outdated. Two summers ago, Bethany had been only seven. She had still been missing a front tooth when the picture had been taken. Lisa had been eleven and he had been thirteen and in the eighth grade. It seemed like a lifetime had gone by since he had been in the eighth grade. And his Mom had missed it all.

Greg found himself wanting to fill her room with life, with news, with noise. He opened the blinds a little more and let the sunlight stream in across her bed.

He turned on the stereo. And then even that didn't seem to be enough, so he flipped on the television, too. There was a soap opera on, one called "Guiding Light," and Greg paused to watch the teary-eyed blond on the screen. "It's over between us, Kyle," she was saying. "It has to be. I've fought and scratched my way away from you. Don't come back now and say these things."

"It will never be over between us, Reva." The man named Kyle searched her face, and it struck Greg as funny that an actor's face could register so much visible pain and confusion. Was real life ever that intense and that visible? Greg didn't think so.

He went to his mother's side and gazed down at her for a long while before he picked up her hand and squeezed it in his. He wanted to squeeze her hand hard enough so she would feel it. But she didn't move. Looking at her closely made Greg sad. She was so thin and her skin was so sallow that she looked almost transparent to him. It seemed as if he could see the sheets below her almost through her arms. "Oh, Mom." He said it loud so she could hear him over the stereo and the television set. "Hurry up and come home. We can't wait much longer."

Greg turned from her then and walked out of her room without looking back. He knew that now he would do nothing but think of her like this, lying here, silent and sallow, looking like a stranger. And when he climbed into the Studebaker and turned the key to start the ignition, he knew he wasn't ready to face everyone at home. He needed to be alone.

He drove the Studebaker out of the hospital parking lot and turned on the radio to a station he liked.

But even the wildly pulsating beat of the rock music did nothing to take his pain away. He just drove around on country roads around Waxahachie for a while, thinking of everything that had happened during the past months and mostly thinking about his father. Every moment in that hospital room bore testimony to how much Clint loved Manderly, how much he needed her, how much he had lost.

The familiar anger came welling up and stuck in Greg's throat. This time, it threatened to overtake him. What right did his father have to deny the rest of them the chance to love her, to be with her, too? His mother needed all of them.

"I could have done some of that, Dad." He was talking to the car, the sky, the road, the radio. "I could have been strong enough to handle it. Why didn't you let me?" As he talked, his foot eased down on the accelerator. It was as if all of him, his arms, his legs, his heart, was struggling against some unknown enemy. And he didn't notice it when the speedometer began creeping up and then edged on past eighty. "I could have done it. Why didn't Dad let any of us be there for him?" Greg let a wave of self-pity wash over him. And for one split second and that was all, he almost wished that his mother had died. Then it would have all been over. They could have mourned and they could have told her goodbye and then his father could have let go of the searing edge of hope that was always present, always ready to tear parts of their hearts away. It would have been over. And none of them would have to be strong anymore.

Greg was ashamed of even thinking about his mother's death. As long as there was any thread of hope at all, the family would cling to it. And he drove on, wondering if he should turn back toward home, not daring to let himself feel anything, letting the pulse of the music on the radio take him away from all of it. He was in a vacuum. For a moment, it was as if he didn't have a mother or a father or anyone else who could hurt him. He squeezed his eyes shut to force his mind full of nothingness. And when he opened them, the curve on the road to Maypearl loomed up at him.

Greg had already driven this curve three times during the past two hours, but he had been ready for it when he hit it. He wasn't ready for it now. His body and his mind were filled with a numbness that affected his reflexes. When he tried to negotiate the curve, a sharp picture came into focus in his mind. He saw his Uncle Philip and Emily bending over an unmoving tiny calf lying in the dust of the corral. And his mind told him instantly what was wrong. He hadn't reacted quickly enough. And even if he had, the Studebaker was going too fast to negotiate the curve. The car veered wildly to the right and then, for one or two seconds, the vehicle itself seemed to hover in the air as if it would turn back onto the road. Then it spun onto the road shoulder and the rear right tire struck a ditch, and the last thing Greg remembered was the car flipping over and over and then all was blackness as the dust around him settled. From somewhere that seemed to be far, far away in a meadow, the song on the car radio was still blaring.

MEMBERS OF THE ELLIS COUNTY Sheriff's Department traced the license plate on the Studebaker to Clint Manning only moments after two sheriff's deputies arrived on the scene of the accident. The dispatcher at the sheriff's department in town called Clint's office but couldn't get an answer. Clint had given his secretary the day off so she could spend a few days with her grandchildren in Corsicana.

The dispatcher called Clint Manning's residence and couldn't get anyone there, either. Twice when she called, the telephone line was busy. The third time she called, an answering machine bleeped at her. The dispatcher didn't feel it was appropriate to leave a message like this one on an answering machine for an unsuspecting person to hear. So she hung up and did some quick research in the sheriff's files and found that Clint Manning had a brother.

The trial had recessed two hours before the dispatcher's first call, and Emily had been anxious to go back to Waxahachie. Philip had stayed at the office to finish paperwork on a new listing.

When Emily had arrived at the farm, the house seemed strangely silent.

"Where is everybody?" she asked Bethany when her youngest charge came downstairs.

"Oh, they're around," Bethany said vaguely. The girl looked worried and maybe a bit guilty. Her expression made Emily wonder if she was deliberately being evasive. If she was, Emily was surprised at her. Bethany was a loving, honest person. Emily couldn't believe that Bethany would be deliberately dishonest.

Nevertheless, she decided to take an individual inventory of the family. "Where's Lisa?"

"She's in the pecan grove." Bethany perked up. "She's climbing trees again. She said she'd be back at the house in a little while."

"What's Greg doing?"

Bethany hesitated for a long time before she answered. "He's with the Studebaker." Bethany wanted to cry. She loved Emily and she hated not telling the whole truth. But Greg had made both of his sisters promise to cover for him. Bethany was torn because she loved her brother and she thought he was doing something he needed to do. And she hadn't exactly lied to Emily. Greg *was* with the Studebaker. She just hadn't told Emily exactly where the Studebaker was.

Emily heard the confusion in Bethany's voice. She almost rephrased her question, but in the end she changed her mind. It wasn't fair to put a little sister on the spot for something her older brother might be doing. Emily made a mental note to check on Greg in the garage as soon as she checked the telephone answering machine.

Emily went into Clint's study and flipped on the machine. There was one loud beep that indicated someone had telephoned while she was out but had not left a message.

There was only one message on the machine, and Emily flipped the tape on so she could listen to it. As the familiar hum of long distance came on the line, she grabbed a pencil and bent to jot down information for Clint.

"I am calling to speak with Emily Lattrell," a very professional-sounding woman's voice said. "This is Sylvia Ressling, senior editor for the children's division at Hudson Publishing. We are interested in your Baby Sprout book series. We like the tentative illustrations you submitted with your work. I would like to talk to you personally about this. Please call me collect at..." The voice droned on with an area code, a phone number and an extension. Emily wrote the information down. They had done it! She and Philip were going to sell their work! She was shaking so hard that she could hardly stand up and she felt like weeping and giggling all at the same time. A publisher wanted her Baby Sprout books! Emily's heart was racing.

In the end, she had to play the tape over three times to get the area code, phone number and extension down correctly. Then she went outside and sat on the rickety steps beside the porch and stroked one of the old barn cats that habitually wandered in and out from under the house. She did everything she knew to do to calm herself down and then she tried to remember what time it was in New York. She thought there was only a two-hour time difference between Texas and Hudson Publishing, but it could be three and, if that was so, it was nearing four o'clock there. Emily took a deep breath, and when the secretary answered at Hudson Publishing in New York, Emily's voice sounded every bit as calm and professional as Sylvia Ressling's voice had sounded to Emily.

"Hello, this is Emily Lattrell," she said simply when the editor answered. She was praying that the woman wouldn't have already forgotten who she was.

"Hello, Emily." Syliva's voice was friendly, and as she began explaining her call in more detail, Emily could scarcely believe the things she was saying. She said that she loved the Baby Sprout series. In her opinion, it was light, fun reading for younger readers and it had an easygoing, obvious moral message without being preachy. She and her colleagues could see a definite slot for it in their younger children's list for the upcoming year. And they loved the illustrations. Was her illustrator a professional, she wanted to know.

Emily sat staring at Clint's metal file cabinet in the corner of his office, trying to sort everything out in her mind. Here she was on this farm in Waxahachie, Texas, floundering around in a huge sea of sudden possibilities. When she hung up the telephone, Emily felt like a dam inside her had burst. She was a children's author. Almost. She would be as soon as the contract was signed.

Emily picked up the phone and dialed her father's number at the bank in Decatur. Then she called her brother. And finally she called Lloyd. "Holy moly" was all he could say over and over again when she told him. She stopped her former employer by laughing at him and asking, "Can't you say something nicer than that?"

"I'm overwhelmed." If anything, he had noticed her writing improving since she had become an Absolutely Mom. He had trained her and he had always expected her to be successful with her writing, but maybe not to this extent. "And I'm proud."

"I guess this means I'm deserting you," she teased him. Then her tone became serious. "I hope I can write books for the rest of my life."

"You deserted me a long time ago when you took that silly professional mother position," he teased back. Then his tone sobered, too. "Congratulations, Emily. I'd like an autographed copy of your first printing."

"You'll get one." She was grinning at him even though he couldn't see her. His was her first autograph request.

After Emily hung up the telephone, she sat at the kitchen table by herself and let the reality of her good fortune sink in. There was so much to comprehend that she couldn't do it all in one sitting. She would be an author, contracted to a publisher. She'd be negotiating with an editor. Her words would be printed in a real book and distributed across the world with Philip's drawings on every page. How many children would see Baby Sprout? How many children would love him? As Emily thought about that and about the responsibilities God had seen fit to give her, it was enough to make her weep.

The back screen door banged open a few minutes later and the girls came inside. "Emily? What's wrong?" Lisa asked her when she saw the tears streaming down her face.

Emily did her best to explain why she was crying. Lisa just smiled knowingly.

"That means we have a calf with an almost-famous name," Bethany piped up.

"I guess that's right," Emily said, chuckling. She hadn't even considered the sudden celebrity of Honey Snookems's baby.

"I think we should celebrate," Lisa suggested. "What can we do? This is really exciting."

"I don't know." Emily bit her lip. It suddenly seemed very important to her, sharing this time with the girls. She could call Philip and tell him later. That was going to be very special for her, too. Philip was going to be as excited as she was. "I've got it." She grabbed Lisa in one arm and Bethany in the other and squeezed them to her. "I love y'all so much," she said. "Why don't we go shopping? I'm in the mood to spend money on clothes. I'll buy each of you something."

"Sounds like a good way to celebrate to me," Lisa replied.

"Can I get a red Hawaiian shirt?" Bethany asked, her eyes wide. It had been ages since the sisters had been shopping together, not since before their mother had gone to the hospital.

"If that's the thing you would like to buy, then that would be fine with me," Emily agreed.

So the three of them piled into the car and Emily drove them into Dallas. They spent the next three hours having fun. They tried on outlandish fashions and added up price tags and not one of them, not Lisa or Emily or Bethany, thought about Greg or wondered where he might be.

AS PHILIP LISTENED to the Ellis county officer on the other end of the line, his face went ashen. He was being asked to identify the driver of a 1960 Studebaker.

His voice remained steady, but Philip felt like his insides had been torn out. "That would be my nephew, Greg Manning." He almost added, he's fifteen. Too young to have his driver's license. But that didn't seem to really matter. What had happened to Greg? Filled with dread, he couldn't bring himself to ask the question. He only sat silently on the phone and waited for the deputy to tell him.

"We tried to locate your brother at his office and at his residence, but we couldn't find him. Do you have any idea where he might be?"

"No."

"The boy needs to go into surgery at the hospital for internal injuries. It's imperative. Are you willing, as his uncle, to take the responsibility for that decision?"

They were taking him into surgery, Philip thought, relieved. Well, at least he was still alive. He glanced at his watch. It was 2:15 p.m., and it would take him forty-five minutes to get there. "Can the doctors take my consent over the phone? I'm coming immediately, but I'm still in Dallas and it's going to take me just under an hour to get there."

"I'll have the surgeon call you from the hospital now," the officer confirmed. "I can radio into Dallas county and arrange for an escort for you through the city. Once you get into Ellis County, you'll be fine. Our officers won't stop you. They'll know who you are."

"Thank you." Philip waited by the phone for the surgeon to call. After he had, Philip practically ran to his car. He hadn't bothered to ask the surgeon the specifics of Greg's condition. Philip knew that if he had internal injuries, things were bad. And any other injuries were secondary to that. They had to find the bleeding and get it stopped.

As Philip sped south of Dallas, he was joined by a Dallas County sheriff's vehicle with two officers inside. They led him on through the traffic and set the traveling speed at ninety miles per hour. At that speed, the worst part of Philip's Dallas driving was finished before it had hardly begun. It was odd, he thought, that at a time like this he could still think of such mundane concerns.

Once Philip crossed the county line, his escort vehicle pulled off the road and he was alone. He maintained the same speed, even without an escort. As he thought about it, Philip was relieved he had been the one to receive the first information about Greg. Although Clint would have had no other choice but to approve Greg's surgery, this way his brother had not been faced with the decision. There was nothing else left to do now except find Clint and Emily. And pray.

When Philip arrived at the hospital, Greg was still in surgery. Philip put a call through to Clint's office, but there was still no answer. He put a call through to the house, but he only got Clint's voice on the answering machine. Because he didn't want to alarm anyone he left an intentionally vague message. And half an hour later, after Philip had taken a few minutes to stop in and see Amanda, he heard the pay phone ring in the waiting room and he guessed it was for him.

Emily and the girls had just arrived home from shopping. All their arms were full of crumpled packages, and they were all three dizzy from the lively discussion and the laughter they had shared in the car while Emily drove them home. She had been humming television-show theme songs and the girls had been trying to guess what shows they were. And that game had degenerated further into silliness when Lisa had tried to remember all the words to the theme song for "The Flintstones." They had all marched into the house singing "...they're the modern stone-age fa...a...mi...ly..."

But the mood changed abruptly when Emily heard Philip's voice over the machine. She knew immediately that something was terribly wrong. At first she thought his call had something to do with the trial. But then she realized that she was dialing a local number. Was it the hospital? Immediately, she thought of Amanda.

"Hello?" she said, her body rigid with fear. He answered on the fifth ring and she was suddenly even more frightened, just hearing his voice. Emily thought Amanda had died.

"Philip? It's me. What's wrong?"

"Are you home? Where's Clint? He hasn't been in his office all afternoon." Philip's voice sounded as if he was overcome with desperate sadness.

"He's showing property this afternoon."

"Do you know what he's showing? Can you find him for me?"

Emily had heard her employer on the phone just yesterday morning discussing properties with his new client. "I can try. I'll get Greg, too. We'll split the territory. Greg must still be working on the Studebaker in the garage. I think he's got a crush on his car." She did her best to add a touch of humor to this conversation. "I feel sorry for any girl who falls in love with him. The poor thing doesn't stand a chance with all the competition she'll get from that Studebaker."

"Emily." Philip's voice was husky. He hated to tell her this. She hadn't even missed Greg yet. And she was his adopted mother. He already knew she was going to hold herself responsible for what had happened.

"Greg's here. In the hospital." He stopped talking. He had wanted to say, Greg's here with me. That would have made receiving this news easier for her. But he couldn't hedge the truth. Greg wasn't with him. Greg was in surgery. He had been on the operating table for two hours.

"What's he doing there? Did you come by and pick him up?"

If Emily had been watching Bethany's face just then, she would have seen the girl pale.

"He's in surgery. He's had a car accident."

"No!" Her voice was thin and fragile, as if something inside her was on the verge of snapping. And it was. She had been responsible for Greg today. And she had been so excited about the telephone call from Sylvia Ressling at Hudson Publishing in New York City that she had forgotten to even check on him. "I'm coming now. I'm bringing the girls with me. And I'll find Clint on the way. Is Greg...?" But she stopped. She couldn't ask the question Philip had failed to ask earlier either.

She hung up and turned toward the girls. She didn't have to say anything to them. They had heard enough to understand that the situation was grave. They threw their new clothes on the kitchen table and the three of them ran back to the car. This time, there was no singing as they drove back toward town.

They found Clint showing a property to his client at the second executive home they drove by. Emily jumped out of the car and ran to him. She grasped his arm and spoke to him in a hushed voice. He turned to his clients, a man and his wife, and his face was gray but his voice was composed. "I have an emergency with my son," he told them. He was glad the man had followed him to these listings in his own car. Thankfully, he didn't have to worry about leaving them stranded. "Let me get a colleague to continue showing you these homes." He made a quick call on the phone inside the house and the couple agreed to wait in their car. Then he followed Emily and the girls in his own vehicle and they all just managed to keep to the speed limit. At the hospital, they walked into the lobby and went upstairs to the surgery waiting room without having to ask anyone where to go. They didn't have to. They followed Clint, who had done this once before.

Clint was clutching Bethany in his arms when they reached the top of the stairs and Lisa was clinging to Emily. When Philip saw all of them finally appear, he thought he had never been so glad to see anyone before in his life. He had taken the responsibility for Greg's surgery because no one else could be reached, and the decision was starting to weigh on him. He spoke to all of them quietly, even the girls, and told them that he had given the doctors his permission to operate. Clint sank into a chair and buried his face in his hands just as the surgeon came through the swinging operating room door.

"Are you Greg's father?" The doctor reached out his hand to Clint. He already knew who Philip was. He knew about Amanda, too. Everyone at the hospital did. And he had assisted on her surgery a year ago. One couldn't easily forget a case like that.

The doctor continued speaking, and his voice was warm and kind and full of relief. "Your son is going to be fine. His injuries were not extensive and we got him mended easily, once we found out what the problem was. He's got a broken leg and three broken ribs and a punctured stomach, so it's going to take a while for him to get back on his feet. But he's in recovery now, and I've listed his condition as stable. You can see him in about an hour, after the anesthetic wears off.''

Clint flinched visibly. *Greg was still unconscious.* But the doctor hadn't seen anything unusual during the surgery. And Greg was young and strong. He couldn't end up like his mother, Clint reasoned. Clint hugged both his girls to him and rocked them slightly as Emily stood beside them. For a moment, Philip felt like an outsider. The circles under his eyes were deep and creased and he sat down and held his head in his hands, on the verge of crying. But he couldn't let the tears come, he couldn't release himself and surrender to his feelings. Instead, he looked up at Emily who was standing there, pale and steadfast beside his brother and his nieces.

She saw the look in his eyes, and she knew him so well now that she understood what he needed. She stooped beside him and wrapped him in her arms, and he laid his head on her shoulder as she stroked his head and held him.

IT WAS AFTER SIX in the evening when Clint glanced at his watch and suggested they go downstairs for a bite to eat in the cafeteria. The girls were both tired and hungry and Greg wasn't out of recovery yet, so when they left the physician on duty promised to send a nurse downstairs to find them if the boy awoke while they were eating.

Philip was the only one who didn't want to leave the waiting room, but Emily convinced him to come, too. And while they ate, they talked. Together, they began to piece together the events of Greg's day. Emily remembered the comment Bethany had made this morning. "He's with the Studebaker." She turned to the girl and spoke gently to her.

Bethany told them everything they needed to know. She wouldn't cover for Greg now, not with everything that had happened. "He came here. He said he was coming to visit Mom."

"What?" Clint slammed his fist on the Formica table, spilling his coffee out of the cup into the saucer. "What did he mean by doing that without my permission?"

Bethany began to cry at Clint's reaction, and Lisa bent forward to hug her little sister. Even Emily was alarmed at his rage. Emily wanted to blame herself but she resisted the temptation to do so. She had been trying to help Greg and Clint for months. "Clint, I'm sorry," she said simply.

Although he didn't know her thoughts, Philip's hand shot across the table and grasped her arm just above the elbow. "Don't you dare apologize." There was a chain of circumstances that brought Greg to the hospital, first as a visitor and now as a patient. Emily couldn't distance herself from this family now by feeling that in some way she had caused this tragic turn of events. He wouldn't let her feel devastated by guilt. If this was anybody's fault, it was Clint's. "Don't blame yourself for this." He was almost growling at her.

"No wonder he was driving around the county like a maniac," Clint said, his head in his hands. As Clint kept talking, Emily realized he was in a different world, analyzing his son's emotions and his own. "I never wanted any of you kids to see her." Emily knew he had wanted to protect them from some horrible injustice and pain. It was the same thing Greg had realized earlier as he'd stood in Amanda's room and noticed the homey things his father had gathered for her. Clint had wanted to carry the weight of the constant worry on his own shoulders. He didn't want the consequences of all that hurt to rest on the shoulders of the people he loved, too.

Philip turned to Emily and grasped her other arm. Despite her fears and her worry over Greg and her sadness, the very act of him holding on to her so forcefully was enough to send a new wonderful feeling pulsing up in a place where before there had been only regret and loneliness and confusion. And when Philip spoke, his eyes were glued to Emily, but he was speaking to the entire family.

"I've figured out what you've been trying to do, Clint. And it's admirable. All this time, I've been thinking you were being hardhearted to the kids. Sure, it came across as if you were trying to protect them. But it came across as more than that, too. Maybe you didn't think they were strong enough to handle this. Or maybe you thought you could keep Amanda closer to you by not sharing your grief with the kids."

Emily was surprised that Philip was speaking so honestly to his brother. But these were things that desperately needed to be said, and she knew it, too. As she listened to him, she was proud of him.

"It's more than that, isn't it?" Philip asked his brother. "You never had any serious doubts about their capabilities, did you? You know all of us, even Bethany—" here, he tore his eyes away from Emily and glanced at his niece "—every one of us, if push comes to shove, is strong enough to handle this. But you love these crazy kids so much that you don't want them to have to feel the same things that you feel. You're doing your darndest to feel everything for them." His eyes were riveted on Clint's. "You can't do that, bud. It doesn't work. In loving these kids so much, Clint, you're denying them a part of themselves. You're denying them their individual grief and their individual hope. And, in the end, sir, you are going to be denying them their chance to grow and their front-row seat to a miracle. Because Manderly *is* coming home to this family. Right now, Clint, you're trying to play the game as if she was never gone. But she is gone, bud. And if these kids don't truly realize that fact, if you don't let them feel the grief, then they won't get to feel the hope and the wonder, either."

All was silent around the table. Clint stared at his brother and wondered where that long, incredible speech had come from. It wasn't Philip's style to launch into a long monologue. Clint grinned at his brother to break the tension between them. "I'll call my secretary right now and get her to book you on an extensive lecture tour, Philip. You're very good."

The speech had been an accurate, soul-searching one. As Clint analyzed his brother's points and considered some of his own opinions from a different angle, he began to understand what Philip was telling him. His brother's words, in addition to what Greg had done—sneaking the car out of the garage once more and driving here to see his mother alone because he had been so desperate to see her—made Clint begin to pinpoint the mistakes he had made.

He just sat for a moment with tears in his eyes watching his two children whom he loved more than anything in the world, and thinking about the third, his firstborn son, lying upstairs in the recovery room. And he realized as he looked at the girls that Philip was right, that he owed all three of his children much more than what he had been able to give them on his own.

Silently, he stood and extended both hands to them, one to each of his daughters.

"Come on," he said to them. "It's time we went to see your mother."

It was Lisa who understood the complete significance of this moment more than Bethany. Their father had decided it was time to share something important with them. She still had hold of her little sister's hand. The three of them formed a small, simple semicircle as they left the table in the cafeteria and went to retrieve something that the three of them had lost a long, long time before.

CHAPTER THIRTEEN

EMILY TURNED TO PHILIP and watched him. She tried to think of the right words she could say to make him know how grateful she was to him for turning such a negative experience into a positive one. The things he had said were so gentle and true. She loved the way he had metaphorically taken Clint's hand and had led him to a place where he could see the truth about all of them. He'd been so tender and loving in the way he had guided his brother, and as Emily thought of it, she realized that during the past few months he had done the same thing with her, too. Philip had come to her in friendship and had touched her with his kindness. He had said the things he needed to say to make her forget what she perceived as her inadequacies. And because of that, the guilt and the empty places in her life had stopped haunting her. Philip had taught her how to trust him, and in doing that she had learned to trust other people and herself, too.

Philip had given her his trust the same way Santa Claus left his gifts beneath the tree at Christmas, without ever expecting anything in return. And because of that, Philip Manning had set her free. Philip was an anchor to her. He was the first person in her life who hadn't been inconsistent or abandoned her or caused her to seek life's meaning in cold gold plaques and empty awards. He was everything she had prayed for a long, long time ago when she'd needed someone in her life who was stable and steadfast.

She didn't know how to tell him that, but without being told, Philip saw the things that were written in her eyes.

"Let's get out of this hospital." He dropped his hold on her and stood up from the table. "I can't stand this place."

Wordlessly, she stood, too, and the two of them walked outside together. The sun was just disappearing behind the horizon and they walked along, side by side, finally coming to a halt in the dusk. They stopped below a huge live oak tree that stood gnarled and ageless on the hospital lawn. And it was then that Emily reached across to Philip and took his hand in hers. He turned to her. "I'm so proud of you," she whispered as she touched one of his fingers with her own. Everything that she was feeling for him—the gratitude, the trust, the immense respect—welled up within her.

Philip didn't say anything. He just held her hand as if he needed to absorb those feelings, as if he needed her strength and support for the things he had said to his brother. It was the only thing he needed now, to feel close to her. When he tried to talk, the words simply wouldn't come. He just looked at her and shook his head. And somehow she understood.

Emily looked up at him, suddenly animated as she remembered something she had forgotten to tell him. *Baby Sprout*. She had been so concerned about Greg that she had forgotten all about her conversation with Sylvia Ressling. It seemed to her, as she stood in front of him thinking of it, that the things she and Philip had shared, the things he had taught her to believe in, had become tangible in this project. Now they would work on all their books together.

"I have an interesting professional assignment for you," she said to him, and he didn't quite understand the glint he saw in her eyes. He didn't understand why she would mention anything about working right now. They were at the hospital. And they still didn't know much about Greg's condition. But there was something in her eyes, a certain tenderness that was a natural consequence of what they had shared today. Philip realized suddenly that she was going to tell him something very, very important.

"What is my interesting assignment?"

"Well..." Emily looked down at the ground. She was enjoying dragging this out. "How about illustrating some work that I've done?"

"Oh, no," he teased her. "What is it this time? Let me guess. Something else that girls shouldn't know anything about. Baby armadillos. Baby catfish and crawdads."

"No." She was shaking her head at him and laughing. "We haven't progressed that far yet. We're still on possums."

Philip didn't say anything. He couldn't understand what she was driving at.

She stood on her tiptoes and spoke softly into his ear. "Maybe you'll figure it out when I show you the contract."

"Emily?" His eyes were wide now. "What are you telling me?"

She locked her hands around the back of his neck. "I'm telling you, sir, that Hudson Publishing is sending us a contract. They like my stories. And they love the way you illustrate them."

"Oh, Emily." Philip grabbed her around the waist and lifted her high in the air. He twirled her around as he laughed with her. "You did it."

"No." She shook her head down at him. "We did it. We're going to be famous together, Mr. Manning."

Philip had the feeling as he watched her laughing down at him that she had come along and had blessed all their lives by the strength and the magic she had brought to them. And only this morning, she had told him that she loved him. Philip knew now what it felt like to be the victor. He realized that there was no place he would rather be than with Emily, right here, beneath the live oak tree at the hospital, while her dreams were coming true.

TWENTY MINUTES LATER, Greg awoke after his surgery and the doctors authorized a move to a private room. He was weak but feeling fine and glad to see the people who loved him. Philip noticed the boy tiring soon after they arrived and he offered to drive the girls back to the farm so Greg and Clint could have some time alone together.

"How are you feeling, son?" Clint asked the boy when everyone had left the room.

"I'm okay, Dad." Greg glanced at the broken leg ruefully. "This cast is really neat. I'll have to get every girl in the school to autograph it for me."

"I'm sure your sisters will oblige," Clint kidded his son. "I don't know about the rest of the girls in Waxahachie."

Greg shook his head at his father. "I intend to make this worth the hassle. I'll bet this thing starts itching."

"I'm sure it will, son."

A nurse came in then to change Greg's bed. She helped him into a wheelchair while she worked.

Greg bit his lip and wrinkled his forehead at the nurse. She was blond and pretty and he was willing to bet that she was just out of college. "Will you autograph my cast?"

"Certainly," she told him, and Greg winked at his father across the room.

Greg looked at the nurse seriously then. "It feels good to be up for a while. Would it be okay if I took this chair and we went for a walk?"

"It wouldn't hurt," she told him. "Leave the chair reclining and your father can push you. And don't go far."

Greg turned and looked at his father. "I'd like to visit my mother's room."

Clint's face darkened. But he didn't say no. He stood from where he was sitting and pushed his son down the hall.

"Thank you, Dad."

"Your sisters went in to see her this afternoon," Clint told him.

"How did they do?"

"Fine," Clint told Greg. "It didn't upset them as much as I'd thought it would." They had come to

Manderly's room. Clint pulled open the door and pushed his son's wheelchair inside.

"See." Greg craned his neck and looked up at his father. "Dad, you can always depend on us kids."

"Yeah." Clint glanced down at his son's cast. "Sometimes I can depend on you to be real dumb."

"Did I mess up the Studebaker real badly?"

"I'm afraid so, son," Clint answered him. "I don't know if it can be restored or not."

"Dad, I'm sorry."

Neither of them noticed the slight movement in the bed beside them. They were both too intent on the things they had to say to each other.

"I need to apologize, too, son," Clint said. "That's one reason I went ahead and brought the girls up to see your mother today. Your Uncle Philip made me realize..." His voice trailed off.

Amanda's body had rolled over. She was on her side, eyeing her son and her husband. "Say, y'all..." The comment came from the bed to their left. Amanda's voice was sluggish but no more so than if she had only been awakened from a heavy sleep after twelve hours...twelve hours, instead of twelve months. "If you two are going to have one of these deep discussions, why don't you both go downstairs? I'm tired. I've had a hard day. Bethany..." Manderly stopped speaking. She was totally confused. What had Bethany done today, she asked herself. She couldn't quite remember. It seemed suddenly as if that had been a long, long time ago. The anesthetic from her operation must have messed up her sense of timing, she reasoned because she certainly felt strange.

Clint and Greg were almost too stunned to move. Almost. Their eyes locked and the color drained from Clint's face. Everything seemed to be happening in slow motion, as if every second was an eternity and every movement had been choreographed as a freeze-frame pantomime. Clint turned to face his wife, and then he moved toward her. And Greg tried to move the wheelchair forward without much success. Tears welled up in his eyes, but his hands found the controls and he gradually inched forward.

As he struggled to get to his mother, Greg felt like a chair with four legs that hadn't been glued together yet. All the parts he needed to move together to get to his mother's bedside were going in opposite directions. His father was already over there beside her while he was still trying to get to her side. And then, when he finally gave up his struggle and sat long enough for the truth to sink in, he realized what this was going to mean to all of them. His mother had come back.

Amanda was staring up at the ceiling thinking it looked odd. She was thinking that the ceiling was unfamiliar, all bumpy, with sparkly things in it, and that it was strange because a minute ago she had awakened and had heard Clint and Greg talking and she'd thought she was at home in their bed, with a fire in the fireplace, waiting for Clint to come climb in beside her and hold her. But now she remembered she was in the hospital.

"Clint?" She turned to her husband and grasped his hand. Then she saw her son sitting in the wheelchair across the room. "Greg? What did you do to your leg?"

"I broke it."

She couldn't understand why Greg was staring at her.

Clint spoke to her and his words were slow and deliberate. He didn't want to frighten her. He was addressing his son without once letting his eyes waver from his wife's. "Greg? Why don't I push you outside and we'll let somebody important out there know what's going on in here?" He didn't want to say doctors or nurses. He had no idea if Manderly could remember anything. And he wondered if she even knew where she was.

Give us another few days and none of us will be worried about doctors or nurses, he thought. Doctors or nurses. It seemed to Clint that doctors and nurses had been ruling all their lives forever.

"Manderly." He stroked her arm as he spoke to her. He didn't know how much he should tell her, how much she was capable of comprehending. "Before I go outside, try to remember something for me, will you? Do you remember getting ready to come to the hospital? For surgery?"

"That's right." Amanda looked pleased. She had checked in yesterday morning—or had it been this morning—for gynecological surgery. Slowly, she raised her torso and swiveled her hips beneath the blankets. "It must have gone pretty well." Her eyes were wide. Maybe the local anesthetic just hasn't worn off yet, she thought. "I'm stiff but I certainly don't feel an incision. When do I get to go home to the farm? I feel ready to get out of here."

"What is this?" Clint smiled down at her. "You sound just like your son. Why does everybody want to go home?"

"Because we like it there," she told him, winking at Greg. And Clint just stared down at her. She was glad to see him, too, but she couldn't understand why he was looking at her that way. She had just gone in to have a simple cyst removed yesterday. The doctors had told her there was nothing she should worry about. And now Clint was hovering over her, looking as if a miracle had happened because she was awake and speaking to him. And there was Greg, sitting in a wheelchair.

She remembered something then, about the meals she had prepared for them before she left the hospital. "How were those chicken enchiladas? I tried one of Mom's recipes. Did y'all like them?"

Clint was smiling at her now, and she didn't understand the gleam of amusement in his eyes. "They were wonderful." He couldn't even remember them.

"Is the food holding out okay? Do y'all have enough to last another day or two until they let me out of here? Are you really in here too, Greg? What happened?" Clint was laughing now, laughing at life and at miracles and at her menu. How could they have possibly survived for twelve months on one pot roast, a pan of chicken enchiladas, a tuna casserole and a pound of meat loaf?

"I love you, Manderly." He bent over her and kissed her.

"What's so funny?" She didn't kiss him back. She wanted to know why he was laughing at her. But when he moved back, she saw that there were tears in his eyes, and Greg's too, great pools of them glittering there, and she reached up and kissed Clint's hand even though she didn't understand why it was that he was crying.

CHAPTER FOURTEEN

PHILIP RAN HIS EYES down the list he had made.

    (1) Mow lawn.
    (2) Trim grape arbor.
    (3) Paint fence.

It was an odd list. If anybody back at the office were to see this one, they would laugh. But as Philip ran his eyes down it once more, he decided that it was probably the most important list he had ever made. These were things Clint had asked him to do at the farm before Manderly arrived home.

Clint was spending his every waking minute at the hospital with his wife. The doctors were observing Manderly carefully. All indications were that she would be coming home within the week. Clint wanted everything to be perfect for her.

The entire family had started to make ready for her arrival. Greg was home now and his body was mending nicely. Even though the doctors had told him to rest, he had spent time in his closet straightening his clothes and organizing his sports paraphernalia on the shelves. When Emily had found him in his room working, she had ordered him back to bed, all the time clucking at him like an enraged mother hen. The thought of her like that, herding his nieces and nephews around the house, made Philip laugh. She was taking so much responsibility for them. She wanted things to be perfect for Manderly almost as much as Clint did. Emily was outside now, washing windows when she could have been inside relaxing and watching the Saturday afternoon Texas Rangers' baseball game on television. He could hear her scrubbing on the panes outside Clint's study. Philip rose from the sofa and went into the room so that he could watch her working. She was outside polishing the glass with ammonia water and old newspapers. Her hair was tied away from her face with a faded navy-blue-and-white bandana, and she was so intent on her work that she didn't see him enter the room. Philip watched her while she stepped back from the window and frowned up at a smudge she had missed on the left-hand side. He decided, as he watched her, that he loved her most of all because she never did anything halfheartedly. When she made a decision, she remained totally and enthusiastically committed to it.

Philip moved closer to the window as she wiped over the smudge a second time, and she caught the reflection of his movement in the glass. She grinned at him and waved.

He moved closer still and pressed his face against the pane. "I think you are beautiful," he mouthed to her through the glass. He couldn't resist telling her that. She had newsprint on her nose.

Emily reached one hand up and touched a strand of hair where it had snuck out from beneath the bandana. Just being around Philip made her feel beautiful. And she felt as if she might feel that way forever, she was so full of joy. Manderly was coming home.

Soon Emily wouldn't be a mother for the children anymore, but she couldn't feel sad yet, she was so happy for them. More than ever, she needed to know Philip was being strong for her. "Thank you," she mouthed back.

"Need help washing?"

She shook her head at him and he leaned his forehead against the glass.

"Don't!" she shrieked from outside as she waved one of her cleaning rags at him. "You're smearing my window!"

"Sorry." He jumped back and started laughing. "I didn't know you had already washed the inside." He touched the glass with one finger and she swatted at him again. "I'm coming out there."

"Don't," she called to him. "Then I really won't get any work done."

"That's okay," he called back. He turned from the window and went outside to where she was working. When he walked up to her, she flopped her cleaning rag over his shoulder and she grasped both of his arms. She had an uncanny way of reading his mind lately. And she wasn't afraid of the things he had to offer her.

She leaned against him and whispered to him, "Kiss me. I deserve it. I've washed twenty windows this morning." She wanted him to know how glad she was that after knowing Morgan he trusted her.

"Okay." His voice was husky. He cradled her face in both his hands, and her hair fell through his fingers in tendrils. He couldn't resist winking at her. "I will." Slowly he bent toward her and his lips found her hair, her eyelids and finally her lips. And when she kissed him back, Emily felt as if she were weightless as he held her. She pulled away from him when she heard a car pulling into the gravel driveway. "Is that Clint?" Emily hadn't expected him back so soon. He had been at the hospital with Manderly all day long every day since she'd come out of the coma.

Philip squinted his eyes into the sun so he could see the approaching car. "It isn't Clint. I don't know who it is. I don't recognize the car."

They stood beside the house and watched as a maroon Ford pulled up beside the house and parked. When a tall wiry man opened the door on the driver's side and climbed out, Emily gasped. "Philip," she turned back to the man who stood beside her. "It's my brother. It's Jim."

"Jimmy?" she called out as she ran toward the driveway.

"Emily," he called back. "Wow, what a place! Is this where you live?"

She reached him, and she was breathless as she flung her arms around her younger brother and hugged him. It had been months since she had seen him and years since they'd been close. "Yes." She gazed up at him while Philip watched the two of them from the side of the house. He wondered if he should move forward so Emily could introduce him. He was fascinated by the prospect of meeting a member of Emily's family. The entire time he had known her, it had seemed as if the sadness of Emily's mother had overshadowed whatever bond the Lattrell family might share. Now, here was Emily's brother.

Jim was tall and happy and handsome, with kind dark eyes the same color as Emily's and thick curly sandy-blond hair.

"I'm sorry I didn't write much," Jim apologized. "How's my little sister doing?" He loved to tease Emily. She was six years his senior, and he stood a good head taller than she did.

"I'm great. I can't wait to show you around. Philip," she called as she glanced over her shoulder. "Come meet my baby brother." She turned back to Jim. "Are you finished with classes at A&M? What are you doing here?"

Jim's face darkened at her question. "I came because I wanted to bring someone out to see you."

Philip was beside her now, and he extended his hand to the young man. "This is my brother," Emily told him quietly. She turned to Jim. "This is Philip Manning." But Emily wasn't watching the exchange. She was peering at the car. She hadn't noticed that there was another person in the front seat of the car until Jim drew her attention to the fact.

"Jim? Who is it?"

Jim turned from Philip and looked anxious. He didn't say anything then. He just moved back to the car and opened the door. Then he stared at his sister while a look of disbelief registered on her face. Emily gasped audibly when she recognized the woman in the car.

"Mother?"

"She wanted to see you." Jim's voice was soft. "It's been a long time."

Emily moved to the car and grasped her brother's arm while a stricken-looking older woman stared at them without moving from the front seat. Philip discreetly moved away from them and made his way to the house. "What's she doing here?"

Jim didn't answer. Instead the woman got out of the car and then approached her daughter.

"Darling, hello."

For an instant, Emily felt totally lost. She wheeled around to find Philip, but he had already disappeared. She was going to have to face this reunion on her own. And suddenly, as she stared at her mother, she thought what a miracle it was, that here were the three of them, standing together in a gravel driveway, when they'd been estranged for so long. It was a beginning of sorts to her, just realizing that loving them was worth the pain she'd endured all her life.

"Hello, Mother."

"I'm sorry to shock you." The woman became more animated. "I wanted to see you. I've missed you, Emily."

"I've missed you, too." She had been missing her mother for a very long time.

"Your father tells me that you wrote a book. He tells me you're having it published."

"You've talked to Daddy?" Emily asked.

"Last week." The woman paused. Her eyes were full of pride. "He told me all about it. It made me very proud of you."

"Thank you." Emily was still confused. She didn't know why her mother had come.

"Are you going to write several of them?"

"I'd like to." She paused. "I have an illustrator I like. I'm hoping we can work together on a children's series."

"Are you going to quit your job on the farm because of this?"

"My job here on the farm is over. I'm leaving, but not because I sold my book." Emily chose her words carefully. She had almost finished her responsibilities here. She was proud of what she'd been able to do, but leaving the farm would be painful. "The children's mother is coming home soon. Then they won't need me any longer." Emily braced herself for a reprimand. She was certain her mother would find something unsatisfactory with the situation. But the negative comments didn't materialize.

"You like it here, don't you? It's beautiful."

"Yes. It is."

"Did you write your book here?" her mother asked.

Emily wondered why she was interested. She couldn't remember her mother ever being interested in anything she had done, ever.

"I wrote it at the agency. Living here gave me the bravery to send it in, though."

Emily studied her mother. There was something subtly different about her. Even though her mother's face was almost devoid of color it was so entirely pale and powdery she looked happy. She was wearing a stroller-length black sable coat. And it was almost seventy degrees outside this time of year, even in the evening.

"What's this?" The coat looked so soft that Emily wanted to touch it. But she couldn't quite decide whether it was the coat she wanted to touch or the woman who was wearing it. Emily reached a tentative finger out to the collar and stroked it. "This coat is lovely."

"It's a victory present to myself." Emily's mother grinned and Emily thought when she did that this woman looked like a stranger. She was beautiful when she smiled sincerely. "They had a postseason fur sale at Joske's this week. So I just stopped by and picked it up. What do you think? I've never owned anything like this in my entire life." She turned around slowly so Emily could see the coat from every angle.

"It's beautiful, Mother." Emily was shaking her head. It seemed crazy to wear a heavy fur coat on a warm spring day like today. "But it's warm outside."

"I don't care," her mother explained, shrugging. "I know it's warm out. That's why I'm traveling to Vail for a week. I have to go somewhere cold so I can wear this thing," she said, her eyes sparkling.

Emily glanced at her brother. Jim was the skier in the family. Vail was perhaps the most prestigious and expensive ski resort in Colorado. Emily was impressed. "Jimmy, did you talk her into a trip like this? I'm jealous."

Jim shook his head.

Emily's mother was laughing. "I want everybody to be jealous. I deserve this trip."

"Is Jim taking you?" Emily glanced at her brother once more. Seeing her brother and her mother together so suddenly was unnerving.

"No, I'm not," Jim answered her this time. "She just wanted me to bring her over here this afternoon so she could talk to you."

Jim felt funny saying anything more. He didn't want to tell Emily how frightened her mother had been about the visit. It had taken every ounce of strength the woman had to go to her husband and her son to tell them the things she needed to say. Now it was her turn to talk to Emily. Jim knew what an emotional toll this trip to the farm was taking on his mother. Emily was the one in their family who still harbored the most resentment, the most guilty remorse for the things that had happened during their childhood. Because of that, Jim had agreed to come today. He had wanted to see Emily. But he had come mainly to protect his mother and his sister from each other. He had come to give both of them moral support.

"Are you making the trip with friends?"

"I am," her mother replied. "I have a job at a flower shop in Dallas now. I have two or three new friends. We decided to go to the mountains together and celebrate."

"Tell me about the victory you're celebrating." Emily whispered the question. She was hoping that she would learn something important from the things her mother had to say to her. She scarcely dared to look up at her for fear that she might be mistaken. The thought struck her, suddenly, as she walked along beside her brother and the woman in the fancy mink coat, that she was with the people who had once been her family. It was an incredible feeling, having them here, and she had to swallow a sudden burst of exhilaration.

"I'm celebrating..." Her mother's voice was soft but that didn't keep her pride from coming through as she spoke. "I'm celebrating the fact that I finally found a drinking rehabilitation program that works. I'm celebrating the fact that I finally found the willpower within myself to make my recovery happen."

Emily's mother went on to explain that she had admitted herself to a lock-in alcohol treatment center almost four months ago. She didn't dare tell her daughter that she had called the treatment center the afternoon Emily had called to thank her for the journal. She didn't quite know how to tell her daughter what an impact the few words of thanks had had on her life. She only wanted Emily to know that she had done it. "I'm sober."

Emily's eyes were huge. She had dreamed of hearing those words from her mother for years now. "Mother? Are you saying that you aren't an alcoholic anymore?"

Her mother looked wistful. "I'll always be an alcoholic. Now I'm a reformed one. I've been wanting to tell you my news for weeks, Emily." She had picked up the telephone to call her daughter at least five times since her release. But she hadn't quite been brave enough to let the call ring through.

"Mother?" There were tears welling up in Emily's eyes.

"There are a great many things I've been wanting to tell you." Emily's mother's voice was quavering now, too. "I realize there a big chunks of your childhood that I don't remember. I only wish..." She started to say, that I could bring some of those years back. But that wasn't what was important to her any longer. She knew she had no right to the past. But she had a right to the future. "I wish you could forgive me, Emily. As part of my treatment, I have learned to take the responsibility for the terrible things my alcoholism did to my family. I know that doesn't make it any easier for you and Jimmy and your father but I—"

"You're taking responsibility for that?" Emily interrupted her mother. She could scarcely believe what was happening. She had been hoping to hear these words for so long. There was a rush of happiness from somewhere deep within her. "But I take responsibility for it, too. I always knew that I did something to you. I always knew that there was some reason that you weren't proud of me."

"You blamed yourself."

"Who else could I blame?"

"Me," the woman said frankly. "I'm the one who created the situation for all of us." She paused and sucked in her breath. "I need your forgiveness, Emily. I need to know that you'll start trying to forget the things that I did to you. And I need you to know that I love you more than anything else on this earth. You are my only daughter."

Emily's eyes were wide. "You love me?"

"I always have."

The silence was awkward between them for a moment. Neither one of them knew what to say next. A great wall had come tumbling down between them, but neither of them knew how to deal with the open space. Emily did not move to embrace her mother. And her mother understood why. These feelings were so new to both of them.

Jim walked to his sister and slipped an arm around her shoulders. "I guess we should be getting back to the city. Mother has a plane to catch this afternoon."

"You're leaving today?"

Emily's mother nodded. "I just wanted to come out here and see you before I left. I've been afraid. But I decided I didn't want to wait any longer."

"Thank you, Mother."

The woman didn't say anything more to her daughter. She only held her arms out to her.

Emily reached out to her mother and hugged her close. Then Emily stepped back and stared at her. There were a thousand things she wanted to say to her mother, but only one thing really mattered. "I do forgive you, Mother." She paused. "I love you."

Jim put his arm around his mother's shoulders and guided her toward the car. Emily said nothing more. She just stood beside the house and watched them go. And as the car drove away, she leaned against the house siding and let her breath come out in a rush. She had a family, too. She was sad to be leaving the Mannings' farm. But she suddenly had people who loved her. Her brother. Her mother. And Philip.

Emily leaned her head against the windowpane that she had been washing, and she watched as the car her brother was driving disappeared on the Maypearl Road. And then at last tears of victory, tears that were as genuine and precious as her mother's sable victory coat, began to slip down her cheeks in earnest.

THERE WERE SO MANY subtle changes around the farm now that Manderly was coming home. Emily and the girls had washed windows and ironed curtains until Emily thought her arms would break. The geraniums were back in their places on the balcony and the railing had been painted with a fresh coat of white. The bed in Clint's room upstairs was covered with clean sheets and a fresh quilt. The girls had been out all morning picking wildflowers in the meadow and they were everywhere, now, in huge weedy clusters; they made the whole house smell fragrant and fresh.

Emily straightened her back and looked around the front room for the last time. This place was so beautiful and it had come to be such a special home for her. But now it was time for her to go to another home, to the place where she had belonged before she had come here. This was going to Manderly's home again. The children didn't need an Absolutely Mom any longer.

Emily thought, as she looked around, that nothing could ever really stay the same. And it struck her how much her own life was changing, too. This was the part of being an adopted mother Abbie Carson had told her about months ago...the part where Manderly Manning came home to her family...the part where Emily would be asked to leave the family. This was the part where she would have to learn her hardest lesson about love. This was the part where she would have to learn how to let it go.

Emily thought of her mother and her father and her brother. Her own family was scattered all across Texas. But she had learned something about them from caring for the Mannings. Clint and Amanda had fought to love one another no matter what the cost. They had proved to her that love could last. The Mannings didn't flit around in the middle of a crisis banging into one another and knocking one another off course. They held together and they trusted one another and they held on tightly to the things that really mattered.

"Whoa...Mama... Easy..." Emily heard Philip's voice out in the front yard and she turned to gaze out the window at him. He was running across the front yard chasing Honey Snookems and her calf. The girls had decided Honey needed to be waiting in the front yard when their mother came home, so Philip had agreed to do the cattle herding this morning. She couldn't resist just watching him. He was such a strong, sensitive man and she loved to see him here, where he belonged, herding cows and growling up into trees. Philip had given all of them so much.

Emily shut her eyes to squeeze back her tears. How she was going to miss being a part of all this.

"I'm turning them over to you now, Manderly," she whispered to the sky. "Take good care of them for me."

As if on cue, Emily heard Clint's car turn off the roadway and cross the cattle guard.

"They're here!" one of the girls shrieked from upstairs. Emily gripped the windowsill as two pairs of legs pounded down the stairs. Greg was outside already, waiting on the front porch in his wheelchair. Philip stopped chasing Honey and he stood by the cow while Clint drove the car up and parked it as close as he could to the front sidewalk. Philip hurried toward the car and opened the door on the passenger side. Then he reached into the back seat and pulled out Amanda's suitcase.

As Emily watched him, it struck her what an important part of this homecoming Philip was. He looked so good and familiar and steadfast to her. As they all stood together in the driveway hugging, Emily wanted to freeze the scene as if on film and hold the picture in her mind forever.

Everyone walked toward the house, and Clint helped Manderly along with one arm around her waist. As the front screen door swung open, Emily felt that perhaps she should run away. But the dark-headed, frail beauty who walked in the front door stopped her. "You're Emily." Amanda's voice was soft and melodic. Emily was entranced by it.

"Hello, Manderly." She stood before the woman who was a stranger to her yet not a stranger, too. Then she hugged her.

Manderly looked at the petite, spunky blond woman who was standing in her living room and felt a strange kinship with her. This was Emily, the Emily who had run her household for months while she had been sleeping. At first, when Manderly had found out about Emily, she had almost been jealous. Emily had shared a part of her family's lifetime that she would never be able to share. But as the days had worn on and the children and Clint had told her stories about Emily, Manderly began to feel as if they knew each other well, as if they had somehow talked. And perhaps they had, in Emily's dreams and prayers.

"A woman's family is the most precious thing she can lay claim to," Manderly said to her. "Thank you for taking care of mine."

"You're welcome," Emily almost whispered. "Thank you for sharing them with me. I've grown to love them all." She had to choke back her tears then. "It's going to be very hard not to be a part of this family any longer."

Clint wrapped his arm around Manderly's waist. She was still weak, and it was time to help her upstairs to her room. As Emily watched the two of them climbing the stairs together, she suddenly felt very alone. The tears poured down her face, and she made no attempt to hide them any longer.

As she cried silently, Emily felt a strong arm slip around her waist.

"Little one," Philip whispered into her hair, and as he held her, it was the first time today Emily felt that she didn't have to be brave. "This has been a hard day, hasn't it?"

She turned to him and surrendered to him as he bundled her into his arms. She needed him desperately.

"I hate myself for feeling this way," she sobbed into his shoulder. "I feel selfish." She turned her head up toward his. "I'm so happy that Manderly's home. It's just hard for me to let go of them. They've become my family, too."

Philip bent toward her and kissed her on the forehead. "I certainly hope that you aren't worried about letting go of me. We still have work to do together."

"I know that," she whispered. She and Philip still had so much to share. He was already working on several new sketches for *Baby Sprout and Priscilla*. But Emily knew it wouldn't be the same any longer. It couldn't be. She didn't belong here the way she once had, when they'd first worked on the book.

"I wonder..." Philip stopped talking and grinned mysteriously.

"What?" she asked him. "What are you wondering?"

"I wonder whether this little creation of ours will have your hair or my hair," Philip commented flippantly. "It could be either, you know."

Emily gave him an elfin grin. It was funny that he was in the mood to tease her today. "Baby Sprout doesn't have my hair. And I don't think you gave him yours."

Philip chuckled. His smile grew wider. He looked at Emily, and the love he felt for her welled up so intensely within him that he scarcely could contain it.

"For heaven's sake," he said nonchalantly as he traced the tip of her nose with his finger. "I hope his hair isn't gray. Wouldn't he be an abnormal baby if he was born with gray hair?"

"A baby?" Emily was still confused.

"Our baby." Philip's voice was soft now. "I'm not talking about Baby Sprout, little one, I'm talking about the other work you and I have left to do. I'm talking about building a family together."

Emily lifted her face to his in wonder.

He cupped her chin in his hand. "I want you to marry me, Emily." Philip's voice was thick with conviction. "I want you to stay a part of this family forever."

She was crying again now, and she stretched her arms up to his face and pulled him down to kiss her. Afterward, she looked at him as he stood above her, so solid, so steadfast, and she knew he was all she would ever need. And she was willing to make a commitment to him. She was willing to fight to make that love last a lifetime.

"Yes." She nodded her head at him as all the things she felt for this man poured forth from her eyes. "I love you, Philip and I want to be your wife more than anything in the world.

"Oh, Philip," Emily said, laughing as she stood on tiptoe and trailed her lips across the bridge of his nose to his cheekbone, and then she stretched higher to kiss his brow. "Do you think building a family together will be work?"

"Yes. It will be." He kissed her full on the lips. "But I'm expecting it to be fun work." And then he laughed, too. "Only I'm wondering if all of our children are going to look like Baby Sprout."

"I wouldn't care if they did." She reached a finger up to his face and followed his jawline from his shirt collar to his ear. "I love you that much."

He bent to kiss her, and when he did, Emily reveled in the sensation that his embrace aroused in her. She felt totally protected, totally anchored to the man who had come to mean everything to her. And as the two of them clung together in the middle of a place that had become a home of sorts to both of them, they felt, at last, the warmth, the all-encompassing peace that comes from having faith in each other...from hanging on...from believing in love's distant promise.

ATTRACTIVE, SPACE SAVING BOOK RACK

Display your most prized novels on this handsome and sturdy book rack. The hand-rubbed walnut finish will blend into your library decor with quiet elegance, providing a practical organizer for your favorite hard- or soft-covered books.

Only $9.95

Approximately 16" x 8" when assembled

Assembles in seconds!

To order, rush your name, address and zip code, along with a check or money order for $10.70 ($9.95 plus 75¢ postage and handling) (New York residents add appropriate sales tax), payable to *Harlequin Reader Service* to:

In the U.S.

Harlequin Reader Service
Book Rack Offer
901 Fuhrmann Blvd.
P.O. Box 1325
Buffalo, NY 14269-1325

Offer not available in Canada.

BKR-1

Harlequin Superromance

COMING NEXT MONTH

#242 LOVE CHILD • Janice Kaiser
Jessica Brandon desperately needs money to care for her crippled son. Chase Hamilton desperately wants a child of his own. Surrogate motherhood seems the perfect solution for them both—until love creates a whole new set of problems.

#243 WEAVER OF DREAMS • Sally Garrett
Growing up dirt-poor on a Kentucky farm has instilled in professional weaver Abbie Hardesty the need for financial independence. She dreams of overseeing every aspect of her own crafts business, but she needs to learn about wool production first. So she becomes Montana sheep rancher Dane Grasten's intern student, and they both end up learning more than they'd bargained for...in each other's arms!

#244 TIME WILL TELL • Karen Field
Attorney Corinne Daye no longer knows whom to trust: Derek Moar, the devastatingly attractive stranger who bears an amazing resemblance to her dead husband, or Margaret Krens, her loyal assistant, who insists that Derek is on the wrong side of the law. She only hopes that when the dust finally settles, Derek will be there to fill the emptiness that stretches endlessly before her....

#245 THE FOREVER BOND • Eleni Carr
With her daughter grown up and her career finally established, Eve Raptis is ripe for a change. Carefree Carl Masters supplies it, but the responsibilities of Eve's past unexpectedly reappear to dim her precious freedom....